Gentlemen of the Night
Captain Phantom

Gentlemen of the Night
Captain Phantom

Stage Plays

by

Paul Féval

translated and adapted by

Frank J. Morlock

A Black Coat Press Book

Acknowledgements: We are indebted to Dagny for typing the plays.

This book is dedicated to John Langford for many years of friedship.

Cover and interior illustrations Copyright © 2007 by Fernando Calvi.

Visit our website at www.blackcoatpress.com

Table of Contents

Introduction

Paul Féval (1816-1887)

Paul Féval is, with Alexandre Dumas (1802-1870), Eugène Sue (1805-1857) and Pierre-Alexis Ponson du Terrail (1829-1871), one of the leading authors of *romans feuilletons*, these sprawling popular novels serialized with great success in French newspapers of the 19th century.

Sue is the author of the seminal *Les Mystères de Paris* (*The Mysteries of Paris*, 1842-43) and *Le Juif Errant* (*The Wandering Jew*, 1844-45). Dumas is best remembered for *Les Trois Mousquetaires* (*The Three Musketeers*, 1844) and *Le Comte de Monte-Cristo* (*The Count of Monte-Cristo*, 1845-46). As for Ponson du Terrail, he is the creator of *Rocambole*, whose adventures he began writing in 1857.[1]

Today, Féval is mostly remembered for outdoing Dumas with his perennial swashbuckling bestseller *Le Bossu* (*The Hunchback*, 1857), in which his hero, Lagardère, a prodigious swordsman, disguises himself as a hunchback to seek revenge against his enemies. But Féval's much greater claim to fame is, undoubtedly, to have been one of the fathers of modern crime fiction. Féval developed the concepts of criminal

---

[1] *Rocambole*, two stage play adaptations, is available from Black Coat Press (ISBN 978-1-932983-57-9, 2006).

conspiracies in *Jean Diable* (*John Devil*, 1862) [2] and *Les Habits Noirs* (*The Black Coats*, 1863-75).[3]

In *John Devil*, he created the character of Scotland Yard Chief Superintendent Gregory Temple, arguably the first modern detective in literature. In *The Black Coats: The Invisible Weapon*, [4] he gave us Rémy d'art, a fearless investigative magistrate–also among the first of its kind. In *L'Affaire Lerouge* (*The Widow Lerouge*, 1866), Féval's own secretary, Emile Gaboriau, went on to create the character of Monsieur Lecoq (a hero seemingly unconnected to the villainous Lecoq of the Black Coats), which later influenced Conan Doyle's creation of Sherlock Holmes.

In 1875, after writing his seventh *Black Coats* novel, Féval lost nearly all his fortune in a financial scandal. As a result, he became what we would call today "born-again" and stopped writing crime novels, which he considered to be sinful. Féval died on March 8, 1887.

The Mysteries of London:

Féval's first bestseller was a serialized novel entitled *Les Mystères de Londres* (*The Mysteries of London*) which was serialized in *Le Courrier Français* from December 20, 1843 to September 12, 1844. It was first credited to "Sir Francis Trolopp" (!) in an attempt to make the readers believe it was a genuine work translated from the English. *Les Mystères de Londres* was commissioned by *Le Courrier*'s editor Anténor Joly to cash in on Eugene Sue's *Les Mystères de Paris*. Originally, Joly had commissioned the project from another writer, but did not like the results and turned to Féval, whose historical *Le Loup Blanc* (*The White Wolf*, 1843) he had

---

[2] Available from Black Coat Press (ISBN 978-1-932983-15-9, 2005).

[3] Available from Black Coat Press (ISBN 978-1-932983-46-3, 2005).

[4] Available from Black Coat Press (ISBN 978-1-932983-80-7, 2006).

previously serialized, and liked, to hastily produce a new version.

Twenty years later, Féval would blame Joly to have taken him away from perhaps a nobler and more respectable type of literature and turned him into a successful *feuilletoniste*. For, in the space of a mere few months, *Les Mystères de Londres* made Féval the equal in popularity of Sue and Dumas. Indeed, anyone tempted to compare the revenge-driven plot of the better-known *Comte de Monte-Cristo* to *Les Mystères de Londres* should remember that it was Féval who pioneered it, not Dumas.

Les Mystères de Londres were first collected in 11 smallish volumes in 1844, and in a more definitive, three-volume edition by M. Lévy in 1848. Féval later retroactively incorporated its criminal organization, the "Gentlemen of the Night," into the saga of the Black Coats. Other aspects of the story, such as a meeting between Rio Santo and Napoleon in Saint Helena, also found their way into later books, such as *John Devil*. As to the Irish theme, it is worth nothing that Féval had actually visited London to research the book and there, had met the notorious nationalist leader, Daniel O'Connell. It is likely that Féval's treatment of the Irish situation later influenced Ponson du Terrail who drew inspiration from *Les Mystères de Londres* and reused the theme in the chapter of the *Rocambole* saga transparently entitled *Les Misères de Londres* (*The Miseries of London*, 1867-68).

In 1848, perhaps because of the popularity of the new Lévy edition, Féval wrote a stage play adaptation of *Les Mystères de Londres*, sub-titled *Gentlemen of the Night*, [5] which was performed at the Théâtre Historique in Paris from December 28, 1848 until February 11, 1849.

---

[5] *Les Mystères de Londres, ou les Gentilhommes de la Nuit.* We have used the alternate title for this volume to better differentiate the play from the original novel, which we hope to publish someday.

9

Captain Phantom

Le Capitaine Fantôme, sub-titled "*Aventures Espagnoles*" (Spanish Adventures), was originally serialized in *Le Pays* from February 25 to August 12, 1862. *Le Pays* had previously published some of Féval's best gothic historical dramas such as *La Louve* (*The She-Wolf*, 1855-56) and *Le Livre des Mystères* (*Revenants*, 1852),[6] and was therefore an obvious choice. That 700-page novel was then collected as two volumes entitled *Les Grenadiers Ecossais* (*The Scottish Grenadiers*) and *Les Filles de Cabanil* (*The Daughters of Cabanil*) by Dentu that same year.

The 1864 stage play version presented here was co-written with Auguste Anicet-Bourgeois, with whom Féval had already worked two years prior on a stage adaptation of *Le Bossu*, and who also adapted *Rocambole* (q.v.). It launched on March 26 of that year at the Théâtre de la Porte Saint-Martin in Paris. Despite initial poor reviews, the play was reasonably successful and lasted until April 30.

Féval would go on to collaborate three more times with Anicet-Bourgeois: in 1865 on *Le Mousquetaire du Roi* (*The King's Musketeer*), in 1866 on *La Reine Cotillon* (*Queen Cotillon*) and in 1874 on *Cocagne*.

Jean-Marc Lofficier

---

[6] Available from Black Coat Press (ISBN 978-1-932983-70-8, 2006).

Gentlemen of the Night

Characters

Marquis de Rio Santo
and in order of appearance:
Mr. Gruff, innkeeper of King George's Tavern
Mistress Gruff, his wife
Bob Lantern
Suzannah d'Arleigh
Clary d'Arleigh, her younger sister
Mother Jacobs, an old woman
Captain Paddy O'Chrane
Mr. Snail
Mr. Turnbull
"Mr. Handcuffs," a Policeman
Donnor d'Arleigh, Suzannah and Clary's father
Doctor Edmund Moore
Frank Percival
Fanny Bertram, Rio Santo's sister
"La Maudlin"
Lady Mordaunt
Mrs. Bloomberry
Lady Stanley
Gerard
Lord Trevor
Lady Campbell, Lord Trevor's sister
Mary Trevor, Lord Trevor's daughter
Prince Dimitri Tolstoy
Lady Brompton

Owen Falkstone
Walter Brown
Nick Smith
Peter Wood (a.k.a. The Practice)
Daniel O'Connell
Mr. Johnstone
Sir Picott
Mr. Harrison
Mitch
Bert
The Police Commissioner of Saint Giles
His Clerk
Jane, a servant
Phegor, another servant
and:
A Passerby at the Queen's Theater
A Customer at King George's Tavern
An Usher at King James' Palace
The Halberdiers at King James' Palace
The Constables of Saint Giles
An oarsman

The story takes place in London in the 1830s.

Act I

Scene I

(The stage represents the square before the Queen's Theater in London. To the right, there is the theater's colonnade; to the left, King George's Tavern. The cabaret is at an angle and its interior can be seen in a cut-away. Behind the theater one sees the fog-shrouded skyline of London.

(AT RISE, we open on a crowded time–6 p.m. Buses drive by. Cabs drop off spectators who then go to wait in line in front of the theater. Inside the tavern, Bob Lantern is snoozing at a table in a corner. The two owners, Mr. Gruff and Mistress Gruff, are talking.)

MR. GRUFF: Ah, there's a line forming in front of the theater. We'll soon have company.

MISTRESS GRUFF (*angrily*): You don't know what you're talking about, Mr. Gruff. No one's coming. Don't you see? It's almost six, and Captain O'Chrane should already be here to escort me to the performance as he promised.

MR. GRUFF: Undeceive yourself, my dear Mistress Gruff. It's only a quarter to six, and Captain O'Chrane won't fail to be here on the dot. No one instructs the Captain when it comes to punctuality (*with a touch of malice*) –and gallantry as well.

MISTRESS GRUFF (*still angry*): Leave me alone!

BOB LANTERN (*dreaming*): I dug through the Earth in twelve hours. The ditch is deep, but the work is progressing. It's hard and tiring!

(Mr. Gruff walks to Bob's table and watches him.)

MR. GRUFF (*concerned*): What's he saying, that one? Should I wake him?

MISTRESS GRUFF: Coward! You wouldn't dare.
BOB LANTERN (*still asleep*): Sharpen my pickaxe, Snail. I'm strong enough to dig a ditch so large that the city will look like a molehill.

(*Mr. Gruff finally decides to shake Bob awake.*)

MR. GRUFF: Wake up, Bob Lantern! Wake up!
BOB LANTERN (*waking up*): What? What? What's the matter? I'm not afraid of anything or anyone. I know the *name.*

(*Mr. Gruff and Mistress Gruff look at each other in astonishment.*)

MR. GRUFF: Lower! My God, Mr. Lantern! Speak lower!
BOB: I know you. I know to whom I'm speaking. Gruff, get your long ear a little closer.
MISTRESS GRUFF (*to her husband*): Go on, then!

(*Mr. Gruff steps forward, then stops as Suzannah enters from the rear, carrying a pot of beer. She is accompanied by her younger sister, Clary, and an old woman.*)

SUZANNAH (*to Clary*): I must leave you here, my poor little Clary. I'm already very late. Mistress Gruff will scold me, you see.
CLARY: But your eyes are still red, sis. You've been crying.
SUZANNAH: No, no–that's nothing. Be very well behaved, sis. Now that you're in the home of good folks, work hard for the love of our poor father. Goodbye, my little Clary. It'll be some time until we see each other again. (*to the old woman*) Mother Jacobs, watch over her!

(*She hugs Clary passionately. Then, the old woman leaves with Clary in tow.*)

MR. GRUFF (*to Bob, after the two women have gone*): Now, you were saying?

(*Suzannah crosses the tavern with her pot of beer and silently places it and some change on the counter. She then remains still.*)

BOB LANTERN (*to Gruff*): The *name* that will make you sell real gin, you, old poisoner! The *name* that will open your purse to the poor, old miser! The *name* which will make you polite and friendly, Mistress Gruff.
MISTRESS GRUFF: Mr. Gruff, your wife is being insulted!
BOB LANTERN: The *name* that will get all three of us hanged, my good friends.
MR. GRUFF: Hush! Suzannah!

(*Mistress Gruff at last understands that her husband is scared of being overheard by Suzannah.*)

MISTRESS GRUFF (*to Suzannah*): What are you doing here? Are you spying on us, girl?
SUZANNAH: No, Mistress Gruff. Here's the pot of beer you sent me to fetch, and the change.
MISTRESS GRUFF (*after having carefully counted the coins*): The amount isn't right. There's a penny missing.
SUZANNAH: Oh no, Mistress Gruff!
MISTRESS GRUFF: Oh yes, missy! Count yourself, you stupid girl.
SUZANNAH (*fumbling in her pocket*): Well, then here's a penny, Mistress Gruff.
MISTRESS GRUFF: Impertinent girl! Go to the backroom now!
MR. GRUFF (*musing*): There's going to be a storm tonight.

(*Suzannah leaves.*)

MR. GRUFF: Don't get angry, Mistress Gruff, and listen to what I'm going to tell you.

MISTRESS GRUFF: Speak then, but speak quickly, Mr. Gruff.

MR. GRUFF: Bob Lantern's right. I fear some misfortune is going to befall us.

MISTRESS GRUFF: Pah! In a few months, we'll retire–rich.

MR. GRUFF: In a few months, yes. But who knows what might happen until then?

MISTRESS GRUFF: Those men are powerful–and they need us.

MR. GRUFF: Oh, yes! Very powerful.

MISTRESS GRUFF: More powerful than the Queen with her two Parliaments! I listened to them the other night. There's all sorts of folks among them–doctors, magistrates, even lords– lords of the High Chamber. Their brotherhood is wrapped around London like a net–and it extends from here to all over the Continent. I was trembling to merely hear their schemes. Thousands of villains of all walks of life, of all nations.

MR. GRUFF (*fearful*): Silence, woman! In the name of the Lord!

MISTRESS GRUFF (*pointing to Bob Lantern*): He's asleep. They're everywhere. Their *name* is like a talisman that opens all doors and bends all wills. The man who can pronounce that *name* is master everywhere.

BOB LANTERN (*in his sleep*): *Gentlemen of the night*!

MISTRESS GRUFF (*shivering*): Even this one is the master here!

MR. GRUFF: Ah! The comfort we're amassing for our old age will cost us dearly, Mistress Gruff.

MISTRESS GRUFF: Shut up–someone's coming.

MR. GRUFF: It's Captain Paddy O'Chrane!

(*Paddy O'Chrane enters.*)

PADDY O'CHRANE: In the flesh! My good Mr. Gruff, 'tis I indeed. (*approaches Mistress Gruff*) Our amiable hostess, beautiful as ever, still rosy as a plum! As God Almighty is my witness, I'm here at your service–or I deserve to be hanged, dearest Mistress Gruff.

MISTRESS GRUFF: You're late, Captain.

PADDY O'CHRANE: Captain Paddy O'Chrane, late to a meeting with such a beautiful girl? Never! Listen, my friends, listen–the bells are just tolling six. (*we hear the bells; to Mistress Gruff*) See? Was I wrong?

MISTRESS GRUFF (*with a small smile*): I'm going to put on my hat.

(*Mistress Gruff leaves. Paddy notices Bob Lantern.*)

PADDY O'CHRANE: Hey! There's Bob Lantern! The dear lad. (*shaking him*) Bob Lantern, my fine fellow–wake up!

BOB LANTERN (*waking up again*): Huh?

PADDY O'CHRANE: You're asleep–while, in front of the theater, there's a collection of gentlemen and ladies whose pockets are full of money. (*as he says these words, he unfolds a large, beautiful handkerchief and wipes his face solemnly.*)

BOB LANTERN: That's a fine handkerchief, Captain. Well, goodbye, Captain. I feel better, much better. To your health. A very fine handkerchief indeed.

(*Bob Lantern exits the tavern and goes to mingle amongst the crowd outside.*)

PADDY O'CHRANE: Suzannah, my heart, mix me a tuppence' worth of gin with cold water, no sugar.

MR. GRUFF (*shouting*): Suzannah!

PADDY O'CHRANE: With a snip of lemon, Suzannah!

MR. GRUFF: Suzannah! I'll be damned if she hears me!

PADDY O'CHRANE: Please, Mr. Gruff, don't swear. I've got bad nerves–may the Devil take me! I can't stand blaspheming!

(*Mistress Gruff returns, properly dressed for her outing.*)

MISTRESS GRUFF (*complaining about Suzannah*): Well, go and give bread to a beggar. Take a moocher into your home and to thank you, she'll annoy your customers and ruin your establishment.

PADDY O'CHRANE: Mistress Gruff, my sweet friend, the Devil take me if I would be the cause of a row! Leave the poor girl alone or, by God, you'll make yourself sick and we'll miss the play. Come, come. (*pulling her*) Oh, how pink you are and how I lucky I am!

(*They exit the tavern and go to take their place in the line at front of the theater. Bob Lantern watches them. At that moment, two other disreputable-looking characters appear outside: the diminutive Mr. Snail and the burly Mr. Turnbull.*)

MR. SNAIL: Please, Mr. Turnbull, my dear brother-in-law, will you go in first? I'm a man of the world–I know my manners.

(*They enter the tavern and go to sit by the window; Mr. Gruff remains unobtrusively behind the counter.*)

MR. SNAIL: Hello, Mr. Gruff. We've come for refreshments. And I'm paying.

MR. GRUFF: If it isn't Little Snail!

MR. SNAIL (*furious*): I'm not little, I'm bigger than my sister, who's Mr. Turnbull's wife, and he's big.

MR. TURNBULL (*laughing*): That's true enough! Look, look, don't get angry, Mr. Snail. Mr. Gruff didn't mean to offend you.

MR. SNAIL: Then, let him proffer his apologies and I'll see if I accept them. (*to Turnbull*) I was letting you know that I intend to provide for you, since you're my sister's husband.

MR. TURNBULL (*after having been served a beer*): And what will that entail, Little Snail?

MR. SNAIL: First, to never call me Little Snail again, brother-in-law. If you do so, I'll ruin you. That being understood, I propose to give you a job...

MR. TURNBULL: A job?

MR. SNAIL: Do you know how to howl?

MR. TURNBULL: Howl?

MR. SNAIL: Yes. Me, I know how to meow. (*starts meowing*)

MR. TURNBULL: Meowing. That's not a job.

MR. SNAIL: Really? How much do you make unloading ships at the harbor?

MR. TURNBULL: Two shillings, by Jove! You know that.

MR. SNAIL: Two shillings, fine. And how much do you earn as a thief, pilfering from the same ships?

MR. TURNBULL: Keep it down, you little toad.

MR. SNAIL: I already told you not to call me "little." Answer me: how much do you earn from your thieving?

MR. TURNBULL: It depends. Not much.

MR. SNAIL (*pulling some bank notes from his pocket*): Well, as for me, this is what I make from meowing, my dear brother-in-law, not counting extras.

MR. TURNBULL: From meowing?

MR. SNAIL: Like a tomcat in March! It's a signal–to warn friends. When you learn how to howl, my recommendation will be worth gold to you.

MR. TURNBULL: It's agreed–I will learn to howl.

(*Outside, there's some movement in the line of customers outside the theater.*)

MR. SNAIL (*observing the line through the window*): Oh! oh! The line's moving. The time has come. Go meet my sister at the house, brother-in-law. She's ill, the poor girl. Here, give her this on my behalf. (*giving him some money.*)

(*Snail exits the tavern and mingles in with the crowd in front of the theater.*)

MR. TURNBULL: That little fellow may be nasty–but he's got a good heart! How prodigal these sons of a good family are!

(*Turnbull exits through the tavern's back entrance. The action now moves to the front of the theater.*)

PADDY O'CHRANE (*to Mistress Gruff*): Patience, my dear Mistress Gruff! Patience! A few more moments and we'll be comfortably ensconced in two fine seats in the gallery that I've rented at the cost of three shillings, may God take me!

MISTRESS GRUFF: Oh! Captain O'Chrane! The crowd! I'm suffocating. I'd give six pence to get some air.

PADDY O'CHRANE: Why the Devil do you assume that air is lacking here, Mistress Gruff? The wind is blowing strong enough to remove the horns from cattle.

(*At this moment, Bob Lantern, who's been sneaking behind the couple, steals the Captain's handkerchief. But Paddy grasps his hand from the rear.*)

PADDY O'CHRANE: Ah, wretched man! But I've got you. Police! Police! Arrest that rogue!

(*But Bob squirms loose and runs away.*)

PADDY O'CHRANE: To the Devil–he's escaped! (*to Mistress Gruff*) My love, the filthy little thief stole my beautiful silk handkerchief. I'd bought it in Field Lane.

MISTRESS GRUFF: Then God is punishing you, Captain O'Chrane, for all the handkerchiefs sold in Field Lane are stolen. Ah! I'm suffocating here, I'm suffocating!

PADDY O'CHRANE: Courage, Mistress Gruff! We're almost there.

(*They enter the Queen's Theater. A small distance away, Bob Lantern unfolds the stolen handkerchief, looks at it and, after having carefully inspected it, wipes himself gravely with it.*)

MR. SNAIL (*arriving*): I didn't see you. Good evening, Master Bob Lantern.
BOB LANTERN: Ah, it's you, Mr. Snail? Good evening.
MR. SNAIL: A pretty handkerchief, my dear colleague, a very pretty handkerchief.

(*Snail turns around and notices a Policeman who's watching them suspiciously. Snail meows and scurries away. Bob Lantern immediately hides the handkerchief, without turning towards the Policeman.*)

BOB LANTERN: Snail's meowed. I get it. The Police.
POLICEMAN (*to Bob*): I saw you.
BOB LANTERN: Very pleased to meet you, Mr. Handcuffs. I hope that Mrs. Handcuffs is in good health too. I'll have a little present for you next week, but in the meantime.... (*he discreetly slips him a coin*) Really nice to see you–and all my respects to your lovely wife.

(*Bob Lantern exits left; Snail returns and follows him. Donnor, an old beggar dressed as an Irishman, steps out of the crowd and stops a Passerby.*)

DONNOR: Sir. Milord.
PASSERBY: What do you want? I'm in a hurry.
DONNOR: Please, Good Sir, have pity on me! Look upon my misery. Doesn't it touch your soul?
PASSERBY: Misery, misery. That's the only folks like you seem to know. Why don't you see your parish?
DONNOR: I would, sir, but I'm Irish.
PASSERBY: A Catholic? Then what do you want from me? You're not my concern.

(*The Passerby leaves. Donnor goes to lean in a corner. Snail returns to the front of the stage and unfolds the same handkerchief, which he has obviously stolen from Bob Lantern. After having examined it, he wipes himself with it. The Policeman quietly comes up behind Snail.*)

POLICEMAN: I saw you.
MR. SNAIL (*aside*): Caught. (*aloud*) Ah, Mr. Handcuffs. (*bows and puts his hand in his pocket*) How is your lovely wife? My word, all things considered– (*throwing him the handkerchief*) Good-bye, Mr. Handcuffs.

(Snail escapes by the back.)

POLICEMAN (*examining the kerchief*): A fine handkerchief.

(*He puts it in his pocket and leaves. Paddy O'Chrane comes out of the theater, then stops suddenly.*)

PADDY O'CHRANE: Where will I find oranges? Mistress Gruff, my love, may the Devil take you and your fancies!

(*Suddenly, a new arrival, Doctor Edmund Moore, steps out of the crowd, walks behind Paddy and places his hands on the Captain's shoulders*).

MOORE: I forbid you to turn and look at me.
PADDY O'CHRANE: Give me the *name*.
MOORE: *Gentlemen of the night.*
PADDY O'CHRANE: I am still.
MOORE: Do you know Lady Brompton?
PADDY O'CHRANE: Yes. She's the mistress of the Russian Ambassador, Prince Tolstoy.
MOORE: Excellent. If she comes to the theater tonight, find a way to approach her–use any kind of excuse–between the third and fourth acts. See how she is adorned–then, go tell a man

who will be waiting for you in the lobby. You will do what he orders you.

PADDY O'CHRANE: Yes, sir. Is that all?

MOORE: No. You'll need a helper.

PADDY O'CHRANE: I'll find one.

MOORE: He must be a skilful man.

PADDY O'CHRANE: An Eel. Don't be concerned, sir. But what will I do with him?

MOORE: The man in the lobby will give you your instructions. Go find your helper now. Have him wait at the door of the theater. But first, give me time to get away. Don't turn around. Don't look at me.

(*Moore takes his hands off Paddy's shoulders and heads toward the tavern, which he enters.*)

PADDY O'CHRANE (*aside*): The Devil if I wouldn't give a shilling or two to see this rogue's face. Too many secrets. Ah! If I didn't know that our dear masters were powerful enough to see me hanged, I'd find a way to get to the bottom of it all. (*aloud*) Sir, sir, are you gone? (*looking around him*) Nobody. Now, it's a question of following orders. Find a skilful man! The Devil if that's hard to find at this hour in this neighborhood–but one who's reliable, that's another thing. There's my old friend Bob Lantern, who would steal the tongue of a gossipy woman before she has time to say "Good Lord." That is, on my faith, the pure truth. But to ask him to return that tongue, or whatever else he's stolen, could be like asking for my handkerchief back...

(*At this moment, Paddy sees the Policeman wiping his face with his handkerchief.*)

PADDY O'CHRANE: Ha-ha! I now know where my handkerchief has gone. It's in the hands of the law. As for Little Snail, he's surely the nastiest ne'er-do-well that I know–but he's still a bit young. Bah! Let's go for Snail. But what will Mistress Gruff say when she doesn't see me return with her oranges? I can imagine the frightful rage of that sweet dove.

(*Paddy leaves, going to look for Snail. From his corner, Donnor watches him go.*)

DONNOR: I didn't dare ask that man. Come on, come on. Courage. I must make another attempt, but this will be the last.

(*Donnor goes after Paddy and leaves. Moore comes out of the tavern. Fanny enters and positions herself behind him, just as he had done with Paddy earlier.*)

MOORE: That idiot is gone, so I can leave too. I bet he didn't understand the reasons for the order which I gave him, but then, neither do I.

(*Fanny places her hands on Sir Edmund's shoulders.*)

FANNY (*mysteriously*): Doctor Moore?
MOORE: Who are you?
FANNY: I forbid you to turn and look at me.
MOORE: Oh, come on! Well, fine! Me, too–but–
FANNY: Do you understand? *Lady of the night–*
MOORE: Yes, yes! But, a beautiful lady, were she of the night, would not be giving orders to a *gentleman of the night–*
FANNY (*showing him a seal*): Do you recognize this?
MOORE: Ah! His Lordship's seal–that's different, then.
FANNY: That is adequate proof for you, right?
MOORE: Perfectly so. What is your wish?
FANNY: The Council needs a young girl, beautiful, unfortunate, obedient.
MOORE: Beautiful–that can be found. Poor–that's not rare. Obedient–it's more difficult.

FANNY: I didn't say poor, Sir Edmund, I said unfortunate. One can be proud and lacking in docility in one's poverty; but misfortune brings obedience.

MOORE: I will search, Milady.

FANNY: I've already found her for you.

MOORE: Ah?

FANNY: In that tavern.

MOORE: King George's Tavern?

FANNY: Yes. The girl we need is there.

MOORE: What's her name?

FANNY: Suzannah. She is a servant.

MOORE: Since you've already found the quarry, Milady–in what other ways could I be of service to the Council?

FANNY: The girl must be ours tonight. You're a clever man, Sir Edmund, very clever. Win Suzannah over to us this very night. That's what the Council wants of you.

MOORE: The means?

FANNY: I told you–she's unfortunate. I will add that she's got heart. For a clever man, isn't that enough?

MOORE: That's more than enough.

FANNY: To work then!

MOORE: I am but a slave of the Council of the Night. Milady has nothing more to order me?

FANNY: Don't turn around until I've reached my carriage.

(*Fanny leaves.*)

MOORE (*aside*): When will I be Master so that I, alone, know what all the others are doing?

(*Donnor returns and approaches Moore.*)

DONNOR: Charity, if you please?

MOORE (*rebuffing him*): I already have my poor.

(*Moore leaves. Percival enters. Donnor approaches him.*)

DONNOR: Your Honor! Your Honor!
PERCIVAL: What do you want?
DONNOR: Oh! I'm hungry!
PERCIVAL: Is that really true?
DONNOR: Oh, sir!
PERCIVAL: Then you are an honest man!
DONNOR: Why's that?
PERCIVAL: Because, in London, where every vice becomes a profession, one must be an honest man to be dying of hunger.
DONNOR: Well, in that case I must be honest–for I am dying of hunger.
PERCIVAL: It's hurts me to hear it. Let's go in.

(*They go into the tavern.*)

PERCIVAL (*to Gruff*): Serve this man something to eat.
MR. GRUFF: Right away, Your Honor.
PERCIVAL: And make it that we're alone and undisturbed, if that's possible.
MR. GRUFF: Of course, Milord.

(*Gruff serves them, then moves to the farthest recesses of the tavern.*)

PERCIVAL (*to Donnor*): Let's sit over there. Eat a little, first of all. What misery! How can such distress exists in our city? Here, my good man, drink. How do you feel?
DONNOR: Much better–thank you, Milord!
PERCIVAL: Now, tell me your name.
DONNOR: I'm Irish; my name's Donnor d'Arleigh. My story is not unusual, Milord. You see, we Irish have a passion to come to London and then, London kills us.
PERCIVAL: But who forced you to come here?
DONNOR: Alas, Milord, I no longer have anyone to love in Ireland, but I have two daughters in London. One who must be big and strong by now; the other, still quite young. My beautiful Suzannah and my poor little Clary. Oh! You don't

know what misery exists among us, Milord! One day, long ago, my Suzannah took her little sister by the hand and kneeled before me. There was a colony of Irish who were about to leave for London. Suzannah demanded my blessing and embraced me, weeping. I really wanted her to stay, because she was my consolation and my joy, but there was no bread in our hovel. So she left–on foot–with Clary in her arms. The poor little child.

PERCIVAL: Why didn't you go with them?

DONNOR: My wife–Helen–was sick, so very weak–she already had the fever which ultimately killed her.

PERCIVAL: Please continue, my good man.

DONNOR: At first, I received news from Suzannah. She had quickly learned to write to console us–to speak of Clary, whom she was protecting like a mother. It seemed that she was earning some money working, because she sent us a half-guinea with each letter. Thanks to her, my poor wife died on a wool mattress. But, after a year, misfortune must have fallen on my daughter, because the letters stopped. After my wife's death, despair seized me. The sight of the deserted cottage broke my heart. I fled–where? I don't know. I think I was mad. Perhaps Suzannah still wrote, but I never saw her letters.

PERCIVAL: Poor man.

DONNOR: I regret that time. It was like a long sleep. I no longer remembered who I was. But finally, I woke up and regained my senses. Then, I felt a desire to go to London, where I knew my children were. London is quite far, Milord, and I had nothing to pay for the trip. O, how I suffered. What cruel nights and long days! Many times, I thought I would die before reaching the end of my journey. But God doesn't completely abandon the wretched, since finally I made it here. And thanks to your kindness, I have now enough strength to wait for Him to reunite me with my children.

PERCIVAL: Do you know where to find them?

DONNOR: If I knew, would I be here?

PERCIVAL: Indeed. Well, here's my card. Come and see me. Search for your daughters but know that, in the meanwhile, you will lack for nothing at my home.
DONNOR: Oh! Thank you, Milord! Oh, good and kind sir! Oh, brave heart who took pity on me! May the Virgin and my patron saint protect you and watch over you–and over my daughters.

(*Outside, the theater is letting out; people are leaving. Some enter the tavern. Suzannah comes out to help Mr. Gruff serve the customers. Outside, Mistress Gruff seems in a very bad mood.*)

MISTRESS GRUFF (*calling*): Captain O'Chrane! Captain O'Chrane! (*aside*) He's not here! To leave a woman alone at a performance, exposed to the unwanted attentions of the first comer–and under the pretext of going to find oranges! It's shocking!

CUSTOMER (*to Gruff*): Hey! You didn't give me back my full change.
MR. GRUFF: Yes, I did.
CUSTOMER: No, you didn't!

(*A quarrel begins. Tumult ensues just as Mistress Gruff enters the tavern.*)

MISTRESS GRUFF (*screaming*): What's going on in here?
MR. GRUFF (*aside*): My wife! (*to her*) Nothing, my dove. Nothing at all. A trifle mistake.
MISTRESS GRUFF: Whose mistake?
MR. GRUFF (*timidly*): Er, Suzannah's. I think.
MISTRESS GRUFF (*shouting*): Suzannah! Always, Suzannah!
SUZANNAH (*to Gruff, reproachfully*): Oh, sir!
MISTRESS GRUFF (*to Suzannah*): Well, girl, will you say something? Are you at least going to apologize? (*Suzannah is*

quiet) (*raising her hand*) I don't know what's stopping me from... (*Suzannah assumes a pose of sad resignation.*)

MR. GRUFF: Dorothy–calm down! There's company.

MISTRESS GRUFF: Me, calm down? So now I should be insulted by a girl who–Ah! You wretched girl! Go away! Leave here at once!

(*Mistress Gruff hits Suzannah, who recoils with a look of anger, quickly repressed. After a moment's hesitation, Suzannah slowly leaves, her head lowered, without saying anything.*

(*As some of the customers step back to let her through, Moore appears at the back of the stage and intercepts the servant girl.*)

MOORE: Are you Suzannah?

SUZANNAH (*raising her head and looking at Moore*): What do you want?

MOORE: I wish you well. Trust me–where are you going?

SUZANNAH: Where am I going?

MOORE: Yes.

SUZANNAH: I'm going to the Thames!

MOORE: To the Thames? Why, my child, why?

SUZANNAH: Because I have neither hope for the future, nor refuge for the present.

MOORE: I will give you refuge, Suzannah–and I will bring back hope.

SUZANNAH: Often in the past, men have talked to me like this. They want to buy me. You're like them, no doubt! But I'm not for sale.

MOORE: May God be my witness, my child, I don't–

SUZANNAH: Don't call me "your child." I don't want to be reminded of my father.

MOORE: Ah! You have a father?

31

SUZANNAH: A poor man who's suffered much. I have a sister, too. A poor child who will be left alone on Earth. Let's not speak of them. That rips my heart apart.

MOORE: And you are thinking of abandoning them? In that case, you don't love them.

SUZANNAH: My God! My God!–but what can I do for them now? My sister has been placed with a merchant's wife in the City. When she sees her without any family in the world, she will come to love her, my poor little Clary. Alive, I can't do anything for her–and but dying, I secure her fate. Leave me alone, I go to drown myself.

MOORE: What if you could do something for your father–and for your sister?

SUZANNAH: Oh! My father! My sister!

MOORE: If they were to be redeemed–given money?

SUZANNAH: My God! My God!

MOORE: Well?

SUZANNAH: No! Too many have already spoken to me like this. No! I can't! I don't want to. Leave me alone! Ah! Leave me alone, I tell you!

MOORE: You are free to go, Suzannah!

(*Moore steps back.*)

SUZANNAH (*aside*): I must write a final goodbye to my father–and to Clary–and to him

(*She sits down at a table and begins to write a note.*)

SUZANNAH: They'll find this on my heart.

(*Suzannah exits the tavern, but Moore reappears from behind her and snatches the note.*)

SUZANNAH: Why did you do that for?

MOORE (*reading*): You lied to me. Your father and your sister don't occupy your thoughts alone. You love–

SUZANNAH: Well! yes! I love–I love a man whose name I don't even know–but he's very high–and me, very low–so low that, in my obscurity, he's never noticed me! So low that, powerless as I am to reveal myself to him, I best throw myself from London Bridge–and by dying young, maybe he'll learn my name!

(*At this moment, an elegant carriage stops on the square. A liveried servant opens the door to a young man who has just come out of the theater.*)

SUZANNAH (*uttering a scream*): Ah! It's him!
MOORE: Him? That's the man you love?
SUZANNAH: Yes.
MOORE: You were right, girl. There is much distance between you and this man!
SUZANNAH: An abyss! Goodbye.
MOORE: Wait–what if I filled that abyss?
SUZANNAH: That's impossible!
MOORE: Not to me.
SUZANNAH: Truly?
MOORE: I can do it.
SUZANNAH: What will you want from me?
MOORE: Your obedience.
SUZANNAH: My obedience?
MOORE: Yes–listen carefully. I want you not for me, who is weak, but for a brotherhood that is strong and terrible. I know you better than you know yourself–and I know what you can do. Loyalty, obedience, discretion–those will be your duties! Take this (*giving her a card*)–take it. Tomorrow, at noon, rap on the door at this address. It will open. You will enter and take possession of it–for this house will be yours.
SUZANNAH: And I will again see my father and my sister–and they will be rich, happy?
MOORE: You will see them–and they will be rich, happy.
SUZANNAH: And him? What about him?

MOORE: Tomorrow, you will see him at your knees. Goodbye, Suzannah, goodbye!

(*Moore walks away as the carriage passes by Suzannah who remains still while more spectators come out of the theater.*)

Scene II

(*The house of the Princess de Longueville. A crafty older woman, a.k.a. La Maudlin, bizarrely wrapped in a silk garment with a garish flower pattern, is taking tea in the corner by the fire.*)

LA MAUDLIN (*shivering*): How cold it is in England! How sad and unpleasant to watch is this oil fire! If I were the Queen, I'd sell my three kingdoms to purchase a mansion in Paris.

(*Jane enters.*)

LA MAUDLIN: Is the princess dressed?
JANE: Yes, Madame, here she is.
LA MAUDLIN: Fine. Leave us then.

(*As Jane leaves, Suzannah enters; she is richly dressed. La Maudlin observes her through a lorgnette.*)

LA MAUDLIN: Beautiful! Very beautiful! My angel, you know you are at home here.
SUZANNAH (*coldly*): Yes, I know.
LA MAUDLIN (*somewhat surprised*): Right. And how do you like your new home?
SUZANNAH (*glancing around the room calmly*): It's fine.

LA MAUDLIN: Marvelous! You're playing your part ravishingly, my dear child–I have little to teach you. Do you know your new name?

SUZANNAH: No.

LA MAUDLIN: You'll be my niece. And I, I'm the Dowager Duchess of Gesires. I left France because I couldn't stand the Bourgeois Court any longer. Your husband was Prince Philippe de Longueville, my unfortunate nephew, who died in the flower of youth–and you wept over him for a year. Can you remember all this?

SUZANNAH: Yes.

LA MAUDLIN: What beautiful eyes you have, Madame Suzanne de Longueville!

(Suzannah rises. La Maudlin takes her hand with a caressing gesture.)

LA MAUDLIN: Since you're my niece and I'm your aunt, we must love each other. The Laws of Nature are rather strict about such things. Will you love me, Suzannah?

SUZANNAH (*pulling her hand away*): I don't know.

LA MAUDLIN: I'm so sweet and so nice! And as for me, I will love you very much.

SUZANNAH (*sighing*): No one has ever loved me.

LA MAUDLIN (*low*): Not even the one who smiles at the bottom of every young girl's heart?

SUZANNAH (*sadly*): No.

LA MAUDLIN (*astonished*): But you're so beautiful. (*changing tone*) But let's return to business–

SUZANNAH (*interrupting her*): So be it! I belong to you and I will obey. But I was told that you'd return my father to me– and my sister–where are they? You promised to make them rich, happy. My obedience is at that price–don't you forget it.

LA MAUDLIN: Patience! Patience, my sweet! (*aside*) A pox on that girl! (*aloud*) What you were promised will be done. The men you now serve hold all of London in their hands. If you obey them faithfully, you will be happy.

(*La Maudlin takes a newspaper and reads it with the help of her lorgnette.*)

SUZANNAH (*wistfully*): Happy!

LA MAUDLIN (*emphatic*): They can do everything! Your father's in Ireland; it will take time to fetch him. As for your sister, that's another matter–she's going to be here soon.

SUZANNAH: And–him?

LA MAUDLIN: Ah! Yes! Him! (*rises*) You see plainly that he exists. Ah, indeed, we all love him. Don't blush! I know you do. I was 18 once, just like you, my niece. I recall loving a young lad, whom I thought was as handsome as Apollo. But after a short time–three weeks or a month–when I no longer loved him–I noticed that he had big, insipid eyes, red hair and was shaped like a drum major–

SUZANNAH (*interrupting haughtily*): Don't jest, Madame.

LA MAUDLIN (*backtracking*): I didn't mean to offend you, my sweet! (*aside*) A pox on that girl! (*aloud*) I'm confident of your taste–he must indeed be a perfect gentleman. What's his name?

SUZANNAH: Edward.

LA MAUDLIN: Edward who?

SUZANNAH: I love him by that name and I don't know the other.

LA MAUDLIN: Have you spoken to him?

SUZANNAH: Never–

LA MAUDLIN (*smiling*): Young girls! Young girls!

(*There's a rapping on the door.*)

LA MAUDLIN: Who's there?

(*Jane enters.*)

JANE: A pretty child, escorted by an old woman.

SUZANNAH: It's my sister–

LA MAUDLIN (*to Jane*): Show them in–quick, quick–
JANE: Here she is–

(*Clary enters, followed by Mother Jacobs; Jane leaves.*)

CLARY: Sis! Sis!
SUZANNAH: My Clary, my beloved child (*to La Maudlin*) Thank you, Madame, thank you (*to Mother Jacobs*) Sit down, Mother Jacobs.
CLARY: Well, naughty sister, you said to me only yesterday that we would be a long while without seeing each other again. That was to torture me, right? You wanted to surprise me?
SUZANNAH: No–I didn't want to deceive you, my Clary. I would never do so. If I don't tell you the truth, the whole truth–it's that... (*looking at La Maudlin who casts a meaningful glance at her*) –it's because it's impossible.
CLARY (*looking around*): How beautiful you are! And how nice it is here! What a difference from that villainous tavern where you were so badly treated! Is this all yours?
LA MAUDLIN: Yes, all this belongs to Mademoiselle de–
SUZANNAH (*to La Maudlin*) Oh! Do respect this child–don't lie to her!
CLARY (*leading her sister aside*): Tell me, my good sister, does that woman over there treat you the same way Mistress Gruff did?
SUZANNAH: No, my Clary, no. No one here is mistreating me. And if someone dared, there would still remains to me the supreme remedy that I was about to use yesterday.
CLARY: What remedy would that be, sis?
SUZANNAH (*hugging her*): Let's not think any more about that. Let's talk about you instead–let's talk of our poor father.
CLARY: Oh, yes, let's.
SUZANNAH: He's going to come–
CLARY: Here?
SUZANNAH: Yes–here.
CLARY: Today? Right away?

SUZANNAH: Ah! Soon enough–crazy girl! There has to be time for a voyage. Ireland is really far away–and even further is our poor village of Arleigh.

CLARY: Which delays me from embracing him! That is, if I recognize him. Is he really handsome, tell me, sis?

SUZANNAH: He's really nice-looking! But you know what else, Clary? You're going to go into a boarding school.

CLARY: What! We're going to separated again?

SUZANNAH: It's necessary, my Clary. Don't look so sad. Won't you be better off being educated? Won't you be happy to be able to write to our father if he leaves us again?

CLARY: Write to him! To our good father? And to you, too, Suzannah!

SUZANNAH: To me, too. And I will go and see you as often as I can.

CLARY: If you don't come, I'll write to you–all the time.

SUZANNAH: That's it. (*aside*) Excellent little sister.

(*There is a knock on the door.*)

LA MAUDLIN (*to Suzannah*): They're knocking downstairs. Kiss your sister.

SUZANNAH: Goodbye, sis. Goodbye, Mother Jacobs!

(*Jane enters.*)

JANE (*announcing*): Mr. Edward!

SUZANNAH: Heavens!

(*Mother Jacobs leads Clary away; they go out just as the Marquis de Rio Santo enters, and look at him with curiosity. Suzannah is visibly shy, not daring to look in the newcomer's eyes.*)

RIO SANTO: Who is that child?

LA MAUDLIN: Her little sister.

RIO SANTO: Ah. Leave us.

(La Maudlin leaves. Suzannah keeps her head lowered. There is a moment of silence. Then, Rio Santo kneels before Suzannah, kisses her hand and leads her to a seat. He deposits his hat on a chair at the back, then returns, leaning over the back of Suzannah's chair.)

RIO SANTO: You are beautiful, Mademoiselle! Quite beautiful.

(Suzannah gently raises her head and rests her gaze on Rio Santo. After a new silence, he continues.)

RIO SANTO: They tell me that you're in love with me. Answer me. Is it true?

SUZANNAH: Yes, I do love you!

RIO SANTO *(aside)*: That is strange.

SUZANNAH: In your turn, will you look at me?

RIO SANTO: I am looking at you, Mademoiselle; I admire you. But still, this is strange. Where have I seen you before?

SUZANNAH: Do my feelings cause you regrets?

RIO SANTO: I don't want to fall in love, Madame–and despite myself–perhaps–

SUZANNAH *(joining her hands)*: Listen! One month! One week! One day. Let God give me a day of your thoughts and I will bless him until my last hour.

RIO SANTO: Do you know what I can give of my heart to a woman? Do you know that my nights and my days belong to a mysterious project on which I lavish all my strength and my intelligence, all the passions of my soul, all the power of my will? What will remain for you?

SUZANNAH: A smile today. Tomorrow, perhaps, a memory.

RIO SANTO: You are beautiful. And your heart is as beautiful as your face!

SUZANNAH: My heart! I felt it the day when I saw you for the first time. My heart–it's yours! There's nothing in my heart but your image and the echo of your voice, Milord.

RIO SANTO: Oh! I see it plainly! You want to be loved. (*kisses her hand*) Your name?

SUZANNAH: Suzannah.

RIO SANTO: I will never forget it. But where did you see me?

SUZANNAH: In the home of a rich and celebrated man whose servant I was. He lived in Goodman's Fields–and his name was Ishmael Spencer.

RIO SANTO (*recoiling*): Ishmael Spencer!

SUZANNAH: Ishmael the forger, Milord, who was executed at Newgate.

RIO SANTO: Ishmael. He had a daughter called the Siren...

SUZANNAH: I was she, Milord. Ishmael made me pass for his daughter.

RIO SANTO: You! But they say that she was involved in an infamous traffic...

SUZANNAH: Milord, I am but a poor girl and you are much above me. But I can look at you without blushing.

RIO SANTO: I believe you! How not to believe you? I must know who you really are. So many women have helped me plait this long garland that is my life! So many women–all beautiful and worthy of being adored! But you are the first before whom my heart is dismayed. I don't know what I'm feeling, but I don't want to blindly cross the threshold of an unknown temple yet. Kings don't drink any wine that hasn't been tasted. Suzannah–I want to see your whole soul.

SUZANNAH: And you will be my judge

RIO SANTO: I will be our conscience.

(*They sit down.*)

SUZANNAH: It's been a long time since I've looked back upon my past. When I light my memory, I find so many tears and so little joy. But I am yours, Milord, in the past as well as in the present. (*concentrates her thoughts*) Arriving from Ireland, poor, abandoned, my eyes filled with tears, with my Clary still a child, chance opened the door of Ishmael's house.

RIO SANTO: An angel into this Hell!

SUZANNAH: I was his servant; yet Ishmael made me learn music and dance with tutors who were instructed to not answer my questions. I also learned languages. We took long trips abroad and I saw nothing except men who talked of millions. During these trips, Ishmael introduced me as his daughter. I couldn't stop him because he was sending money to my poor parents–and he took care of my sister. But I never called him father.

RIO SANTO: And then–?

SUZANNAH: When I turned sixteen, Ishmael said to me: "Suky, now you're grown up. You're a woman. Since you've been here, you and your family have cost me a lot of money. Now you must pay me back." I replied, "I have nothing." "You have a fortune, Suzannah," he continued, "a fortune in your big eyes which already know how to burn or languish. A fortune in your supple and charming figure. A fortune in your blonde hair which falls on your pale cheeks in long rings of gold." I didn't understand.

RIO SANTO: Oh! The wretch!

SUZANNAH: He's dead now. Perhaps you know, Milord, that Ishmael owned a gaming salon in Sloane Square. All the Lords of London met there to gamble. One night, Ishmael put my harp on my shoulders and put me in a carriage. We went to his house in Sloane Square. A stage had been erected in the main salon. I sat on a throne, my golden harp at my feet. Around the stage hung a thick gauze. The people only saw me though a cloud.

RIO SANTO: And you wore rich clothes, Suzannah?

SUZANNAH (*lowering her head*): Have pity on me, Milord.

RIO SANTO: Pity–why?

SUZANNAH: Because the words stop in my breast. I want to tell you everything but I can't.

RIO SANTO: Continue–continue, Suzannah!

SUZANNAH: Ishmael ordered me to sing–and so, I sang!

RIO SANTO: Ah!

SUZANNAH: I sang. The salon exploded in bravos! I couldn't find any joy in it. They were applauding a lifeless body! Worshipping a statue!

RIO SANTO: And you returned the next day?

SUZANNAH: Yes, milord. I sat at the same place. Once more, Ishmael told me to sing–but this time, my fingers trembled on the cords of the harp. My voice died out in my breast, choked by my tears.

RIO SANTO: Your tears?

SUZANNAH: I felt as if I were dying.

RIO SANTO: What happened next?

SUZANNAH (*softly*): Then I saw a man–for a moment–through the window. He looked proud, strong and decent, Milord–and suddenly a new anguish seized my poor heart! I was a woman–a blindfold fell from my eyes. Henceforth, I had a shield against Ishmael's designs. The love I felt for that man became my guardian; he saved me from evil–unknown to him. It's God who showed him to me, for his very sight illuminated my night–it was he who taught me modesty.

RIO SANTO: And this man–?

SUZANNAH: Yes, it was you, Milord.

RIO SANTO (*kissing her hand with passion*): Suzannah! Continue–

SUZANNAH: I never returned to the house in Sloane Square. Never!

RIO SANTO: But Spencer's died within the year. What became of you after that?

SUZANNAH: I suffered.

RIO SANTO: And no one came to your aid?

SUZANNAH: One time, one single time, I was able to say thank you from the depths of my heart. It was a beautiful young girl in a rich neighborhood, not far from Regent's Park. I was thinking of my father and my sister, both without resources. I was in so much pain that I had no more tears. The girl got down from her carriage and came to me. I don't know her name, but I pray to God for her every night. She gave me a purse; she did better than that, she kissed my face, me, the poor girl, and gave me her address, telling me to go to see her.

RIO SANTO: Well–what did you do with it?

SUZANNAH: I lost it one day when I saw you ride by in a carriage.

RIO SANTO: Poor Suzannah!

SUZANNAH: What more shall I tell you? I fell from misery to misery, until I ended up at King George's Tavern.

RIO SANTO: I know the place.

SUZANNAH: You do? Do you also know that strange things occur there, and–

RIO SANTO: I don't wish to hear of them now, Suzannah. You have suffered. The pure gold of your heart has not been tarnished despite being exposed to so much villainy. That's all I wanted to know. This interview, which I dreaded, has reopened my heart to hope, perhaps to love. Yes, I will love you, Suzannah. My soul was dead, but it's now reborn. You will be my support, my faith, my courage.

(*La Maudlin comes in.*)

RIO SANTO: What do you want?

LA MAUDLIN: Doctor Moore is waiting for the Mademoiselle.

RIO SANTO: Moore!

(*Rio Santo turns and notices Moore, who has just entered the room and who bows to him gravely.*)

SUZANNAH (*to La Maudlin*): The time has come, isn't it? What does he want from me? Speak, I'm ready, even if it were a matter of life or death!

LA MAUDLIN (*laughing*): A matter of life or death. Come, come! Get dressed!

SUZANNAH: Where's he taking me?

LA MAUDLIN: To a ball, where else? Come!

43

(*La Maudlin drags Suzannah away. Moore is about to leave.*)

RIO SANTO (*to Moore*): Doctor, I forbid you. It's no longer necessary that this girl serve our projects.
MOORE: But necessity requires–
RIO SANTO: I said, I forbid you. Don't forget it who I am, sir.

(*Rio Santo leaves.*)

MOORE (*alone*): You forbid me! You forbid me! Ah! Will this man always be our master?

CURTAIN

Act II

Scene III

(A hall at Saint James' Palace, during a great party. The ordinary people, curious to see the guests, enter by a side door at the back and remain on stage. The Lords and Ladies enter on the left, announced by an Usher, then cross the stage and exit right.)

USHER: Their lordships, Lord and Lady Stuart of Dundee! His Grace the Duke of Northumberland! The very noble Marquis of Exeter. Her Ladyship the Countess of Derby! The Lord Archbishop of Canterbury.

(The characters cross the stage as they are announced.)

LADY MORDAUNT: His Grace, the Lord Archbishop, is more often seen at parties than at his office.
MRS. BLOOMBERRY: Since when does a Countess of Derby have precedence over the Primate of England, Scotland and Ireland? Truly, it's anarchy.
LADY STANLEY: My dear ladies, have you been forgotten, like me?
LADY MORDAUNT: Now that mere bourgeois are admitted to Royal parties, true Ladies must give way.
MRS. BLOOMBERRY: Are you referring to me, Lady Mordaunt?
LADY MORDAUNT: No, Madame, since you clearly are not invited!
LADY STANLEY: Dear ladies! Please! Not in Saint James' Palace. But the fact is that these parties are now horribly attended. One sees adventurers there! Even Frenchmen!
ALL (*shocked*): Oh!

(They salute Gerard who passes by. Meanwhile, Percival enters through the small door at the back and goes to present his card to the Usher.)

PERCIVAL: Here's my card, sir.
USHER (*after having examined it*): You may enter.

(Percival then notices Gerard who is leaning against a column.):

PERCIVAL: Gerard!
GERARD: Percival!
PERCIVAL: By what stroke of luck–luck for me–do I find you here at Saint James' Palace?
GERARD: By the luck that leads tourists where there is something unfamiliar and interesting to observe. I learned that, today, there was to be a Royal reception at Saint James' and–my word!–I didn't want to miss such a fine opportunity. The rest of us, French, have so perfectly broken with ceremonial monarchic traditions that it's necessary cross the Channel and come to London to rediscover the pomps of Royalty.
PERCIVAL: As a Frenchman–and an artist–you may be disappointed. Our ceremonies may not please you. We're not like you, we preserve our customs and the ritual of kissing the King's hand at functions such as these has not changed for the last two centuries. It's still reserved for the highest dignitaries only–of which this man here is a fair example... (*points out a Lord passing by who is overdressed in a caricatural fashion*) For the Ladies, there are always the opportunity to display their interminable dresses, which often require the help of a page hired at a half-guinea for the evening.
GERARD (*looking through his lorgnette*): Why that's wonderful!
PERCIVAL: As for the staff, it's pure farce. His Majesty does like his faithful subjects: he hires by the hour the actors required to mount this old comedy. Did you see the Halberdiers and the mace-bearers beneath the peristyle?

GERARD: They make a handsome chorus.

PERCIVAL: They'll come in to form a double line after the carriages have arrived. Some of their costumes date back to King James II.

GERARD: That's what I like: color! My word, I doubly congratulate myself for having come here, and having met you, Percival. But I thought you were still traveling?

PERCIVAL: I just got back the day before yesterday. And what about you, my dear Gerard? Have you been in London long? Do you like it? Have you frequented our fashionable salons?

GERARD: Yes, indeed! Thanks to some good friends, the very best. For example, yesterday, I was invited at Lord Trevor's ball.

PERCIVAL (*shaken*): Lord Trevor!

GERARD: What's the matter with you?

PERCIVAL (*grasping his arm*): Then, you don't know?

GERARD: Know what?

PERCIVAL: Nothing. Continue, my friend. You went to Lord Trevor's ball. His daughter was present, no doubt?

GERARD: Certainly! Why wouldn't Miss Trevor be present at a ball given by her father? An engagement ball, especially!

PERCIVAL: Did you say, engagement?

GERARD: Yes! Where've you been, Percival? Switzerland? What do they talk about there? In London, all the gossip has been about the impending marriage of the beautiful, wealthy Mary Trevor to the Marquis de Rio Santo!

PERCIVAL (*aside*): A marriage! Ah! Mary! Mary! (*to Gerard*) Pardon me, my friend, I must seem strange to you? Soon, you'll understand. But first, tell me—who is this Marquis de Rio Santo?

GERARD: Rio Santo! You ask me who Rio Santo is—why Rio Santo is—Rio Santo, by Jove! That's all there is to say! That's not enough for you?

PERCIVAL: No!

GERARD: Well! He's a Marquis! But as one seldom sees—a handsome, young, rich, elegant Marquis.

PERCIVAL (*bitter*): An Adonis.

GERARD: No, not quite–but seriously, a remarkable man. A man who, by his splendor, even in this splendid city, with his army of servants, hounds and devoted coterie of a dozen of the most beautiful ladies in town, consumed with love for him, has become the subject of all the conversations in London. In the parks, he is the object of all the glances. If he enters a room, his name raises a murmur in the crowd. Finally, he is without peers in the realm of fashion...

(*The Halberdiers enter.*)

GERARD: Why here are the Halberdiers. The show's started! They are fine–very fine–My word–pure Louis XIV!

PERCIVAL (*aside*): Rio Santo! There's the one she prefers to me. And yet–no, it's impossible! Mary couldn't perjure herself that way!

(*The Halberdiers take places at the doors.*)

USHER (*announcing*): His Lordship, Count Trevor, Peer of England, Lady Campbell and the honorable Miss Mary Trevor.

PERCIVAL (*aside*): It's she! Oh, I knew I would see her here!

(*Lord Trevor enters with Lady Campbell and Mary. He is immediately mobbed by the other Ladies.*)

LORD TREVOR: Excuse me, ladies, I have a word to say to the Chief Usher.

(*Lord Trevor moves back to talk to the Usher.*)

PERCIVAL (*to Gerard*): Did you hear? Lord Trevor and his daughter. I'm going to–

GERARD (*holding him back*): Wait– My God! How pale she is!

LADY CAMPBELL (*to Mary*): Come, my niece, get hold of yourself–don't tremble, child, perhaps this presentation to the King terrifies you. Don't worry. The King loves our family. He desires to learn from your father's very mouth the name of your lucky fiancé. The Marquis de Rio Santo! (*Mary nods*) Aren't you marrying him of your own free will? Don't you love him? Why, then, this apprehensive look? No childishness, Mary, I entreat you. (*going close to her*) Perhaps, you're still thinking of Frank Percival? But you know quite well he's forgotten you. For the last year that he's traveled on the continent–not one word–not one letter!

(*Gerard, holding Percival by the hand, approaches the two women.*)

GERARD: Madame!
LADY CAMPBELL (*noticing Percival*): Heavens!
MARY TREVOR (*barely repressing a shock*): Frank!
PERCIVAL: Your Ladyship, I–
LADY CAMPBELL (low, close to him): Not here–not now, I entreat you. People are looking at us.
PERCIVAL: Your Ladyship! I must know–
LADY CAMPBELL: Tomorrow! I will explain it all to you, but tomorrow. The poor child resisted a lot, has suffered enough.
PERCIVAL: Your Ladyship–
LADY CAMPBELL: I entreat you, Mr. Percival, let's wait until tomorrow.
PERCIVAL: Miss Mary, please–

(*Lady Campbell drags Mary off and quickly takes the arm of Lord Trevor who, after having chatted with the Usher, walks towards the door of the Lords without having noticed Percival. The latter attempts to follow but is blocked by the Usher.*)

USHER: No one can pass. Close the doors to the public.

(The doors can be heard closing. Suddenly, Captain O'Chrane appears at one of the doors just before closes.)

HALBERDIER: No one can enter.
PADDY O'CHRANE: Ah! The Devil! I must've made a mistake. Excuse me, my good man.

(He disappears. Percival returns to Gerard's side.)

PERCIVAL: Gerard–now, I can tell you–
GERARD: Oh! You don't have to tell me. I understand everything. We, French, have a knack for that sort of things. You love Miss Trevor. Prior to your absence, she loved you. And I believe she still does.
PERCIVAL(*hopeful*): Do you really?
GERARD: I'd bet a fortune on it! Her emotion when she saw you–her silence–all that tells me that, despite the irresistible prestige of the Marquis de Rio Santo, she hasn't forgotten you.
PERCIVAL: My God! My God! If that's true–if it's possible– I haven't returned too late.
GERARD: Ah! My poor friend, I mustn't hide it from you. You face two formidable adversaries. Rio Santo, first of all. Then, the aunt, Lady Campbell. As for Lord Trevor, we have no need to speak of him. My guess is that he will blindly obey his sister.
PERCIVAL: What to do? I should have suspected Lady Campbell. It was she who advised me to take this trip, at the return of which Mary and I were to be wed. I had Lord Trevor's word –Lady Campbell's word, too.
GERARD: Perhaps she was sincere then. But she hadn't met Rio Santo yet.
PERCIVAL: Yes. I understand. After my departure, Rio Santo cast a spell on Lady Campbell. That's the way of things. The appearance of being the heir to an immense fortune, being surrounded by an innumerable court... I thought I had left all my rivals behind; I could believe the battle was over. But I

wasn't counting on the arrival of a Rio Santo–and Lady Campbell's perfidy.

GERARD: Well, if you are defeated today, don't forget what happens after the marriage is over–

PERCIVAL: What do you mean?

GERARD: What happens is that the humble and the strong live to fight–and conquer–another day. A star may henceforth belong to a single man, but her rays are the property of all.

PERCIVAL: Gerard, don't jest with my heart! I love Mary with deep, ardent, invincible passion–and if it's true, as you have said, that she hasn't forgotten me, then I will conquer–I swear to you–all the obstacles, whatever they may be, in the path to my happiness. And if not–

GERARD: If not?

PERCIVAL: If not, I will die. Gerard, since chance has placed you in this matter–

GERARD: Don't say chance–say friendship.

PERCIVAL: Very well! In the name of friendship, then, stay with me tonight.

GERARD: With all my heart. But what do you plan to do?

PERCIVAL: Wait for Mary, obtain from her one word, a single word that will decide my fate. She's going to cross this hall to enter the Queen's–

GERARD: What, before the whole world–you intend to–?

PERCIVAL: Yes! I require only one word, a single word! Is it too much to exact one word when the life of a man is at stake–perhaps, two men?

GERARD: So it's come to that? Oh! oh! Rest assured, my friend, I won't leave you.

(*They go toward the rear.*)

USHER (*announcing*): Her Ladyship Lady Anna, Baroness Brompton. His Grace, Prince Dimitri Tolstoy, Ambassador from Russia.

(*Lady Brompton enters and crosses the stage; Prince Tolstoy follows, first at some distance, then joins her mid-stage.*)

TOLSTOY (*to Lady Brompton*): Delicious! Adorable! I've never seen you so beautiful. This outfit suits you ravishingly.

LADY BROMPTON: I owe you the most beautiful adornment. These magnificent diamonds–these jewels ought to adorn an Imperial face...

TOLSTOY: Silence! If someone suspected–

LADY BROMPTON: You've braved a great danger to please me, Prince.

TOLSTOY: Please, let's not speak of that.

LADY BROMPTON: But I do intend to thank you–with all my heart. No one here can match the richness of my finery.

TOLSTOY: Aren't you still the most beautiful?

LADY BROMPTON: Please come soon to take your diamonds back. Come by yourself, I'll be more at ease.

TOLSTOY (*with heart*): I will–and I can't wait to tell you–

LADY BROMPTON: Hush, dear heart! We're being observed–

TOLSTOY: Till this evening then.

(*Tolstoy goes into the room where the Lords and Ladies went. A new Halberdier replaces the one who stopped Captain O'Chrane earlier. We recognize him: it's Bob Lantern. Almost immediately, Paddy O'Chrane returns.*)

PADDY O'CHRANE: Let me through!

BOB LANTERN: No one can enter.

PADDY O'CHRANE: Shut up, imbecile! Don't you recognize me?

BOB LANTERN: Oh, right! I get it now–it's clever! Go on, go on!

(*Paddy lets Suzannah in; she is wearing a fancy gown and Mr. Snail, dressed as a page, follows her, holding her train.*)

PADDY O'CHRANE: Here we are then, in the abode of Lords.

MR. SNAIL: Ah! It's nice–very nice here! I wish that my sister could see all this. And my brother-in-law, Mr. Turnbull, too. And my wife, Madge. And all my family. Did you see Bob Lantern? What a funny figure he makes in that costume!

PADDY O'CHRANE (*taking him by the ear*): Do you think we've come to Saint James' only to make fun of Bob? Pay attention, young whippersnapper!

MR. SNAIL: I'm listening, old man, I'm listening

SUZANNAH (*to Paddy*): Where are we and why have you brought me here in these clothes that are too sumptuous for me?

PADDY O'CHRANE: We're at Saint James' Palace, my dear.

SUZANNAH: The Queen's Palace. Why have we come here?

PADDY O'CHRANE: You will see, by Jove. Your role is confined to a small thing. But don't forget your oath: whatever you may see, whatever you may hear–no foolishness! (*to Snail*) Come here, you!

(*Now, Paddy approaches the Halberdier who guards the door leading to the salon where the Lords are.*)

HALBERDIER: No one enters.

PADDY O'CHRANE: My worthy sir, your honorable colleague over there (*pointing to Bob*) begs you to allow this handsome child (*pointing to Snail*) to look through the keyhole to see the Lords and Ladies.

HALBERDIER: Do it fast!

PADDY O'CHRANE (*to Snail*): My son, this excellent gentleman allows you to look.

MR. SNAIL (*at the door*): I'm looking.

PADDY O'CHRANE (*low*): What do you see?

MR. SNAIL: A lot of fat gentlemen and villainous-looking ladies–they have lace and jewels on all seams–

PADDY O'CHRANE: Is that all?

MR. SNAIL: My word–yes. (*leaving the door*)

PADDY O'CHRANE (*pushing him back*): No, that's not all.

MR. SNAIL: Gently, gentle, my dear Captain. How you go on!

PADDY O'CHRANE: Fool! Don't you recognize Lady Brompton whom I asked you to observe the night before last, at the Queen's Theater? Remember, we only left her after becoming convinced that she wasn't wearing the diamonds.

MR. SNAIL: Yes! The diamonds that the Russian Ambassador purchased for the Czar, and that he's had the foolishness of letting his mistress wear. Wait, now I see her. She has them.

PADDY O'CHRANE: What?

MR. SNAIL: The diamonds! Lady Brompton! I recognize her now! Captain, how they shine! They dazzle my eyes.

PADDY O'CHRANE: Now that you've seen them, I'll explain to you what remains to be done.

MR. SNAIL (*rubbing his eyes*): Just like the Sun they are!

(*Paddy pulls Snail aside. The two talk. Suddenly, the Chief Usher shouts:*)

USHER: Open the doors! My Lords and Ladies–the King!

(*A line begins to form; the Lords and Ladies cross the stage, clamber up the stairs and enter the King's room. When Lord Trevor walks by, Lady Campbell on his arm, followed by Mary, Percival approaches her and speaks to her urgently.*)

PERCIVAL: Mary! A word–a single word of hope!

(*But Mary looks at him with fright.*)

SUZANNAH (*recognizing Mary from afar*): It's her. The girl who helped me–as sweet and pretty as the day she saved me from misery.

(*At this moment the door at the right opens.*)

USHER (*announcing*): Don Jose Maria Tellez, Marquis de Rio Santo.

(*General movement of curiosity. Everyone looks at Rio Santo.*)

SUZANNAH (*recognizing Rio Santo*): It's him! My God!
MARY (*to Percival*): Goodbye, Frank, goodbye.

(*She lets her handkerchief fall. Percival picks it up.*)

PERCIVAL (*to Gerard*): She was weeping.
GERARD: She loves you.

(*Rio Santo, at the back of the stage, bows gravely to Lord Trevor, Lady Campbell and Mary, who return his greeting. Meanwhile, other characters have emerged from the Lords' chamber, among them, Prince Tolstoy, then Lady Brompton, whose train is carried by a page. The delay causes Lady Brompton to remain momentarily with her page near the door of the Lords.*)

PADDY O'CHRANE (*to Snail*): She's stopped– Your move!
MR. SNAIL (*approaching the other page, aside*): Heavens! It's Bobby! What luck! (*aloud*) Bobby, my son, here's a crown–go amuse yourself and give me the train of this noble lady. Go, I tell you–if she notices the change of page–that's my concern. I'll say that I'm your brother and I'm replacing you. Go!

(*Lady Brompton's page moves away. Paddy makes him leave by the door guarded by Bob Lantern. Snail takes Lady Brompton's train and walks gravely behind her. At the moment the line is almost over, Rio Santo approaches Percival.*)

PERCIVAL (*aside*): The man who's my rival.

RIO SANTO (*to Percival*): Excuse me, sir. You were near Miss Trevor when she lost her handkerchief...

PERCIVAL: That question is–

RIO SANTO: That question is quite natural. Were you, yes or no, near Miss Trevor when she lost her handkerchief?

PERCIVAL: Once again, sir, what is it to you?

RIO SANTO: It matters greatly, sir, since you picked it up. No one has the right to pick up Miss Trevor's handkerchief and especially to keep it–other than I.

PERCIVAL: Other than you?

RIO SANTO: Yes, other than I, her fiancé.

SUZANNAH (*aside*): My God! Did I really hear that?

RIO SANTO: Consequently, sir, I'm begging you to return this handkerchief to me. After the explanation I've just given you, there would be no reason for you to keep it.

PERCIVAL: You are mistaken, sir, for, like you, I love Miss Trevor, and like you, I was her fiancé.

RIO SANTO: Ah! I beg your pardon! You are Mr. Percival?

PERCIVAL: Himself.

RIO SANTO: I know everything, sir. Lady Campbell apprised me. I was hoping–we hoped–that your absence–

PERCIVAL: For whom are you speaking, sir?

RIO SANTO: I'm speaking for myself–and for Lady Campbell and–

PERCIVAL: Enough, sir! I will call you a liar if you dare pronounce any other name.

RIO SANTO (*deliberately*): –And also for Miss Trevor.

PERCIVAL: Liar!

GERARD (*grabbing his arm*): Stop! In the name of Heaven, what are you doing?

RIO SANTO: Mr. Percival, it's enough. You have succeeded in provoking me. Let it therefore be done according to your will.

PERCIVAL: My will is that one of us die, and I thank God that you have the heart of a gentleman. Till tomorrow?

RIO SANTO: Till tomorrow!

(*Rio Santo follows the line with the greatest calm.*)

SUZANNAH: He loves that young lady–and she is my benefactor. I still feel his kiss on my face–but now it burns me!

MR. SNAIL (*running to Suzannah*): Quick, quick! Hide this in your breast.

PADDY O'CHRANE: It's done! Fine! Let's go! (*to Suzannah*) Move! Move, will you? How pale you are!

SUZANNAH: What's this? Diamonds?

MR. SNAIL: They're getting agitated over there. They're coming–quick–quick!

PADDY O'CHRANE (*dragging Suzannah*): Hide them, by the Devil–and let's leave! There's nothing good for us here. Make way, Bob!

(*Paddy, Snail and Suzannah leave excitedly through the door guarded by Bob Lantern. At the back of the stage, we can see a great agitation.*)

USHER: Halberdiers, close the doors! Let no one leave!

BOB LANTERN (*crossing his halberd*): Don't worry, my good sir! No one will get out of here now!

Scene IV

(*Rio Santo's "Round Room," the secret sanctum of the Gentlemen of the Night. It is a windowless room with six doors. Rio Santo enters through door No. 1, wearing a very elegant riding costume. He carries pistols under his coat, which he removes, to remain dressed in a jacket and soft boots. He throws his pistols on a table and looks at them for a moment. Then, he makes a gesture of boredom and calls.*)

RIO SANTO: Phegor!

(*A black servant appears.*)

RIO SANTO: Strike the gong.
PHEGOR: How many times, Master?
RIO SANTO: Five times.

(*Rio Santo hurls himself in an armchair. Phegor strikes the gong five times. At the fifth blow, the five doors open at once. Owen Falkstone comes out of door No. 2, Walter Brown from door No. 3, Nick Smith from door No. 4, Fanny Bertram from door No. 5 and Peter Wood (a.k.a. The Practice), carrying a huge ledger and wearing green eyeshades, from door No. 6. These comprise the Council of the Night. Phegor advances chairs and leaves. The new arrivals bow respectfully to Rio Santo; he gives them a sign to sit down.*)

RIO SANTO: I need money.
WOOD (*aside*): Always!
SMITH: We're at your disposition, Milord. (*the others bow*) How much does Your Lordship need?
RIO SANTO: 10,000 pounds.
ALL: 10,000 pounds!
RIO SANTO: For tonight.
FALKSTONE: For tonight!
FANNY: I'm ready, Milord. All I have is yours.
RIO SANTO (*softly*): I know it, Fanny. But you, Peter–
WOOD: I'm ready.
BROWN (*after an hesitation*): So I am.
FALKSTONE: I'm ready–ready to say that all this isn't worth the Devil! I know the respect I owe you, Milord, but I've never seen money spent like this! Money which is hard to come by! Here we are, five respected businessmen: Mr. Wood owns a currency exchange office which does some good business; Mistress Bertram's stores offer cashmeres of a quality not seen even in India, and lace and other fineries– what do I know!–worth millions! Mr. Brown furnishes drapes

to all the rich houses of England and France. Mr. Smith rivals the India Company. And I am the richest goldsmith in the City! Well, to our misfortune, our five shops are built around this cursed room, which leaks money like the barrel of the Danaids! All that we earn goes into it.

RIO SANTO: By Jove, gentlemen, I admire you! What do you complain about? Do you lack merchandise? Do the police trouble you? How much do your jewels cost, Mr. Falkstone? Your drapes, Mr. Brown? Your bank notes, Mr. Wood?

ALL: True, true...

RIO SANTO: Fanny, you will give me nothing today. These gentlemen will pay for you–that pleases me. (*all bow*) Mr. Smith will furnish 1,000 pounds.

SMITH: Yes, Milord.

RIO SANTO: Mr. Wood, 2,000 pounds.

WOOD: Yes, Milord.

RIO SANTO: Mr. Brown, 3,000 pounds. (*Peter bows*) And Mr. Falkstone, 4,000 pounds.

FALKSTONE: I don't have them.

RIO SANTO: They must be had.

FALKSTONE: Impossible!

RIO SANTO: I wish it!

FALKSTONE (*bowing in his turn*): So be it!

RIO SANTO: Are there any reports this morning?

SMITH: As for me, Milord, nothing new.

RIO SANTO: That's fine. And you, Walter?

BROWN (*giving his*): Here's my report.

RIO SANTO (*reading it*): Ah! why didn't you tell me this, Walter?

BROWN: I was awaiting orders, Milord.

RIO SANTO: This is very serious, gentlemen, very serious! Once suspicion starts being focused on our brotherhood, we are all imperiled. And you say that it's in the parish of Saint Giles they are holding these meetings attended by the police?

BROWN: Yes, Milord.

RIO SANTO: This is serious! Who is the head of the police in Saint Giles?

BROWN: A clever Commissioner.

RIO SANTO (*jesting*): Clever–that suits us fine.

BROWN (*seriously*): Clever and honest. Totally honest, Milord.

RIO SANTO: That's another matter. He must be replaced tomorrow.

BROWN: Replaced! I don't see any way, Milord.

RIO SANTO: It's necessary. Write to the Chief of the Metropolitan Police, tell him that I wish to speak to him. Have him come immediately.

BROWN: His Lordship won't willingly trouble himself.

RIO SANTO: His Lordship *will* trouble himself. What about you, Mr. Falkstone?

FALKSTONE: This is my report on the subject of yesterday's diamonds. I'm proposing to the Council of the Night to send them immediately to Holland where they will be safer than here.

RIO SANTO (*to Brown, who is writing*): Tell his Lordship of the Metropolitan Police that I wish to speak to him on the matter of the diamonds stolen yesterday at Saint James'.

FALKSTONE: Milord, what are you thinking of?

RIO SANTO (*to Brown*): Keep writing. Where are those diamonds, Mr. Falkstone?

FALKSTONE: Milord–

RIO SANTO: You have them?

FALKSTONE: Yes, Milord, but–

RIO SANTO: That's fine–go find them and bring them to me.

FALKSTONE: I don't know...

RIO SANTO: Go, Falkstone. Don't force me to ask you a second time.

FALKSTONE (*reluctantly*): I obey, Milord. I obey.

(*Falkstone leaves. Walter Brown hands the letter he's just written to Rio Santo.*)

RIO SANTO (*reading*): That's fine! Let the letter be delivered immediately.

WOOD: Milord has no further orders to give?

RIO SANTO: No; you can withdraw. Go, gentlemen. Ah! Have someone go to the Russian Embassy and ask His Grace, Prince Dimitri Tolstoy if he can receive me this morning! (*to Fanny*) Stay, Fanny.

(*The other three leave.*)

RIO SANTO: As for you, you're my friend!

FANNY: Your sister, Milord. My mother nourished the two of us. Both poor, we left dear Ireland; my mother died of starvation there, and I would have died here too, if not for your generous protection.

RIO SANTO: The debt that I contracted with your mother, I paid to her daughter.

FANNY: You did more than that, Milord. We'd lost sight of each other when we arrived in London, amidst waves of men, in this maelstrom of misery and crime. I was alone, without work, at the end of my resources. Distress was pushing me towards the abyss at the bottom of which vice awaits its prey. You met me, you recognized me, and as you had become rich and powerful, you called me your sister again. That day, you gave me a guinea, which saved my life. You could have given me a hundred, which would have ruined me. You could have said: take this and dazzle; instead, you said: take this and work. That guinea, and your wise advice, Milord, made me rich–and kept me pure. You've given me a fortune; you've preserved my honor. Your advice is graven upon my soul. Your guinea, I marked with a cross, and much later, I repurchased it for a hundred guineas from Ishmael Spencer. I still have it–on my heart. It's a talisman, a memento. That's why I remain your friend, Milord.

RIO SANTO: The most patient, the most active, the most intrepid of women.

FANNY: For you, for your plans, for your service, yes, Milord.

RIO SANTO: Thanks, Fanny. You're the only heart in whom I trust!

FANNY: But let's speak of you now. You were expecting letters from Ireland today?

RIO SANTO: Yes?

FANNY: But our regular messenger hasn't come.

RIO SANTO: Ah.

FANNY: Another man has presented himself in his place.

RIO SANTO: Another man?

FANNY: Of piercing eyes, austere visage and imperious gesture. I think I know him.

RIO SANTO: How's that?

FANNY: This is the man whom you saw last year, in that small house in Dublin, during the trip we took there.

RIO SANTO: The man from Dublin? Oh! That's impossible! What did he tell you?

FANNY: He looked at me silently at first, then with a voice that no Irishman will ever forget, Milord–

RIO SANTO: Speak lower.

FANNY: –He said: "Tell the Marquis de Rio Santo that I've left Dublin to see him, and that, this very day, I will see him– at his home."

RIO SANTO: Today. He's in London, he's going to come here. He–

(*Phegor enters.*)

RIO SANTO: It must be him!

FANNY: I'm withdrawing.

RIO SANTO: Yes, Fanny–Fanny, if only you knew! Later, much later. Goodbye, my friend, goodbye.

(*She leaves.*)

RIO SANTO (*to Phegor*): Let him in.

(*Phegor departs.*)

RIO SANTO (*alone*): He's in London, and I was unaware of it.

(*Daniel O'Connell enters; Rio Santo treats him with great respect and bows to him.*)

RIO SANTO: Allow me to thank you for the honor you're doing me in coming to visit me here–you, the greatest citizen of Ireland and the father of all the Irish.

O'CONNELL: Milord, I'm coming to you despite my illness, because of your orders calling to London 10,000 young men from our poorest counties. These are like my own children. I must know–what use do you intend to make of their arms?

RIO SANTO: What use?

O'CONNELL: Yes. Ten thousand men for whom you intend to pay passage. You are indeed rich, Milord.

RIO SANTO: I have money for them and for all those who will come to me in the name of Ireland.

O'CONNELL: Are these soldiers you're enlisting? You keep silent, Milord. Still, I must know. Hear me. This would be an unequal war–a mad struggle whose means the world would condemn and that God would not bless.

RIO SANTO: You have the right to speak thus. But open your eyes in the name of our suffering fatherland! See the movements on the marshes. Many have come to help us. You haven't dared to say that this war is unjust. Is it then fear that should delay us? England has filled the cup of oppression and infamy to the brim. How many times in these hallowed halls has your voice resounded, how many times have you shouted: Shame, shame on England!

O'CONNELL: But I have also proclaimed: Peace to Ireland!

RIO SANTO: What is peace to a slave? Is it you who speak now, you whose burning heart got you named the Liberator? Are you now going to regret the drop of blood which will purchase our independence? I've avidly pursued this work. for ten years. I've visited Russia, Spain, Austria, France, always faithful to this austere passion that I hid under the effeminate folds of a Don Juan. To see me thus–asleep at the feet of women–no one could suspect in me the existence of that profound, patient and implacable purpose. And yet, for the last ten years, I've preached our crusade. For ten years, I've consumed the best part of my life in an ungrateful, exhausting labor. I've done more. I've made the greatest of all sacrifices: I've choked the voice of my conscience.

O'CONNELL: I feared so, Milord.

RIO SANTO: Yes, I've descended to the depths of villainy. Yes, I've sought in the misery of London those dark alliances with men whose criminal empire spans the Continent. Yes, I've committed crimes which the sanctity of my cause is barely enough to purify. Yes, I'm the Marquis de Rio Santo, Grandee of Spain, but I'm Irish first and foremost! I know very well that these shadowy mires into which I've plunged my hands to further my task will not soil my heart.

O'CONNELL: Milord, you love Ireland, and that makes me love you. (*extending his hand*) But trust me: don't let your hate dominate your patriotism. Imitate my example–wait!

RIO SANTO: Wait? When a nation is in agony! Wait, when the mine is collapsing! When I already see this odious, invasive, oppressive colossus, shake! I've waited ten years, I tell you–the hour has come. Now, I no longer intend to wait.

O'CONNELL (*rising*): I have waited longer than you–I, who the rest of Europe has long accused of impetuosity and violence. Do you think that I haven't had to make prodigious efforts to still the passion of my heart? Milord, in this century, the law is a sharper weapon than the sword. We must conquer, but in accordance with the law, through the law. My violence, my passion, my impetuosity–these were evil counselors that I crushed under the weight of my will. I waited because I ought to have waited.

RIO SANTO: The future will decide between us two then.

O'CONNELL: Milord, my strength has been exhausted in the cause to which I have devoted myself completely. Look at me–the struggle has broken me. My life is ready to pass away–one foot in the tomb. I want to descend into my grave as calmly as I ascended into this world. I know that another must continue my work by the same means, the same peaceful means. That's why I've come, Milord. I came to know you, for you might be my successor; but before giving you that title, before placing the supreme hope in you, I must be convinced that you won't compromise the sacrifices of my entire life. What am I saying? The heroic sufferings of an entire nation. In the end, you must tell me what you intend to do with my 10,000 Irish children.

RIO SANTO: To explain my plans to you, to unveil my whole soul, I ask two more days.

O'CONNELL: I trust you, Milord–two days, then–so be it! I shall return to Dublin, where my presence is expected–our men will be ready–but think about it: the sword of God must be without stain, and the ways of Providence, while strange and often twisted, never become an evil path. In two days, then, milord, I will know if God is calling you to continue my work. In two days, I will know if my poor Irish children should leave–if they should give you their arms and their hearts, follow your path blindly and die as Christians. Goodbye, Milord.

RIO SANTO: Goodbye, sir.

(*O'Connell leaves.*)

RIO SANTO: That man spoke the truth–the sword of God must be untarnished. But the good I've done, placed in the balance, will perhaps outweigh my sins. And yet, shall I be a redeemed?

(*Falkstone returns.*)

RIO SANTO (*aside*): Come on, come on, no more weakness! (*to Falkstone*) Approach, Mr. Falkstone.

FALKSTONE: Milord, here are the diamonds.

RIO SANTO (*pointing to a table*): Put them there–that's fine–I won't detain you.

FALKSTONE: In the name of Heaven, Milord, consider that I am accountable to the rest of our brotherhood.

RIO SANTO: As I am accountable of the very security of our brotherhood itself, Mr. Falkstone. There's danger over our heads. Do you prefer to keep these diamonds–or your life?

FALKSTONE (*terrified*): Milord!

RIO SANTO (*pointing at a door*): Go in there. When the Chief of the Metropolitan Police comes, lend an ear. I permit it. I desire it.

FALKSTONE: I will listen, Milord, since it is your good pleasure.

(*Falkstone goes to hide.*)

RIO SANTO (*ringing*): Phegor!

(*The black servant appears. Behind him is Doctor Moore*)

RIO SANTO (to Moore): Ah, Doctor Moore. You bring news of the Right Honorable Mr. Percival?

MOORE: Yes, Your Lordship.

RIO SANTO: Have you seen him?

MOORE: I put the first dressing on his wound.

RIO SANTO: And?

MOORE: The bullet passed a mere inches from the heart.

RIO SANTO: Ah!

MOORE: I know you to be an extraordinary shot, Milord. I think that you've been generous.

RIO SANTO: Perhaps. What did you think of the wound?

MOORE: It can be cured.

RIO SANTO: So much the better.

MOORE: So much the better? What about Miss Trevor?

RIO SANTO: No questions–but–

MOORE: This Percival is an obstacle.

RIO SANTO: I know it, which is why I wanted to destroy him.

MOORE: But you no longer intend to?

RIO SANTO: No.

MOORE: Yet, your marriage with Miss Trevor–

RIO SANTO: All this wearies and displeases me.

MOORE: Milord, each of us does certain things unwillingly. And all is not pleasure in the brotherhood of which you are the supreme leader on those islands. The association needs this marriage, which will make you heir to a peerage and give you the most effective protection. The Great Family is counting on you, Milord.

RIO SANTO: Am I slave or free?

MOORE: You are not free.

RIO SANTO: Then I'm a slave!

MOORE: Milord, this marriage is all our hope. The Trevors are almost of royal blood. By this union, we arrive–you arrive, Milord–at the very steps of the throne. Remember that you swore an oath before the assembled Council in Sartene...

RIO SANTO (*interrupting him*): I remember, sir–and I will consider– (*changing tone*) Meanwhile, I am still the Master here, right?

MOORE: Indeed, Milord.

RIO SANTO: How is it then that my orders are not executed?

MOORE: If I know the guilty party–

RIO SANTO: The guilty party–that's you, Doctor!

MOORE: Me!

RIO SANTO: I forbade you earlier to involve that young girl Suzannah in our shadowy maneuvers.

MOORE (*feigning surprise*): The young girl–ah, pardon–I understand now, Milord. I truly didn't expect so much memory on Your Lordship's part–

RIO SANTO (*severely*): You've disobeyed me! (*sits down*)

MOORE (*with feigned humility*): Milord, ordinarily, when it's a question of a woman, I'm astonished that you remember anything. (*in a low voice*) She's very beautiful, this Suzannah!

And might that be the motive for your change of heart? Before seeing her, you were quite prepared to marry Mary Trevor.

RIO SANTO (*rising*): If you disobey me again, I will have your head, Doctor Moore!

MOORE (*standing up abruptly*): I am a member of the Council of the Night.

RIO SANTO: And you would like to rise in rank. My place seems good to you–you're thinking of taking it–don't deny it, I know you–you've already tried to ruin me. You're one of the first practitioners in London. You have much science, much reputation–much future. Yet, between you and the scaffold, there's only my will.

MOORE (*incredulous*): The scaffold! You're going too far, Rio Santo!

RIO SANTO: I say this to you now, because you know how to kill from a distance, and chance might put my life in your hands. I tell you this now because you're my doctor–and that I intend to sleep peacefully, even with you watching my sick bed. Don't be too surprised. I hold more or less all your colleagues the same way. Our colleagues from the Continent call it the *invisible weapon*. Without it, I would need to have a thousand lives.

MOORE: If you please, what then is the crime you hold over my head?

RIO SANTO (*lightly*): Choose between any of your misdeeds. I have proof of one of them. A good proof. Irrefutable evidence. Enough to hang you.

MOORE (*aside*): What does he know? (*aloud*) Milord, I've let you speak, but whatever your prejudices and suspicions against me, there's no need of threats for me to serve you. It's my very fidelity, and it's my profound devotion to the brotherhood, that henceforth will plead my cause to Your Lordship. What are you pleased to order me to do?

RIO SANTO: Cure Percival's wound.

MOORE (*hesitating*): That's your will?

RIO SANTO: That's my will.

MOORE: It will be faithfully done.

RIO SANTO: As for that young girl–
MOORE: The beautiful Suzannah? It suffices, Milord. Henceforth Suzannah is sacred to us. Is that all?
RIO SANTO: That's all– Go!

(*Moore starts to leave, then returns.*)

MOORE: I would have Your Lordship tell me that he holds no rancor against me.
RIO SANTO (*weary*): I am no longer thinking of you. Go! Ah, no! A moment more–would you jot down on a piece of paper the names and addresses of some devoted men–men who can be relied upon–men of a certain world–you understand?
MOORE: Perfectly, Milord. (*writes*) Here–
RIO SANTO: Fine! Goodbye, Doctor Moore.

(*Moore bows deeply and heads toward the door. Rio Santo stretches out on the sofa nonchalantly. Moore stops in the doorway and casts a glance of pure hatred at him.*)

MOORE (*aside*): Your marriage with Miss Trevor will take place, and Suzannah will help me–despite yourself, despite you, Milord.

(*He leaves as Phegor returns.*)

PHEGOR (*announcing*): The Right Honorable Mr. Johnstone, Chief of the Metropolitan Police, Sir Picott, Superintendent of Police and Mr. Harrison, Comptroller of Police.
RIO SANTO (*aside*): Ah! My God! So many agents of the law!

(*The three men enter.*)

JOHNSTONE (*in a dry tone*): Have I the honor of addressing the Marquis de Rio Santo?

RIO SANTO: Himself, sir.

JOHNSTONE: You've asked to make an official report and so I've come to your residence–accompanied by these gentlemen, my subordinates–to hear your statement and, if appropriate, lawfully record it. (*to his men*) Sit down and prepare to write.

RIO SANTO: I see. (*a pause, then gravely*) Sir, do you know that your men have acted very badly?

JOHNSTONE (*indignant*): What do you mean, sir?

RIO SANTO: Did you know, sir, that Lady Brompton–from whom the diamonds were stolen–is Prince Dimitri Tolstoy's mistress–and that the Prince is a dear friend of mine?

JOHNSTONE: Ah! His Grace is–

RIO SANTO: An intimate friend. Now, if the Prince–my friend–lodges an official complaint with the Foreign Office, this can turn into an embarrassing affair. Oh, so very embarrassing–for you–as you also may not know that the diamonds had been purchased by the Prince on behalf of his government.

JOHNSTONE (*low to Picott*): You hear that, Picott?

PICOTT (*low to Harrison*): You hear, Harrison?

HARRISON (*aside*): Ah! If only my deputy were here!

RIO SANTO: If these diamonds are not found, the Prince will be upset, the Russian government will be upset, and no one knows how far things may go. Mr. Johnstone, have you heard of the war which blew up between two great powers over a glass of water?

JOHNSTONE (*dumbfounded*): Over a glass of water?

RIO SANTO: Yes. There are historic precedents. Lady Brompton's diamonds–or I should say, the diamonds of His Majesty the Emperor of all Russia–would make a fine *casus belli*? My God, it would be so much more credible than a glass of water. A war! And whose fault would it be? Yours, Mr. Johnstone.

JOHNSTONE: Mine?

RIO SANTO: Yes, yours–because you haven't clever enough to find the diamonds.

JOHNSTON (*to Picott*): You realize the terrible consequences of your inaction, Picott?

PICOTT (*to Harrison*): Did you hear that, Harrison? See what humiliation I'm enduring all because of you–

HARRISON (*aside*): My deputy will pay dearly for this!

RIO SANTO: So then, war it is, then!

JOHNSTONE: Oh! Milord! Peace! Mercy!

RIO SANTO: Well! So be it–no war. I agree. It's bad for business. Let's suppose that some simple explanation is found–

JOHNSTONE: She lost them!

RIO SANTO: Yes, Lady Brompton lost the diamonds. That's it. In that case, the least action our government can take to appease the Russians–or so I believe–is to sack you, Mr. Johnstone. You would left penniless and destitute.

JOHNSTONE: Milord, had you no other reasons to summon me than to make me feel even more miserable?

RIO SANTO: Not at all! you do right to remind me of the purpose of this meeting. But first, would you send these two gentlemen away?

JOHNSTONE: Mr. Picott–get out. You too, Mr. Harrison.

PICOTT: What! Are we dismissed?

HARRISON: If that's the way it's going to be... (*writes excitedly*)

JOHNSTONE: What are you doing, Harrison?

HARRISON: I'm firing my deputy.

RIO SANTO: Please, gentlemen, you may wait in the next room. This won't take long.

(*Picott and Harrison leave.*)

RIO SANTO (*taking the box that contains the diamonds and opening it*): Mr. Johnstone, do you recognize these stones?

JOHNSTONE (*astounded*): These are Lady Brompton's diamonds. (*pulling out a list*) Item–25 stones mounted. Item–

RIO SANTO: No need of your list. These are indeed her diamonds.

71

JOHNSTONE: How is it possible? And they are in your hands, Milord?

RIO SANTO: No, they are in yours. And they look so comfortable there that I am thinking of letting you keep them.

JOHNSTONE: Milord, this is a mystery–a mystery which causes me to tremble with joy, but for which I must have an explanation.

RIO SANTO: There is one–a very simple one, Mr. Johnstone. The person who committed the theft is a poor devil who allowed himself to be seduced by the dazzle of these jewels. Once the theft was consummated, he became embarrassed with his treasure. He understood–too late–that their very importance would make it very difficult for him to get rid of them. He became afraid and, thinking that news of the theft had not yet been widely publicized, he rushed to the one man he felt might pay him a fair price–myself–this very morning.

JOHNSTONE: Your Lordship has the reputation of being so very rich.

RIO SANTO: I recognized the diamonds right away, of course. I'd seen them several times before at Prince Tolstoy's home. I threatened the wretch to deliver him to justice; in his fright, he abandoned the jewels without even picking up the purse I threw him. I let the poor devil flee. Then, naturally, my first thought was of you, Mr. Johnstone.

JOHNSTONE: Your Lordship is too kind. If there's ever anything in my power–

RIO SANTO: Since you mention it, there are several poor gentlemen who have–I don't really know why–chosen me to be their patron. They recently came to me and asked me to recommend them to you.

JOHNSTONE: To me?

RIO SANTO: Yes, five or six gentlemen. They aspire to work for the police. The conversation turned to you and–oh! if only you had head them, Mr. Johnstone!–they praised you–really praised you–deservedly, I must say. I have their names here.

JOHNSTONE: Give them to me, Milord. I will be pleased to find employment for gentlemen who have spoken of me in such flattering terms to your Lordship.

RIO SANTO: You see, their enthusiasm for you made me think. By Jove, I said to myself, if I return the jewels directly to Prince Tolstoy, no one will benefit. But if it's the worthy Mr. Johnstone who returns them, why, he may profit from such action–a promotion, perhaps.

JOHNSTONE: Does Your Lordship have any ideas what kind of job would his friends require? We actually have a few vacancies–

RIO SANTO: Working in an ordinary police station would be excellent. How about the one located in the Parish of Saint Giles? It would be most convenient.

JOHNSTONE: Ah, yes, but the Commissioner of that station isn't an easy man to deal with. He might take umbrage... He's a man of vigilance, integrity, active as if he were still a young sergeant, despite his 33 years of service.

RIO SANTO (*indignant*): Thirty-three years! Did you say, 33 years of service, Mr. Johnstone? Why, that's a scandal!

JOHNSTONE: What do you mean, sir?

RIO SANTO: A shame! Thirty-three years of service and you don't grant an honorable retirement to an old man who has so nobly and faithfully acquired the right to rest! No, I tell you, sometimes I wonder if governments deserve the zeal and the devotion with which their servants tirelessly lavish on them.

JOHNSTONE: I hadn't looked at the question from that point of view, but you're right.

(*Phegor enters and delivers a letter on a silver platter.*)

RIO SANTO: What is it, Phegor? What's wrong? Ah! A letter from the Prince–Mr. Johnstone, this may concern you– (*reading*) "Dear Marquis: Pardon me for not seeing you this morning. I am rushing about on the matter of which you know. Whatever it cost me, I will tell the truth. If the diamonds are not found, I shall be ruined–but then, I intend at least to have vengeance–"

JOHNSTONE: Vengeance!

RIO SANTO: You are now safe, Mr. Johnstone.

JOHNSTONE: Ah! Milord, thank you–I might have been ruined– or worse! I'm so grateful! Excuse me for leaving you so quickly. I'm now in haste to see the Prince.

RIO SANTO: Go, go, my friend, and spare no modesty! Do value yourself justly.

JOHNSTONE: All the fortune which may fall upon me, I owe to you, Milord. Till I have the honor of seeing you again.

RIO SANTO: Goodbye, sir. Ah! Don't forget my list!

JOHNSTONE: Oh! A thousand pardons. It's the confusion I'm in. Tell your protégés, Milord, that I'll take care of them personally. Tomorrow, they'll be in Saint Giles! It is Saint Giles, right?

RIO SANTO: Yes, but if it causes you any trouble–

JOHNSTONE: Say no more, Milord! I will put them all there myself! (calling) Picott! Harrison!

(*Picott and Harrison enter.*)

JOHNSTONE: Gentlemen, follow me. We have a heady day ahead of us!

HARRISON (*tearing up a sheet of paper*): Right! I'll be merciful towards my deputy!

(*They leave. Falkstone reappears.*)

FALKSTONE: Now I understand, Milord.

RIO SANTO: How fortunate. In that case, you will bring me 500 guineas more for our new installation in the Saint Giles police station.

FALKSTONE (*laughing*): Gladly, Milord.

CURTAIN

Act III

Scene V

(*Frank Percival's lodgings. On the one side, there is a small salon, with a door leading outside; on the other, Frank's bedroom. Gerard enters the salon from the outside.*)

GERARD: Nobody–where is Donnor? Frank's health worries me.

(*Donnor enters, from Frank's bedroom.*)

GERARD: Well–how is our patient?
DONNOR: Better, Monsieur. The first nine days were hard to get through but, since yesterday, the fever has gone–and last night, he slept like a saint.
GERARD: Dear Frank! What a terrible wound!
DONNOR: A shot to the heart! The best heart I've met in this world! You see, Monsieur, it seems to me that I've loved him all my life. If you only knew how good and generous he is!
GERARD: I do know it. Am I not his friend?
DONNOR (*warmly*): His true friend, by Jove! I would take my oath on it. You see, Monsieur, I love him so much that I can intuit those who love him, too. As for you, I would leave you alone with him as much as you like–and I'd sleep comfortably.
GERARD (*smiling*): Is someone tempting you to carry him off, my brave Donnor?
DONNOR: It's obvious to me. If I were a gentleman, knowing how to read and write, perhaps I would say more. But at least, we got him out of it–may God be blessed!
GERARD: We have! Thanks to the worthy and skilled Doctor Moore.

DONNOR: Yes, yes, the worthy and skilled Doctor Moore, as you say! As for me, you see—but perhaps I'm mistaken.

GERARD: What do you mean?

DONNOR: Nothing, nothing worth anything, no question. It's not for a poor ignorant man like me to have the right to speak–still–in the end–never mind–

GERARD: You have something against Doctor Moore?

DONNOR: Well! Actually, no! After all, did saved Mr. Percival. Still, I might–no, I would be saying something stupid–I prefer to inform Mr. Percival of your arrival.

(*He returns to Frank's bedroom.*)

GERARD: Poor, brave man! he's taken an aversion to the Doctor–I wonder why? Very clever is he who would know what to say to him!

(*Frank Percival comes out of the bedroom, leaning on Donnor.*)

GERARD: Oh! Oh!–here we are standing–walking without support–bravo!

PERCIVAL: Still very weak, my dear Gerard.

GERARD (*shaking his hand*): But finally convalescent, from what I see, by Jove! Frank, you don't know how you love people when they're in good health.

(*All three walk back into the bedroom. Percival sits on a chaise lounge and sits by his side.*)

PERCIVAL: And when you're in good health, you don't know who loves you truly. Thanks, Gerard. I'm not unaware of the proofs of attachment you lavished on me when I was there, nailed to my bed.

DONNOR (*giving Percival a tie*): Ah! 'Tis true, he's a famous comrade!

PERCIVAL: I thought myself alone in this world–but misfortune made friends for me. Here, Gerard, this is a worthy man (*points to Donnor*) who has cared for me as if he were my own father.

DONNOR: Oh, sir...

PERCIVAL: Devotion at all hours–at every minute!

DONNOR (*confused*): Don't you go thanking me! If I had had the opportunity, I'd have busted my head for love of you, sir!

GERARD (*slapping him on the shoulder*): Good Donnor!

PERCIVAL: All this because I gave him a slice of bread, by chance, one day when he was hungry.

DONNOR: A scrap of bread–yes–and good words–and consolation–and hope–and, especially, friendship. Oh, for that friendship, I've dedicated my life to you–yes, I have. That's all I've got!

PERCIVAL: He's telling the truth, too. He's given me more than his life, he's given me his only desire, his passion, his paternal concern.

DONNOR: My poor children!

PERCIVAL: Twelve days that he's remained at my bedside, he who traveled 200 leagues on foot to get closer to his daughters. Gerard, you will help me to compensate Donnor, won't you?

DONNOR (*standing upright*): Compensate me!

PERCIVAL: As you deserve to be. We will get your daughters back, won't we, Gerard?

GERARD: If it were only up to me...

PERCIVAL: We will get them back for you, my friend.

DONNOR (*kissing Percival's hand, tears in his eyes*): It would make me happy to find them through your intercession

GERARD (*to Percival*): I know a person who will be almost as happy am.

PERCIVAL (*going pale*): Gerard, I don't dare to ask you news–

GERARD (*smiling*): Good Lord, you seem to want to be forced to endure your happiness!

PERCIVAL: My happiness?

GERARD: So much the worse if the dear Doctor Moore accuses me of indiscretion, or imprudence! I can't keep silent. My friend, from something ill comes something good. Your wound worked wonders! Lord Trevor, that brave and honest man, spent a day at your side. Lady Campbell couldn't do a thing when Miss Trevor learned that you were in danger of death–that broke the spell–
PERCIVAL: She still loves me?
GERARD: Still–more than ever! Rio Santo, who is, on the whole, a true gentleman, felt the blow and kept to the side. There's only that cursed aunt, that very witty, very devoted woman, who will not admit defeat–she has changed tactics. In cahoots with Rio Santo or not, I can't say, but she's opened another trench–

(*Enter Doctor Moore who comes into the salon and listens at Percival's bedroom door.*)

GERARD (*unaware*): There are vague reports of anonymous letters. In short, they've succeeded in making Mary jealous.
PERCIVAL: Jealous?
GERARD: Jealous like Hermione.
PERCIVAL: What slander! Am I then surrounded by snares? But you, Gerard, you who know my entire life, why didn't you tell Miss Trevor?
GERARD: I said all anyone can say–but she pictured constantly a beautiful woman at your bedside, a woman whom you would have had brought from France–
PERCIVAL: Infamous lie! I see plainly that the aunt is very ingenious, very devoted to the Marquis de Rio Santo! But, how to disabuse Mary? If only I could see her...
GERARD: Well, that's not impossible
PERCIVAL: What are you saying, my friend? Oh–don't hide anything from me.
GERARD: Mary loves you–she, too, is burning with desire to see you.

PERCIVAL: Oh! Let her come–let her come! And I'll only need a word to convince her that my thought, my heart, my very love are hers and hers alone.

GERARD: Calm down, your Doctor will scold me for the emotion I'm causing you. Soon, Frank– (*laughing*) Prepare for a surprise–today, perhaps–and if you did bring a beauty from France, hide her well, or look out for yourself!

(*He makes a gesture of mocking threat and walks into the salon.*)

GERARD: Oh! Doctor Moore–

PERCIVAL (*to Donnor*): Mary! Mary! Do you understand, Donnor? To see Mary again?

DONNOR: Your Mary is yours–yes (*noticing Moore through the open door*) When this man comes, I don't know why but my heart is seized.

(*Meanwhile, Gerard crosses the salon, preparing to leave.*)

GERARD: Ah! Doctor Moore, you've got a fine cure there!

MOORE: Except for the fever this morning, it would be all over–

GERARD: Not a shadow of fever now! Miss Trevor will become one of your friends, Doctor! Pardon, but I must leave you. I'm rushing to Lord Trevor's as a matter of fact. Goodbye, goodbye–Dear Doctor–there's not a man who's comparable to you in the whole Royal College!

(*He leaves.*)

MOORE (*alone in the salon*): If one were to put things in good order, the Marquis de Rio Santo would be quickly and easily rid of this marriage. But what to do? Time presses– Let's see.

DONNOR (*in Percival's bedroom*): Who is it talking to himself all alone?

MOORE (*aside*): Jealousy! Miss Trevor is jealous– She must come this very day (*reflecting*) What if when she came, she were to find–Installed here? Why not? Yes–the idea pleases me. (*seems delighted with himself.*)

(*He then walks into Percival's bedroom.*)

PERCIVAL: Eh! Hello, Doctor! I'm feeling better, I am doing admirably well.

MOORE: Your face is radiant (*takes his pulse*) Your pulse is excellent! Come on, Mr. Percival, two or three days of rest, and you'll be fit as a fiddle!

PERCIVAL: Thanks to your good care, dear Doctor, and your unrivaled skill.

MOORE (*in a paternal tone*): And thanks a little to the happiness which has spread like a balm over your wound.

PERCIVAL (*taking his hand*): Well, it's true, Doctor. Joy is even more powerful than your remedies. I feel myself reborn. Life is overflowing in me. The blood which runs in my veins is young and invigorating. I am strong because I am happy.

(*As they talk, Percival gets up and he returns to the salon on Moore's arm. Donnor remains behind, watching them.*)

MOORE: Well, come, come now. I love my patients the way one loves one's children–and I want to try your strength. Now, tell me about your happiness.

PERCIVAL: Why, since you know all about it?

DOCTOR: Gerard has confided everything to me. Even Miss Trevor's jealousy! Jealousy! That's evidence of love, the best evidence!

PERCIVAL: Oh! it's this jealousy which gives me hope, for I still doubt. But do you know how easy it will be to disabuse her?

DONNOR (*aside*): This Doctor remains a long while today. I wish he'd leave–but no–

PERCIVAL: I will only have one word to say to convince her.

MOORE: Right.

PERCIVAL (*warming up*): A single word! And this Rio Santo, my rival, will henceforth slander me in vain–

MOORE (*alarmed*): Don't say any more

PERCIVAL (*surprised*): Why?

MOORE (*pulling a flash from his pocket*): The fever is coming on– (*rises to find a glass, aside*) I've got to stop you from uttering that word. (*he pours the contents of the flask into a glass and leaves the empty flask on the table.*)

DONNOR (*watching*): A flask! That man always gives me a fright. What's he pouring him?

PERCIVAL: Fever? But it seems to me–

MOORE (*returning with the glass full*): Drink this.

DONNOR (*terrified*): He's going to drink it!

(*Donnor rushes into the salon.*)

PERCIVAL (*distracted*): What is it, Donnor?

DONNOR: Nothing. It's just me. (*watches Moore*)

PERCIVAL: It seems to me that I don't have a fever. But my confidence in you is great, Doctor! (*rising*) Wait–I recall that I saw everything, when you thought I was unconscious. I would astonish you if I told you what I remember. One day, your assistant placed a bandage on my wound, on which he'd poured some drops of a liquid whose strange odor gave me something like vertigo.

DONNOR (*aside*): It's all true.

PERCIVAL: Did I dream that?

MOORE: I don't have any recollection of it

DONNOR (*muttering*): He's lying!

(*Moore turns around. Donnor's face becomes expressionless.*)

PERCIVAL: A hand–yours, no doubt–

DONNOR (*aside*): No–not his.

PERCIVAL: A hand grasped the bandage and tore it off. It seemed to me that that saved me from death.

DONNOR (*aside*): My God! Thank you! You really inspired me that day!

PERCIVAL: But I have great confidence in you, Doctor.

MOORE (*presenting the glass*): Drink.

DONNOR (*seizing the glass*): Excuse me.

MOORE: What?

PERCIVAL: What's wrong, Donnor?

DONNOR: It's that–it's that I don't have any confidence in this potion!

PERCIVAL (stopping him): Donnor!

DONNOR: Sir?

PERCIVAL: Not another word! If you love me! give me that glass (*sits and drinks*) Doctor, pardon him on account of his affection for me.

DONNOR (*to Moore*): Sir, excuse me–it seems I was wrong!

MOORE: You are a good servant, and as good servants are rare, I pardon them–even for the excess of their zeal. (*to Percival*) You have no further need of me.

PERCIVAL: No, my good Doctor.

MOORE: In that case, I am going to leave you, but I shall return.

PERCIVAL: I feel a bit numb– Still, I feel fine–very fine. It seems to me that I want to rest now. (*rising*) Donnor, your arm. *Au revoir*, Doctor, *au revoir*.

(*Donnor gives Percival his arm and helps him back to the bedroom, where he starts dozing on his bed.*)

MOORE: So far everything's going well.

(*He leaves.*)

DONNOR (*alone*): He's gone! Despite the assurances of Mr. Percival, my suspicions have not dissipated. Why this deep and rapid sleep? That's not natural. Suppose I wake him? (*he tries to shake him awake*) Mr. Percival! Sir! Nothing! Ah, why this sleep? What was he given? If it was poison!

(*He returns to the salon.*)

DONNOR: Ah! I am crazy! They said I was crazy! How to know what to do? He pulled a flask from his pocket. He poured the contents of his flask in this glass. Nothing! I ought to have told him. I ought to have opposed his departure until he gave me that flask. In the end I ought–Ah! here it is! (*he finds the empty flask which had remained on a table*) Now, I will know the truth! A label! What's it got on it? Misfortune! I don't know how to read! Someone's coming. It's that Doctor again.

(*Doctor Moore returns, followed by a veiled woman– Suzannah. Donnor is hiding behind a chair at the back of the stage. The Doctor crosses the room silently, followed by Suzannah, and they enter the bedroom.*)

DONNOR (*aside*): He brought a woman!
SUZANNAH: Where have you brought me? Who is this young man?
MOORE: Silence! You've sworn to obey.
SUZANNAH: Can I not at least know?
MOORE: You will know everything–later.

(*Gerard returns.*)

GERARD: Donnor, where are–?
DONNOR (*to Gerard*): Ah! It's you! God be praised!
GERARD (happy): She's coming.
DONNOR: I know.
GERARD: What–you know?
DONNOR (*pointing to the flask*): Yes, yes. In the name of Heaven, tell me–what is that?
GERARD: Why–?
DONNOR: Answer–answer!

GERARD: It's another of your suspicions against the Doctor, isn't it? Ah, you think that he wants to poison Frank.

DONNOR: I don't know. If you'd seen the effect that water produced....

GERARD: It produces sleep. It's–

DONNOR: Yes?

GERARD: –laudanum.

DONNOR (*happy*): Ah! I was mistaken! You're quite sure of what you are saying, Monsieur Gerard?

GERARD (*smiling*): Perfectly sure.

DONNOR: It's because I love him so much. After all, perhaps he's a fine man–this Doctor Moore. Speaking of your young lady, he's just brought her.

GERARD: Who?

DONNOR: The Doctor.

GERARD (*astonished*): What young lady?

DONNOR: By Jove, Miss Trevor.

GERARD (*aside*): Ah, indeed. That brave man is becoming quite mad! As if Frank really had some mistress... Unless...

DONNOR: A gentleman and another lady!

(*Lord Trevor and Mary enter.*)

GERARD: Miss Trevor! Milord! You are not made to wait–

DONNOR (Aside): Miss Trevor? Who then is the other woman? (*very agitated and embarrassed*)

LORD TREVOR: You told him?

GERARD: Yes, of course. Will you wait?

MARY TREVOR: Wait? Why? Is he more ill?

GERARD (*confused*): No. Surely– (*aside*) It can't be. If the old man spoke the truth, who is in that bedroom?

SUZANNAH (*in Percival's bedroom*): What must I do now?

MOORE (*listening attentively*): Patience!

MARY TREVOR: Monsieur Gerard! I grow concerned.

GERARD (*trying*): There's nothing to be concerned about, Miss Trevor.

DONNOR (*aside*): That woman? Who is that woman?

GERARD: You must excuse us, Miss Trevor. In the house of a patient, there's always a little worry–uneasiness–

MARY TREVOR: Ah! Sir–something is being hidden from us. I know it. (*rises*)

GERARD (*embarrassed*): Not at all! What would there be to hide? There's not the least mystery.

MARY TREVOR (*exchanging a look with her father*): Since we are causing some disturbance here, we can always return later–come, father.

LORD TREVOR: As you wish, Mary.

GERARD: Milord, please, one more moment of your time. I implore you. (*to Donnor*) Come, help me, you.

DONNOR: Miss, Milord–I don't–

TREVOR: That's fine. A word, brave man.

(*Trevor pulls Donnor aside. Mary and Gerard talk low.*)

MOORE (*in Percival's room, low and rapidly to Suzannah*): Suzannah, get closer to this young man. (*imperiously*) Do what I say!

(*Suzannah gets closer to Percival.*)

LORD TREVOR (*to Donnor*): You're not trying to deceive me, are you?

DONNOR (*awkward*): No, Your Lordship.

SUZANNAH (*to Moore*): What do you want me to do?

MOORE: Pretend to save his life–

LORD TREVOR (*to Donnor*): Well, then, I shall go in.

MOORE (*to Suzannah*): Lean over his face. Kiss him. Obey!

(*Just as Lord Trevor enters the room, Suzannah bends over the sleeping Percival's face and kisses it. Lord Trevor stops. Mary, who has leaned forward to see where her father was going, also catches Suzannah in the act.*)

MARY TREVOR: A woman! Ah! My forebodings were true. Monsieur Gerard! Why did you make me come here? My God! My God! Ah! (*faints*)

GERARD: *Mon Dieu!* She's fainted!

SUZANNAH (*who has turned*): A young girl. My benefactress! My God—what's wrong here?

(*Moore walks into the salon.*)

LORD TREVOR (*to Moore*): Doctor, please help my daughter!

MOORE (*cursorily examining Mary*): That nothing, Milord. She'll be fine. Don't worry.

(*Suzannah comes into the salon. Donnor looks at her attentively.*)

GERARD: She's coming to. She's opening her eyes.

LORD TREVOR (*to Donnor*): Tell my driver to ready my carriage. We're going.

(*But Donnor continues to study Suzannah.*)

GERARD: Go, my friend, do what His Lordship asked!

DONNOR (*tearing himself away*): What? Ah, yes—yes, I'm going.

(*He leaves slowly.*)

SUZANNAH (*going to Mary*): Miss! If I dared to offer you my help—

MARY TREVOR (*looking at her*): Father! (*getting up and pushing Suzannah away*) Father! (*crossing the stage*) It's that woman!

SUZANNAH (*aside*): What have I done?

MARY TREVOR: Father—take me away.

LORD TREVOR: Monsieur Gerard, please take my daughter's arm.

(*Gerard gives his arm to Mary.*)

LORD TREVOR (*to Moore*): Thank you, Doctor. (*looking at Suzannah*) Make way! (*aside*) What impudence.

(*Lord Trevor, Mary and Gerard leave.*)

MOORE (*to Suzannah*): Now, take my arm and come.
SUZANNAH: Sir, what happened here? I want to know.
MOORE (*smiling*): Ah, you want to know?
SUZANNAH: Yes, I insist! That language astonishes you, from I, a servant. Very bold, perhaps? But I've just been insulted to my face, and that wasn't part of our agreement, sir.
MOORE: True.
SUZANNAH (*coming forward*): So, will you answer me? Why did that young girl shrink away from me in horror? Why did her father reject me with contempt? What did I do to them?
MOORE (*sarcastic*): A small thing.
SUZANNAH (*violently*): Don't jest, sir.
MOORE (*cold*): Since you absolutely insist on knowing– here's the key to the enigma–it's really quite simple. Miss Trevor loved Frank Percival and henceforth she will no longer love him.
SUZANNAH: Why's that?
MOORE: Because she now thinks you're his mistress.
SUZANNAH (*indignant*): His mistress! His mistress! Me! That's cowardly and infamous. I sold you my obedience, sir, but not my honor.
MOORE (*disdainfully*): Your honor! What do I care about your honor?
DONNOR (*coming forward*): It matters greatly, Doctor Moore. To her, first of all–then to me.
MOORE: And who are you?

SUZANNAH (amazed): My father!

MOORE: What? What did she just say?

DONNOR: Yes, her father, sir!

MOORE (*bowing*): Very well–the rights of a father take precedence, I suppose. (*to Suzannah*) I will leave you with your father. Please accept my congratulations for this unforeseen reunion. But before I leave–a word, if you please. (*pulls Suzannah aside*) You promised silence (*threateningly*) Remember!

SUZANNAH: I no longer take orders–

MOORE (*with feigned courtesy*): Accept my humble advice, then. Keep your silence–for your sake. And that of–you do love your father, don't you?

SUZANNAH: Sir–

MOORE (*harshly*): Then keep silent for his sake. (*bowing and smiling*) Goodbye, Mr. Donnor.

DONNOR (*to Moore*): I am going to question my daughter–and we will see each other again, Doctor Moore!

MOORE (*jestingly*): Is that a threat? Ordinarily, people like me have no hatred toward people of your sort, but as for me, I have no pride, and I do not choose my enemies. Perhaps we will see each other again indeed, Mr. Donnor!

DONNOR: Get out, sir, get out!

(*Moore leaves slowly.*)

SUZANNAH: Father!

DONNOR (*pushing her away*): Suzannah! What did you come here to do?

SUZANNAH: I was unaware when I came, father.

DONNOR: What rights does that man have over you?

SUZANNAH: I can't tell you.

DONNOR: Suzannah, why these rich clothes?

SUZANNAH: Father–

DONNOR: Suzannah, do you remember your mother?

SUZANNAH: Indeed, I do.

DONNOR: Hers was an honest heart–a soul without blemish. When she died, your name came last to her lips. She said to me: "London is a city where young girls forget the Commandments of God, but our Suzannah is well taught. She loves us too much to listen to evil advice. I'm not afraid. I'm going to the next world with confidence in my heart. May God bless our Suzannah."

SUZANNAH: My mother! My poor, saintly mother!

DONNOR: She's lucky to be dead. As for me, I'm alive–I'm listening to you, daughter! I'm awaiting a word from you–a word which is very long in coming.

SUZANNAH: My God! My God! Please!

DONNOR: You have nothing to tell me?

SUZANNAH: Nothing.

DONNOR: Nothing?

SUZANNAH: I am innocent, but I cannot–

DONNOR: Are there secrets that you cannot tell your father?

SUZANNAH: If you were to know–

DONNOR (*violently*): I *must* know!

SUZANNAH (*aside*): They will kill him!

DONNOR: I intend to know where these expensive clothes came from, clothes which put red on my face when I recognized you. The money that you sent to Ireland rendered less sorrowful my poor wife's–your mother's last days. I want to know if I must regret our distress–and curse the mattress on which your mother slept.

SUZANNAH: The money came from my work.

DONNOR: Was it your work that gave you these brilliant baubles?

SUZANNAH: No, it's–

DONNOR (*pointing at Percival through the door*): Look at this poor young man who's sleeping there–who unsuspectingly placed himself between me and despair–that's the reward for his kindness? I brought evil into his home! Now he sleeps quite happily. But when he awakes–to find the love of his life gone! It's I who will tear his heart apart–poor Mr.

Percival! Him, so kind! Him, who just now said to me, "My poor Donnor, I will help you find your children."

SUZANNAH: This is too much–

DONNOR: He loved you–for the love of me!

SUZANNAH: Father! Father, have mercy!

DONNOR: You dare ask for mercy? You, who keep silent!

SUZANNAH: You see plainly, my soul is tormented. An iron hand clasps my mouth and prevents me from speaking. Father, my good father–I love you! When I saw you again, I felt that I was going to die of joy. During the sad years of absence, I thought of you every day! I love you! What can I say? If I can't speak, it's because I love you!

(*Donnor shakes his head and Suzannah throws herself at his knees.*)

SUZANNAH: Believe me! oh, believe me! I entreat you–in the name of my mother whose name my guilty mouth would not dare to profane.

(*Suzannah tries to take Donnor's hand but he pulls it away.*)

SUZANNAH: What have I done to God? (*joining her hands*) Believe me, Father! I beg you, in the name of Clary, my sister, and your dear child!

DONNOR (*shaking*): Clary–it's true. I have another daughter! I don't want her to remain with you!

SUZANNAH (*broken*): Ah! I am so wretched.

DONNOR: I don't want it! Clary is a child. Once Percival is cured–if he's cured now–I will take her by the hand and the two of us will return to Ireland. We will be poor–but there, at least, I will be able to take her to pray on her mother's tomb.

SUZANNAH: Father, you are killing me.

DONNOR: I still have one daughter–

SUZANNAH: Mercy! Mercy!

DONNOR: No, no, leave me alone.

(*Suzannah drags herself on her knees. Donnor recoils to the drapery and pushes her away, then disappears into Percival's bedroom.*)

SUZANNAH (*alone*): Mercy! (*she remains like that for a moment, then rises*) Oh, Father, I love you. I love you so much. (*with resolve*) Well! I will fight these powerful Gentlemen who stand between me and my father. There is justice down here, and since God has no mercy on me–I will have recourse to human justice!

(*Suddenly, Percival comes to.*)

PERCIVAL: Where am I? There's like a veil over my mind! (*seeing Donnor who has his face in his hands*) Donnor? What's the matter?
DONNOR: There is–sir–we are both really distressed.

(*In the doorway, Suzannah hears.*)

SUZANNAH: Oh! All three of us are, father.

Scene VI

(*The Stage represents a cellar in Saint Giles. There is a large stairway in the back, brick pillars, casks, pitchers, etc. The folks of the Great Family of the Underworld are assembled. Some are drinking. Some dance in the back with women. Near the audience, thirty or forty dubious-looking characters are gathered around a small chest and gold coins can be seen rolling. It is a very animated scene.*)

BOB LANTERN, MR. SNAIL, MR. TURNBULL, MITCH, BERT AND OTHERS (*all singing*):

> *London sees its shops closed*
> *But the passersby wants nothing*
> *Watch it! They are our customers!*
> *Clever thieves, we follow them step by step*
> *But careful–no noise*
> *Think that it's midnight*
> *It's the work hour*
> *Of the Gentlemen of the Night*
> *We scorn police and constables*
> *The future will speak for us–*
> *With a charitable love–*
> *Each of us is concerned about the wealth of all*
> *Old milords with full pockets*
> *Young ladies with expensive jewels*
> *Fine gentlemen, beautiful ladies–*
> *Be careful and take care of yourselves!*

MR. SNAIL: Bravo! Bravo! Now, listen! We're going to have a big to do tonight. We are going to have company!

ALL: Company?

MR. SNAIL: Yes. Visitors completely fashionable–who will pay plenty to see us.

BOB LANTERN: Who? Speak up!

MR. SNAIL: I'd give you a thousand guesses, but you would never guess it. Well! We're going to have the lion of lions–the king of fine linen, the Marquis de Rio Santo himself!

ALL: The Marquis de Rio Santo!

MR. SNAIL: Nothing less than that, my little ones! The Marquis intends to visit our establishment of Saint Gilles–with a friend–and be present at our Family gussying up.

BOB LANTERN: The rich! They can't refuse themselves anything!

MR. SNAIL: I have promised him an extraordinary evening. Something in the carefully prepared vein. A cock fight–and boxers tied together.

BOB LANTERN: *Cristi*! Boxing is easy enough! But the cocks?

MR. SNAIL: Don't get upset, Bob. Everything's thought of. Silence, the rest of you. Here's the company.

BOB LANTERN (*coyly*): Let's try to be distinguished. Necessary to do the honors.

(*Rio Santo and Fanny Bertram enter.*)

ALL (*bowing*): Milady Milord–

RIO SANTO: Ladies, Gentlemen–don't let me disturb you! I beg you to willingly pardon us for the perhaps indiscreet curiosity which brings us amongst you.

MR. SNAIL: There's no offense. Put yourself at ease. You're at home here.

FANNY (*aside*): He doesn't know how well he speaks.

MR. SNAIL (*low*): He seems honest enough–for a Marquis!

BOB LANTERN (*low*): Result of knowing how to live. (*aloud*) Should we present your wife to him?

MR. SNAIL: Not at all, not at all. We must beware the thoughtlessness of women. Imprudent!

FANNY (*to Rio Santo*): What is your plan in coming here?

RIO SANTO: Curiosity and necessity. I want to see for myself. There have always been intermediaries between the people of the Family and myself. I'm cautious, you know. Now, I want to see these characters up close because I'm relying on them to play their parts.

FANNY: Dangerous auxiliaries. Villainous faces!

RIO SANTO: You're not very comfortable in the midst of these rogues?

FANNY: Alone, I'm never afraid. When you're with me, I'm only afraid for you.

RIO SANTO: A good worker must know how to use all kinds of tools.

FANNY: These don't look like very good tools.

BOB LANTERN: Hey, gang–let's prepare the ball room!

MR. TURNBULL (*to Bob*): Say, do we have the right to mess in the pockets of these Toffs?

MR. SNAIL: Fie! Bob! Fie! It's plain to see you're not a gentleman. Me, I am William Snail, Esquire! That's the way I sign my correspondence.

BOB LANTERN: Still–the small needs of the Family–

MR. SNAIL: And, the hospitality, wretch! What about the laws of hospitality!

BOB LANTERN: Bah! They haven't eaten salt with us. Salt, that's what constitutes hospitality.

MR. SNAIL: True, true–they haven't eaten the least grain of salt.

BOB LANTERN (*to Rio Santo*): I have the honor of presenting to you–the brave Mr. Turnbull–here–

MR. SNAIL: My brother-in-law!

BOB LANTERN: And this here is the celebrated Mitch, famous for 17 years of success. Come closer, Mitch, let 'em see you! His eye isn't yet clean from the last blow he received, but that doesn't count. It doesn't prevent him from being one of the greatest ornaments to the sex to which he belongs. These two gentlemen will procure you a great deal of pleasure, milord.

FANNY: No fighting, please–

RIO SANTO: Gentlemen, no fighting.

MR. SNAIL: Your Lordship's really squeamish!

BOB LANTERN: Fine, my little gentleman! You're paying for the evening, you have the right to direct it.

MR. SNAIL: In that case: cocks, cocks! I'm going to set His Grace Lord Wellington against Admiral Nelson! See Wellington, admire Wellington–

BOB LANTERN: Look at Nelson! Admire Nelson! A half guinea for Nelson. I don't like the other one, not me!

MITCH: I go for the Duke–

BERT: Two pounds on Nelson!

MR. TURNBULL: A pound on Wellington.

BOB LANTERN: Go for the betting. Wellington against Nelson!

RIO SANTO: Where do these champions come from?

MR. SNAIL: Wellington is from Jersey. Fine stock, offspring of Marlborough and Sidonia.

BOB LANTERN: Nelson comes from Brussels. Fine stock. Offspring of Clara and Ze-ze-bang-bang! Milord–will you bet? And you, milady?

RIO SANTO: We will both bet–

FANNY: Certainly I will bet–and on both fighters if you like.

ALL: Nelson! Wellington!

RIO SANTO (*looking for his purse*): By Jove. Now, that is odd!

FANNY: What's wrong?

RIO SANTO: I no longer have my purse.

FANNY (*laughing*): I won't offer you mine, for I indeed suspect–it's vanished, too.

MR. SNAIL (*to Bob*): Right. Where are they?

BOB LANTERN: They've just mislaid them. (*pulls two purses from his pocket*)

MR. SNAIL (*to Bob*): Ah! Nasty.

BOB LANTERN (*to Snail*): They haven't eaten salt. (*to Rio Santo*) Milord, I think you've misplaced your purse. (*to Mitch*) Hold Nelson for me. (*to Rio Santo*) If you will allow me to loan you some money–

RIO SANTO: It seems you have confidence in me?

BOB LANTERN: Oh! Milord, all that I have is yours!

RIO SANTO: I am holding all the bets, gentlemen!

MR. SNAIL: Bravo! You'll never have so much fun. Move–so everybody can see! Go Wellington! Go Nelson! Go!

(*Cock fight. Suddenly, Paddy O'Chrane rushes in.*)

PADDY O'CHRANE: Stop that! God damns us all! Silence! Pay attention!

ALL: What's the matter?

MR. SNAIL: Have you ever seen an innocent sport so troubled?

PADDY O'CHRANE: Silence! We're all ruined! Are we all Family here?

ALL: Yes!

BOB LANTERN: One moment. There are two strangers here. (*points to Rio Santo and Fanny*)

PADDY O'CHRANE: The Devil!

RIO SANTO: What's wrong? You appear very uneasy! If it's important news, tell it–perhaps, I'm not a stranger after all.

PADDY O'CHRANE: Do you know *the name*, by chance?

RIO SANTO: Perhaps–

ALL: Ah? (*surrounding Rio Santo and Fanny.*)

RIO SANTO & FANNY (*extending their hands*): *Gentlemen of the Night*!

ALL (*extending their hands*): Newgate and Treadwell!

RIO SANTO (*to Paddy*): You see that you can speak freely.

MR. SNAIL (*to Rio Santo*): Ah! You're in! I pay you my compliments, Milord.

BOB LANTERN: Now, let's hear it!

(*All come together.*)

PADDY O'CHRANE: By Thunder! Let me breathe. I took two minutes to come from Mary-le-Bone to come here (*to Rio Santo*) Listen to me carefully, and let's think fast, because we have only a quarter of an hour before us. I was at the local police station (*all bow*) for some petty little fines incurred by these wise guys–when I saw enter–guess who?–I give you a thousand guesses.

MR. SNAIL (*in jest*): The statue from Trafalgar Square?

PADDY O'CHRANE (*raising his hand, Snail dodges*): You will never guess. I saw the girl that Doctor Moore enrolled walk in.

RIO SANTO: Suzannah?

PADDY O'CHRANE: You know her?

RIO SANTO: By Jove–since I'm one of you–

PADDY O'CHRANE: That's true. This Suzannah–conniving bitch–

BOB LANTERN: What did she do?

PADDY O'CHRANE: You ask? She came quite simply to denounce our little business at Saint James–the diamonds and the whole caboodle. If you'd seen her (*imitating Suzannah*) "These wretches," she said, "these wretches took advantage of my despair. The diamonds you've sought so much..." For all the Police in London have had no rest searching for those jewels. The Russian Prince has threatened war and worse if they're not found!

BOB LANTERN: These Russians can be so narrow-minded.

PADDY O'CHRANE (*resuming in Suzannah's tone*): "The diamonds you've been seeking–these men stole then right in front of me. They used me." "Would you recognize them?" said the Commissioner. "Yes, I would, sir." "Will you denounce them?" "Yes, I would, sir."

BOB LANTERN: Well, well, if she ever falls into our hands...

RIO SANTO: And then what?

PADDY O'CHRANE: And then, the Commissioner called for his men. They're coming. I saw the Constables coming down the stairs and spread in the courtyard like a flight of vultures.

BOB LANTERN: The Devil! The Devil!

PADDY O'CHRANE: They're all going to be here in a few minutes.

BOB LANTERN (*desolate*): I've always had the notion that I'd be hanged.

MR. SNAIL: There's still time to get a little air. (*slips towards the door*)

POLICE (*outside*): Open, in the name of the Law!

(*Snail meows. General action of flight, but there's no place to run. The place is surrounded.*)

FANNY (*to Rio Santo*): Shall we stay?

RIO SANTO: There's no exit.

FANNY: They're here.

RIO SANTO: Don't worry.

PADDY O'CHRANE: Palms!

BOB LANTERN: Chestnuts!

MR. SNAIL: Pinched. Police raid! What a trick!

(*Enter Suzannah, followed by the Commissioner and his Clerk, and a host of Constables. The whole cortege gravely descends the steps of the cellar. The Policemen have not noticed Rio Santo and Fanny, to the side.*)

PADDY O'CHRANE: Is one allowed to ask–

COMMISSIONER (*severely*): You will speak when you are questioned.

PADDY O'CHRANE: Gentleman, I'm a honest seaman–

MR. SNAIL: You've already got the rope around your neck, you old fool. (*Bob mimes being strangled.*)

COMMISSIONER (*to the Clerk*): Sit down and write. (*to Suzannah*) Look at these men. Do you recognize amongst them those whom you accuse?

SUZANNAH: Yes.

COMMISSIONER: Point them out.

SUZANNAH (*pointing to Snail*): He was the one disguised as a page.

COMMISSIONER: The one who carried Her Ladyship's train?

MR. SNAIL: Who are you calling a page? Why, by God! I am William Snail Esquire–a gentleman.

SUZANNAH (*pointing to Paddy O'Chrane*): And this is the man who let me inside Saint James Palace.

COMMISSIONER (*to Paddy*): Your name?

PADDY O'CHRANE: A name without blemish, magistrate. Paddy O'Chrane, Captain, a honest man–retired from the reserves–

COMMISSIONER (*to the Clerk*): Write it all down. (*to Suzannah*) And then–is that all?

SUZANNAH: I don't know. I think so, yes.

BOB LANTERN (*aside*): She didn't recognize me, the dear angel!

MR. SNAIL: Don't move! I am hiding you.

COMMISSIONER (*to Suzannah*): As you accuse them here, you will accuse them in Court?

SUZANNAH: I swear to do so.

COMMISSIONER: Sign your declaration! (*to all*) Gentlemen, this is not the first time this establishment has been reported to us. We are therefore going to profit from this opportunity by taking all your names and descriptions.

(*Rio Santo steps forward.*)

RIO SANTO: I'll begin by giving you mine, sir.

SUZANNAH (aside): Him! My God! It's him!

BOB LANTERN: All honor to the Lord! He doesn't funk it, the Toff.

MR. SNAIL (*softened*): Ah! damn, indeed that's a fine gesture.

SUZANNAH (*aside*): Him! Everywhere! But, what's he going to think of me?

COMMISSIONER (*rising*): You here, Milord? Permit us to humbly address our respects to you–and our acts of thanks.

RIO SANTO (*haughtily*): And why is that, sir?

BOB LANTERN (*to Snail*): The Commissioner is joshing– that's rich!

COMMISSIONER (*to the Constables*): Gentlemen, thank Milord. His Lordship has deigned to employ his lofty influence with Mr. Johnstone–

RIO SANTO: Ah, yes, the good Mr. Johnstone...

COMMISSIONER (*continuing*): –To procure us the positions that we are occupying at the Saint Giles police station.

CONSTABLES (*bowing*): Ah! Milord!

RIO SANTO (*laughing*): Fanny, what do you say to that?

FANNY (*laughing*): Excellent! Perfect!

BOB LANTERN: He's laughing–good, good!

MR. SNAIL: My, my! There go the Commissioner laughing, too. Hey, the rest of you, let's laugh, since they're laughing.

(*Everybody starts laughing.*)

BOB LANTERN: All the same, I'd like to know why we're laughing.

RIO SANTO (*to Bob*): Say *the name*.

BIB LANTERN: *The name!* Before these crows?

RIO SANTO: Go ahead!

BOB LANTERN (*timidly*): *Gentlemen of the Night.*

ALL THE POLICE (*in chorus, extending their hands*): Newgate and Treadwell!

(*All burst into laughter.*)

MR. SNAIL: Ah! That was good! Now there's an evening! I'm amused!

(*Bob and the others slap hands with the police.*)

BOB LANTERN (*laughing*): Ah! The spleen! Ah! The belly! They'll be the cause of my death—that's certain. (*pointing to Rio Santo*) All the same—the worst one of us all—that's him.

SUZANNAH (*aside*): Him! In this den of thieves! Him! Their accomplice! Oh, but me, too, haven't I been their slave?

PADDY O'CHRANE (*to Suzannah*): You wanted to get your friends pinched, eh? Well, it's you who are in the mousetrap now.

BOB LANTERN: My neck will recall you for a long while, little girl.

MR. SNAIL: Naughty!

PADDY O'CHRANE: They told you that our Family was powerful. They told you nothing in the world could save you, if you came to betray us. And you have betrayed us—beware!

FANNY (*low to Suzannah*): Courage—he will save you.

ALL (*in the back*): Long live the Marquis de Rio Santo!

PADDY O'CHRANE: Help me, friends! Do you want to judge this woman?

ALL (*returning*): Yes!

PADDY O'CHRANE: The law of the Family has only one article. That article says: "All treachery will be punished by death!" Does this woman deserve death?

ALL: Yes–yes–

RIO SANTO: One moment! I am taking this woman under my protection.

PADDY O'CHRANE: Milord!

RIO SANTO: I said, I am taking her under my protection.

(*Murmurs.*)

PADDY O'CHRANE: Milord, your protection is great, but our security–

RIO SANTO: I demand from you liberty for this woman. Are you already forgetting that you owe me your freedom, perhaps your life? But for me, the Constables of Saint Gilles would be true Constables.

BOB LANTERN: Indeed, that's true, but it doesn't change–

PADDY O'CHRANE: Come on, come on–let's leave her alone–so as not to upset Milord.

BOB LANTERN: As for me, I say that is not smart. All the Constables of London are not *Gentlemen of the Night*. We will have trouble on account of this, you will see!

RIO SANTO (*to Suzannah*): You are free! If you were to speak henceforth, Suzannah, that would be to repay a good deed with treason. That would be ungrateful and infamous. Do you swear to keep silent?

SUZANNAH: I swear it. (*aside*) Because now, I'd be ruining him.

RIO SANTO (*to the Constables*): Come on, gentlemen– accompany her–then you will resign your duties to Mr. Johnstone. We will have need of you elsewhere.

SUZANNAH (*aside*): My God! My God!

(*She leaves with the policemen.*)

FANNY (*to Rio Santo*): That's fine what you did there–very fine.

RIO SANTO: Gentlemen–bring up a table. And now, Fanny, you will learn the rest of my secret. (*places one foot on a chair and the other on the table*) All, come close, listen! Chance has hurried events! It's time that you know the truth. It's been ten years since your supreme leader–the Lord of the Night–conceived a gigantic project. To execute this project required an immense force–you are part of that force. Our association that you think organized solely for crime conceals another purpose. You can be raised up, you can be absolved of the past. Up to now. your word of order has been–pillage and theft. I am coming to propose to you another word of order. Will you be men? Will you shout with me: Ireland and liberty!

(*Murmurs of astonishment.*)

BOB LANTERN (*to Snail*): Heavens, it seems that we were unsuspecting political swindlers!

MR. SNAIL (*to Bob*): It's been said that politicians are not unlike swindlers.

RIO SANTO: It took ten years to assemble the powder which is soon going to explode. The hour has come–and to decide the fate of the battle, only a blow is needed. The Lord of the Night counted on you–will you be his soldiers?

PADDY O'CHRANE: Sure! Why not?

ALL: Yes–yes!

BOB LANTERN: Soldiers, us? Thanks, but no thanks. As for me, I ask to absolutely abstain.

PADDY O'CHRANE: Poltroon!

MR. SNAIL: As for me, if they make me drum major–I am ready.

RIO SANTO: In an instant, there'll be nothing more to fear–for victory is certain. At the hour in which I am speaking to you, Ireland is awaiting the signal for war. The county of Wales, ready to rise, is furbishing its arms. Birmingham and the manufacturing counties are agitating for a charter of the people. There are 50,000 soldiers there who are awaiting only a shout to close their ranks and march–

ALL: It's true! It's true.

RIO SANTO: –On London. Ah! It's here that we are the strongest. Count with me our arms: Spitalfields will launch into the city a thousands of brave workers, made angry by the recent lowering of wages; Saint Giles will cast out its innumerable hosts, like a furious tide that no dyke could ever hope to contain. Ireland finally–the land of heroic sufferings– Ireland will send us 10,000 soldiers–brothers who will fight with us, conquer with us.

ALL: Bravo! Bravo!

RIO SANTO (*to Fanny*): If I die, let it be sword in hand, face to face with the enemy. But listen! Henceforth time presses– the Liberator of Ireland is in Dublin. He must know that everything is ready. A letter might be lost.

FANNY: I will go.

RIO SANTO (*shaking her hand*): Thanks! Tell him what you have just seen–what you have just heard; that his hesitations cease–that he send his 10,000 men–indeed more, that he return at their head! With them. and with him–we will be invincible.

PADDY O'CHRANE (*to Rio Santo*): We are determined, more than ever. Tell us now what we have to do.

RIO SANTO: Let the members of the Great Family hold themselves ready. Let them arm themselves.

PADDY O'CHRANE: And when will action be necessary? The place? The day?

RIO SANTO: Wait! (*to Fanny*) How much time to go and return?

FANNY: How long for the boldest courier, the most intrepid horse?

RIO SANTO: Six days–but you! a woman! You could be killed by exhaustion!

FANNY: I will return in five days. If exhaustion kills me, well, I will die for you. In five days. you will have a reply from the Liberator–

RIO SANTO: Goodbye–sister.

(*Fanny leaves.*)

PADDY O'CHRANE: Well, Milord?

RIO SANTO (*on the steps*): In five days, my friends, under the windows of the Trevor house–

PADDY O'CHRANE: And the signal? Who will give the signal?

RIO SANTO: Your master–the Lord of the Night!

PADDY O'CHRANE: We've never seen him–

RIO SANTO (*uncovering his head*): Look at me! All! And when the day of combat comes, you will recognize my face!

PADDY O'CHRANE (*recoiling*): You are then the Lord of the Night! (*to the others*) He's the Lord! (*removing his hat*) Give a hurrah for the Lord of the Night!

ALL: Hurrah! For the Lord of the Night

CURTAIN

Act IV

Scene VII

(*A poor bedroom. On the wall, there is a crucifix and images of the saints. It is the home of Mother Jacobs, the old woman who takes care of Clary. There is a door leading outside at the back, and one, to the side, leading to a bedroom.*

(*Suzannah, alone, enters. She tosses her hat on the bed and reveals her disheveled hair. She lets herself fall into a seat. She seems broken with emotion.*)

SUZANNAH: It's like a dream, a terrible, mad dream! And him! Him! The Marquis de Rio Santo–he whose proud nobility evoked my love–him! Him! The King of that Hell! Oh! My poor heart! How alone and desperate I am. Who will pity me now?

(*Suzannah remains depressed for a moment. Then the door to the bedroom half-opens and Clary's blonde head can be seen. Suzannah's back is turned away from her; Clary advances on tip-toe.*)

CLARY: Hello, big sister!

(*Suzannah shivers and turns away. Clary sees tears in her eyes. She rushes to her.*)

CLARY: Tears again! Always! Always! Why, are you unhappy now, sister?
SUZANNAH (*drying her eyes*): Hello, Clary (*hugs her.*)
CLARY: You don't reply?
SUZANNAH: You're going to be really happy–

CLARY: Then, why are you still weeping?

SUZANNAH: I'm not weeping.

CLARY (*reproachfully*): When I lie, you scold me very harshly. (*kissing her*) My good sister–you are in pain and you don't want to tell me. I beg you. Here I am, a young lass–tell me why you are sad, and I will know how to console you, watch and see!

SUZANNAH: I'm not sad, Clary–see me smile.

CLARY: You are smiling through your tears.

SUZANNAH: I'm happy. And when you are here, little sister, I think that God will protect us.

CLARY: Oh, yes, God will protect us because God loves those who are good. And you are so good.

SUZANNAH: Dear child! Have you said your prayer this morning?

CLARY (*lowering her head*): I didn't see you yesterday evening. And I wanted so much to embrace you! I forgot my prayer, sister!

SUZANNAH (*clasping her to her heart*): How I love you!

CLARY: You are not scolding me?

SUZANNAH: Listen, you won't be alone in the world. You will have a friend. Someone will watch over you.

CLARY (*frightened*): Why are you telling me this?

SUZANNAH: Because–because you will be beautiful–what do I know? Because I don't want you to cry like me when you're 20, Clary!

(*Suzannah rises. Clary rises and goes near her sister.*)

CLARY: So it's because you're 20 that you are weeping?

SUZANNAH: Come, say your prayer.

CLARY: You will pray with me?

SUZANNAH: Yes.

(*Suzannah takes Clary by the hand and leads her to the Crucifix where they both kneel.*)

CLARY: My God, our Lord, who calls the children and the weak to you, hear the voice of your children.
SUZANNAH: Hearken to us, Lord.
CLARY: My God Our Savior have pity on our dead mother.
SUZANNAH: Hearken to us, Lord.
CLARY: Watch over my good sister, Suzannah, My God, so she can be happy on Earth and blessed in Heaven. (*Suzannah moves away. Silence.*) Your turn, sis! (*Silence. Clary turns and sees Suzannah, eyes bathed in tears*) What is wrong with you, sister? (*she starts crying, too.*)
SUZANNAH: Continue your prayer. Speak to God all alone. God and the Virgin Mary will hear you better if my voice is not joined to yours–
CLARY: Have you forgotten our Irish prayers?
SUZANNAH: No, for I learned them from our mother.
CLARY: Then, why?
SUZANNAH: Continue.
CLARY (*embarrassed*): They say that those who don't wish to pray–you're the one who told me this–have something to reproach themselves with before God. (*Suzannah covers her face with her hands*) You keep silent? (*with a smile*) Oh, you don't need to reply. God knows quite well that you are as good as an angel.

(*Mother Jacobs enter.*)

MOTHER JACOBS: There's a gentleman at the door who would like to speak to Miss Suzannah.
SUZANNAH (*rising and starting*): Send him away. I don't want–I cannot receive anyone.
MOTHER JACOBS: It's the gentleman at–
SUZANNAH: Who cares what his name is. I want to be alone.
MOTHER JACOBS (*undeterred*): –The gentleman at whose home your father–
SUZANNAH: Mr. Percival.
CLARY: Yes–receive him–and try to know if we will soon see our father–

SUZANNAH: Mr. Percival. Show him in. And take Clary away.
CLARY: I would like to know–
SUZANNAH: Go! I'll tell you everything later.

(*Clary leaves with Mother Jacobs through the bedroom. After a moment, Mt. Percival enters.*)

PERCIVAL: Miss, I beg you to be merciful and to–
SUZANNAH: Sir, are you coming on behalf of my father?
PERCIVAL: I would like to tell you I am coming on behalf of your father. But that would not be the truth.
SUZANNAH: In that case, what do you want from me?
PERCIVAL: One more time, please, pardon me. You are the daughter of an honest and worthy man–who is for me more of a friend than a servant. But it's such a strange thing, your perseverance at the bedside of a stranger–that kiss on my face.
SUZANNAH: Oh! Sir! Your reproaches will break my heart– but they will get nothing out of me. I didn't speak when my father kicked me out, I will not now.
PERCIVAL: Perhaps, you don't know all the harm you did?
SUZANNAH: I saw the young girl faint. You were loved– what more can I know?
PERCIVAL: There are some happy folks who console themselves in the family foyer–the sweet voice of a sister comes to cradle their suffering. They have a brother from whom to ask compassion if they become depressed, a father to press his hand in theirs. Their icy face warms to the kiss of a mother. A mother! As for me, Miss, I am alone. God has left me on the Earth after all those who loved me. I lost my brother–a noble friend; I lost my sister, the holy joy of my youth. My father and mother are dead. Well, amongst all this sorrow, one hope shone. An angelic smile lit the night of my despair. I was no longer alone. I was reborn to joy. I was loved–loved! And that was my last thought before I fainted– my supreme hope which forever fled–
SUZANNAH: Because I came–

PERCIVAL: I am not accusing you.

SUZANNAH: Your lamentations accuse me. Your sorrow punishes me.

PERCIVAL: I am so unhappy.

SUZANNAH: As for me, am I happy?

PERCIVAL: But, with a word, you could–

SUZANNAH (*stopping him*): No–

PERCIVAL: You've never loved, in that case?

SUZANNAH (*coldly*): I do love

PERCIVAL: Oh! that's not the way that word is pronounced.

SUZANNAH: Sir, I don't wish to compare my martyrdom with your misfortune, since you are innocent of my martyrdom and your misfortune is my doing. But all that you are suffering, I am suffering a hundredfold. How can you speak of family, you who know that my father rejects me? How can you speak of love, you who are loved? How can you speak of despair, you who still hope? As for me, I no longer hope–yet, my love is true, stronger than my will–stronger than the thought of my father–stronger than the fear of God. It is there, full of delights and full of tortures–it is there, surviving even hope lost. They broke my soul. Well! I still love. They trampled me underfoot! Yet I still love. Oh! If he were jealous of me as she is jealous of you, it wouldn't be sorrow, it would be joy that would kill me.

PERCIVAL: Suzannah! Pity! Have pity on me. I wrote to Mary. I wrote to Lord Trevor–my letters were rejected with disdain. I have no longer any hope except in you. You know what's at the bottom of this secret. And you refuse to tell me! To save me from the abyss of despair, it would suffice for you to extend your hand to me–and you won't extend it. Oh, don't reject me any further! Or indeed, I will believe that you have nothing in your heart. I will believe that you lied when you said you were suffering like me.

SUZANNAH: Sir–I am condemned. I can do nothing for others and I can do nothing for myself. Leave me alone.

PERCIVAL: I am lost! (*coldly*) And what must I say to your father?

SUZANNAH: Tell him not to pardon me, since I refuse you–

PERCIVAL: Oh! I don't want to believe you. You are deceiving yourself–through it's sheathed in ice, I see your heart–and my voice will know how to open a path. Yes, just now, despite you, a tear was in your eye–you hid it, but I surprised it, and hope has returned to me. Listen further. You have a secret. I don't wish to surprise it. Here I am at your knees–asking your pity for me–and pity for her as well. You are turning away your head. (*Suzannah places her hand on her heart.*) If you reject me after this supreme prayer–I will no longer insist, Miss, I will go intercede for you with your father to whom I will say: "Donnor, don't reproach your daughter with my death–an oath binds her–an oath stronger than her will. Pardon her, as I pardon her." You don't reply? Goodbye, Miss–you are condemning me to misfortune. May God make you happy. (*starts to leave*)

SUZANNAH: Stay, stay a while. You said: "Pity for me and pity for her." Pity for you who gave bread to my father when he was dying on the pavements of London where charity is unknown. Pity for her who before extended her hand to me...

PERCIVAL (*excitedly*): To you?

SUZANNAH: It's been a long time since I knew and loved her. What you did for a poor Irishman, Mary Trevor, a beautiful angel of mercy, did for a poor Irish girl. Oh, if it was only a question of my life!

PERCIVAL: I tell you, I don't want to know your secret. She loves me, you know that very well. They profited by her jealousy to throw her into the arms of that man. Go to her and tell her only that Frank Percival never saw you before, that you're only the daughter of the man who serves him, that Frank Percival loves only her and has never loved anyone but her–

SUZANNAH (*hesitating*): If I thought–

PERCIVAL (*with rapture*): Suzannah! Oh! Suzannah!

SUZANNAH: I am suffering less seeing your joyful hope.

PERCIVAL: Suzannah, a good action, and I will owe you for it all my life.

SUZANNAH: Very well–I will go.
PERCIVAL: Ah!
SUZANNAH: What's wrong with you? Poor man–he's ill–
PERCIVAL: It's nothing–joy–seizure–

(*Suzannah makes Percival sit on a chair.*)

SUZANNAH: You indeed love Miss Trevor? It's nice to love. Goodbye, I'm leaving you–you're going to be happy–
PERCIVAL: Wait!
SUZANNAH: What?
PERCIVAL: There's a proper way to be admitted to the House of Trevor. Write to Miss Mary and ask for her permission to see you.
SUZANNAH: Right away.

(*Suzannah sits at a writing desk.*)

PERCIVAL: Tell her–
SUZANNAH: I know what I must say to her. (*sits and write*) I will take the letter myself to be sure–
PERCIVAL (*going to the table*): No, I don't want you to take this letter.

(*Clary appears in the doorway.*)

PERCIVAL: I brought someone with me. I foresaw that you would give in to my ardent prayers–

(*He goes to the door and opens it. Donnor is revealed. He enters. Clary runs to him. They hug. Meanwhile, Suzannah is still writing. Donnor takes an hesitant step towards her.*)

PERCIVAL (*to Donnor*): She has your good heart.
CLARY (*to Donnor*): Oh, father! father! don't you love both your daughters?
DONNOR: Yes–yes– (*advances softly*)

SUZANNAH (*finishing writing*): You say that you have someone to take the letter?
PERCIVAL (*taking Donnor by the hand*): Yes, I do. Look–

(*Suzannah at first offers the letter without turning; then she turns and utters a scream.*)

SUZANNAH: Father!
PERCIVAL: I was sure of your heart, Miss. I wanted Donnor to be here to hear you–
DONNOR: My daughter! My Suzannah! My children!

(*Donnor clasps both Suzannah and Clary to his breast.*)

SUZANNAH: Father! my poor father! have you pardoned me?
CLARY: Oh, father, I don't know what Sis did–those who do no love her are bad.
DONNOR (*to Suzannah*): You are dark-haired and pale, just like your mother. (*to Clary*) As for you, you resemble an angel. My children!
PERCIVAL: There, they are happy!

(*The door opens and Rio Santo appears. Astonished, he stops and watches, visibly softened.*)

DONNOR: If only your mother could see you.
CLARY (*turning and seeing Rio Santo*): Oh!

(*Suzannah shivers. Donnor looks and recoils. Rio Santo bows respectfully to Suzannah. Percival observes them, astonished.*)

PERCIVAL: He's the gentleman–
DONNOR (*uneasily, to Percival*): Do you know this man?
PERCIVAL (*embarrassed*): Yes, I know him.
DONNOR (*astonished*): Is it you he's come to seek at my daughter's?

PERCIVAL (*looking at Suzannah who gives him a sign*): Perhaps–

DONNOR: Then, he's one of your friends?

PERCIVAL (*after a moment of hesitation extends his hand to Rio Santo*): Yes.

RIO SANTO (*low*): Thanks, Mr. Percival.

DONNOR (*aside, suspicious*): She is staying with Mr. Percival. (*aloud*) I am going to take that letter. Goodbye, Suzannah.

CLARY: You won't be long, father?

DONNOR: I'll be back. Do you hear me, Suzannah? I'll be back!

SUZANNAH: You will find me here, father.

(*Donnor leaves.*)

SUZANNAH (*to Clary*) Leave us alone, little sister (*hugs her.*)

CLARY (*pouting*): They always send me away–and always because of this gentleman.

(*Clary leaves.*)

RIO SANTO (*to Percival*): I thank you again, sir–and I wish you had spoken truly in naming me your friend.

PERCIVAL: Milord, you are a courtly man–when you had cast me to the ground with a pistol shot, you didn't omit either a chivalrous bow or a gracious smile. Just now, I named you my friend to spare the heart of this worthy man–the father of Miss Suzannah. He would have suffered if he'd heard your name mentioned.

RIO SANTO: May I know–?

PERCIVAL: That man spent days and nights at my bedside, Milord. He was able to see that your Lordship didn't wound his adversaries only with weapons of combat–

RIO SANTO: I don't understand, sir. I thought to have acted against you honestly.

113

PERCIVAL: "Honestly?" There were moments when I believed that myself. You gave me good ground on the field, Milord, and if I didn't kill you, it wasn't your fault, I must agree to that. Since that meeting, you've sent for news of my health every morning and evening. Your doctor, the wise Doctor Moore, has given all his care to my case–but–

RIO SANTO: But–?

PERCIVAL: Is it I or Miss Suzannah you come to seek here?

RIO SANTO (*smiling*): Sir, I wouldn't come looking for you at Miss Suzannah's–

PERCIVAL: But you sent Miss Suzannah to my home, Milord.

SUZANNAH (*as if struck by an idea*): It was him!

RIO SANTO: At your home? Miss Suzannah–I am unaware–I don't understand–

SUZANNAH: That would be him!

PERCIVAL (*bitterly*): You were not able to kill me completely. Mary still loved me. You thought that jealousy excited in the poor young girl's heart could separate her from me forever. And then, Milord–a wretched and infamous comedy was played at my bedside–the bedside of a wounded man. A woman came, an innocent instrument of this shameful intrigue. Mary saw this woman kneeling by my bed and–

RIO SANTO: Is this true, Suzannah?

SUZANNAH: Yes, it is.

PERCIVAL: You didn't know it?

RIO SANTO: To anyone else but you, Mr. Percival, I wouldn't permit this question, which is an outrage.

PERCIVAL (*lowering his voice*): I am reassured, Milord, and again at your service.

SUZANNAH (*terrified*): Mr. Percival!

RIO SANTO (*to Suzannah*): Stay out of this! (*to Percival*) I can endure a lot from you, sir, because, without intending it, I have done you a great wrong.

PERCIVAL: You no longer deny it?

RIO SANTO: I affirm that I was completely unaware of it.

PERCIVAL (*interrupting him*): This trick was perfectly odious, right?

RIO SANTO: Infamous!

PERCIVAL: And you are profiting by it, Milord! (*Rio Santo makes no reply.*) For I believe that you are not renouncing your plans to marry Miss Trevor.

(*Suzannah looks at Rio Santo on the sly.*)

RIO SANTO (*after a silence*): I am not renouncing then.

(*Suzannah lowers her head.*)

PERCIVAL (*containing his rage*): I am not your enemy. Why, then, do I always find you in my path? Milord, I don't wish to tell you that, to profit from an infamy, it's necessary to be infamous.

RIO SANTO (*pale*): Sir–!

SUZANNAH (*throwing herself between them and grabbing his arm*): Mr. Percival!

PERCIVAL (*astonished*): Miss!

SUZANNAH: Just now, I told you that I was in love. Well, the one I love–is him!

PERCIVAL (*recoiling*): Him! And it's you they chose as their tool. I am lost. But you love him–despite this marriage which he obstinately insists on–despite–

SUZANNAH: Despite all–despite myself–like a slave.

PERCIVAL: In that case, you would obey him–if he commands–?

SUZANNAH: Like a slave–

PERCIVAL: I am ruined.

SUZANNAH: Why?

PERCIVAL: Because he will order you not to see Miss Trevor! And you won't see her.

(*Suzannah lowers her head.*)

RIO SANTO (*who has kept apart*): Mr. Percival, I needed a few moments to vanquish this brutal enemy called wrath! I've just freed myself from its rough assault. And although I have enslaved my passion to my sovereign will, I am only a man–still, my wrath has been conquered. Mr. Percival, you have given Miss Suzannah a mission. I've grasped that it must be to explain to Miss Trevor the mystery of this infamous comedy played at your sick bed. I've grasped that, once she hears that explanation, Miss Trevor's jealousy ought to collapse–and that her hand, which is presently ready to sign the contract that will unite us will then drop the pen. Well, I give you my word of honor that Miss Suzannah shall fulfill the mission you have confided in her–if none other than myself prevents it.

PERCIVAL: Is it possible?

RIO SANTO: If God wills it that you are ever to know me, Mr. Percival, you will be my friend.

PERCIVAL (*half offering his hand*): Milord, if I was sure–

RIO SANTO: Don't go further. Still, our marriage will take place.

SUZANNAH: To hear that, my God–

PERCIVAL (*pulling back his hand*): Ah! You are playing with my distress.

RIO SANTO: Suzannah will see Miss Trevor. And you can be happy if she loves you.

PERCIVAL (*kissing Suzannah's hand*): Oh! I have confidence in Mary's heart to discern the truth.

RIO SANTO: Suzannah will be free after I've had a moment's conversation with her–without witnesses.

PERCIVAL: I'll withdraw, but–

RIO SANTO (*with dignity*): Fear nothing from this interview, sir. What I just promised you, I promise you a second time on my word of honor.

PERCIVAL: It suffices, Milord. (*bows to Suzannah*) Goodbye, Miss–my only hope is in you.

(*Percival leaves.*)

RIO SANTO (*aside*): Come on, no weaknesses now.

SUZANNAH: Finally, we are alone, Milord. Please, explain yourself. Oh, I beg you–tell me where the dream ends, where reality begins; tell me if I've really understood; tell me that I am not mad.

RIO SANTO: No, Suzannah, you are not mad and what you heard, you understood correctly.

SUZANNAH: In that case, you are married; in that case, you are pushing cruelty to come to me to tell me so yourself, in my home–

RIO SANTO: It's because it's the truth that I just said it myself, here, in your home! Do you think that I esteem you so little as to leave you unaware of this marriage?

SUZANNAH: Oh! You are breaking my heart!

RIO SANTO: I am able to break your heart, but to deceive you by means of a cowardly lie–never!

SUZANNAH: And you–you didn't say that this marriage will be my eternal misfortune?

RIO SANTO: Did I promise to make you happy?

SUZANNAH: Ah! You are right, always right, as right has the law, as right the executioner! Take care! You haven't thought that I could be jealous, that this burning, furious jealousy would overthrow my entire being–that it would rob me of my heart and that it would give me the strength to trample beneath my feet this strange respect, this superstitious fear, this cult that I have vowed to you despite myself! Finally, you didn't foresee that, for the love of you, I would attempt a mindless, but implacable, struggle against you.

RIO SANTO: You may try!

SUZANNAH: A challenge! Ah, don't play with my love! I no longer belong to myself, think of it! My heart is bursting–one word more and I am going to reveal everything to Miss Trevor!

RIO SANTO (*crossing the stage*): Go on!

SUZANNAH (*bitterly*): You will place no obstacles on my path?

RIO SANTO: Me? I gave my word. You're free to leave.

SUZANNAH (*still bitter*): Your word!

RIO SANTO: The word of Rio Santo! A man would pay with his life for a single doubt raised against that word.

SUZANNAH: You don't fear that I will tell Lord Trevor what I saw tonight at Saint Giles? You don't want my submission any more? Why, you're still counting, I can see it, on my generosity–

RIO SANTO: I was expecting that word! That word which betrays the secret of its heart. Generosity! So, you imagined that I have need of clemency! Thus you've doubted me! I was sure of it. Women are always thus! Always! They can love and scorn at the same time! Appearances accuse me! Who cares? Appearances must be ignored! The evidence seems to overwhelm me! Who cares! The eyes must be closed, and the evidence denied. That's the way I want to be loved–and your love is a love mixed with outrageous suspicions! And this would be the love which would impede my progress? It's to this love that I would sacrifice my life and my will? No, no! You've just pronounced your doom! Go, Suzannah, go to the Miss Trevor's home–speak freely–especially, don't fear that I will prevent you from getting to her. As for me, you propose to stir up obstacles–oh! No, no! I don't intend to justify your suspicions. If it's to betray me that you're going to Lord Trevor, then do so. I won't interfere. I wish it.

SUZANNAH: Milord!

RIO SANTO: Nothing more! Goodbye, Suzannah–fight me–I leave you your weapons. Love me, hate me, but respect me! Goodbye, Suzannah, goodbye!

SUZANNAH (*falling into a chair, head in hands*): Oh!

RIO SANTO (*aside, in the doorway*): Poor girl! (*passing a hand over his face*) Ireland! Suzannah, do I really know what I have in my soul? (*straightening up*) Yes, I know. I know, and I will conquer it.

(*Rio Santo leaves. Suzannah remains overwhelmed for a moment, then rises abruptly.*)

SUZANNAH: Whatever happens, I will attempt this last effort. Besides, I promised Mr. Percival and my father. Clary! Clary!

(*Clary comes in running.*)

CLARY: Here I am. Are you happier now?
SUZANNAH: Yes–
CLARY: He's a fine gentleman, then–and I love him well–
SUZANNAH: Help me, Clary. My hat–
CLARY: You're leaving?
SUZANNAH: Yes, immediately but not for long–quick, quick, my hat–

(*Suddenly, Bob Lantern, disguised as a poor Irishman, half-opens the door. Clary immediately hides behind her sister.*)

BOB LANTERN: May I come in? (*aside*) I heard the signal. So, we're now thinking of going to see Miss Trevor. But we'll see about that. We'll see!
SUZANNAH: Who are you?
BOB LANTERN (*winking*): It's I, Owen d'Arleigh. Your papa's cousin. You don't recognize me?
SUZANNAH: I don't know you.
CLARY (*aside*): How ugly this man is! I'm afraid!
BOB LANTERN (*bursting into laughter*): You don't recognize me–Suzannah–the daughter of Old Man Donnor? As for me, I recognize you–although you were indeed small when I last saw you. You were ten–result of the difference in age. As for me, I caught small pox, three years ago, like Saint Patrick's–that changes a lad all the same.
SUZANNAH: It's strange. I don't remember you at all. But, what do you want?
BOB LANTERN: I'm coming on behalf of Old Man Donnor.
SUZANNAH: On behalf of my father?
CLARY (*coming closer*): I no long find him so ugly.
BOB LANTERN: Old Man Donnor wants to see you.

CLARY: Let's go quick.

SUZANNAH: See us? But, it was agreed that I would wait for him here.

BOB LANTERN: Heh! It's because something new has come up. He has to hide for the moment, Old Man Donnor.

SUZANNAH: What do you say?

BOB LANTERN: There are dangers–

SUZANNAH: Dangers! Ah! my God! I fear to understand–

BOB LANTERN: Don't worry. I don't think there's any big thing to fear yet, but you mustn't lose a moment.

CLARY: Sis! Come, come, didn't you hear? We must hurry.

SUZANNAH (*after having hesitated*): Let's go–

CLARY: My poor father! Oh, we will save him, won't we, sis?

BOB LANTERN: Yes, my pretty child, we will save him. Pass, pass, my treasures. Ah, pretty loves. (*to Suzannah*) Well–what's the matter with you? A dagger? What for?

SUZANNAH: To defend our father–and if it comes to that, to defend ourselves, too.

BOB LANTERN (*grimaces, aside*): My word! The Doctor won't be happy–well, that's his business.

SUZANNAH: Go ahead–we are following you, sir.

(*They leave.*)

Scene VIII

(*The interior of the King George Tavern. The stage is divided in two horizontally. On the street level, there is a tavern room; above is a bedroom with a chair. There is a window giving upon the Thames. Beneath the window, there is a trapdoor which opens on the river itself; a ship can be seen by the spectators through the window.*)

MISTRESS GRUFF: So, Bob Lantern is going to come with two little ones.

MR. GRUFF: Yes, my dear Mistress Gruff.

MISTRESS GRUFF: But will he actually pay?

MR. GRUFF: He has paid, my pretty bird.

MISTRESS GRUFF: How much?

MR. GRUFF: Ten pounds sterling–in fine gold–all new. Did I forget to give them to you?

MISTRESS GRUFF: Watch out, Mr. Gruff, this will end very badly.

MR. GRUFF: Mistress Gruff!

MISTRESS GRUFF: Shut up–someone's knocking at the door of the alley. Go open.

MR. GRUFF: I bet it's them.

(Mr. Gruff opens the door; Bob Lantern enters, with Suzannah and Clary.)

MR. GRUFF: Your servant.

BOB LANTERN: Hello, Mr. Gruff. Come in, my little ladies. Greetings, Mistress Gruff. Is papa up above?

SUZANNAH (*recoiling*): The King George Tavern. Why did he bring us here? (*Clary hugs her sister, trembling.*)

MISTRESS GRUFF: The old man waited a short while. He went out with a young gentleman. He's going to return in a minute.

SUZANNAH (*suspicious*): Do you know the name of our father?

BOB LANTERN: By Jove!

MISTRESS GRUFF: Like the name of my own husband, my beauty. It's Mr. Donnor, from d'Arleigh County–a brave honest heart.

CLARY: You see plainly.

MR. GRUFF: Yes, yes, on my faith–

MISTRESS GRUFF: Shut up!

MR. GRUFF: Yes, Mistress Gruff.

SUZANNAH: It's really strange that he chose this house.

MISTRESS GRUFF (*smiling*): Because of what happened the other day–I said right away to Gruff: "I wish my hand had withered for having struck that young girl."

MR. GRUFF: By God! Mistress Gruff, now you are telling me!

MISTRESS GRUFF: Shut up!

MR. GRUFF: Yes, Mistress Gruff.

MISTRESS GRUFF: He's shutting up. (*to Suzannah*) I didn't sleep for two days, not knowing what had become of you. You know quite well how I am, my love–head's a bit excitable, but heart's tender. Will you pardon me?

CLARY: She'll think about it.

SUZANNAH: Of course I've forgiven you, Mistress Gruff– but that doesn't explain why my father–

MISTRESS GRUFF (*giving Clary a pat and embracing her*): Here's a pretty little angel–she will be as beautiful as you, Suzannah.

SUZANNAH: But our father–?

MISTRESS GRUFF: Your father? He didn't want you to return to the home of the young gentleman because there's been–well, he didn't tell me exactly what happened, but I got the idea that your presence was causing some disagreements in that house–

BOB LANTERN (*aside*): Nice touch!

SUZANNAH (*astonished*): My father told you that?

MISTRESS GRUFF (*smiling*): Not in so many words. But while he was chatting with that young gentleman, Mr. Luceval–Perival–

BOB LANTERN: Percival

MISTRESS GRUFF: Yes, Mr. Percival. Frank Percival, by God–you couldn't remind me of the name, Mr. Gruff?

MR. GRUFF: Ah, now she wants me to speak!

MISTRESS GRUFF: He's impossible! (*to Suzannah*) The certainty, my pretty little beauty, is that we have not sought your father out to force him to come to us. This was indeed an honor for us, but if you still have some rancor towards me, and if you are not pleased to wait for him here–

122

BOB LANTERN (*low*): What are you thinking of, woman?

MISTRESS GRUFF (*low*): Trust me.

CLARY: But, little sister, since he's going to come...

SUZANNAH: Well, we will wait for him then.

MISTRESS GRUFF (*to Bob*): You see! (*to Suzannah*) In that case, go up, my dear heart. Your father's had a table set in the room above. You know which one–the room that overlooks the Thames. You will be alone together, just as if you were at home. Go light a lamp, Mr. Gruff.

SUZANNAH: Come, Clary.

MISTRESS GRUFF (*caressing Clary*): My God! The sweet creature–

BOB LANTERN (*to Mr. Gruff*): That woman is a treasure.

MR. GRUFF: Would you buy her off me, Mr. Lantern?

(*Bob Lantern grimaces. Suzannah, Clary, and Mistress Gruff climb a stairway and they are seen to reappear in the upper room where a table is set for three.*)

MISTRESS GRUFF: There–the stairs are tough and I'm no longer 20! I would keep you company, my darling children, but your father ordered me to fetch you a pint of good Iris toddy.

CLARY: Sugared toddy, as in Ireland.

MISTRESS GRUFF: As in Ireland indeed! I'm going to go fetch it it. Till later, my little beauties.

CLARY (*to Suzannah*): How could that woman have hit you? She seems to love you so much.

(*Mistress Gruff goes back down the stairway and returns to the lower room.*)

MISTRESS GRUFF: The birds are caged.

BOB LANTERN (*rising*): You are a superior woman, Mistress Gruff. We will do more business together.

MISTRESS GRUFF: Ah, indeed. What will you do with these little ones?

BOB LANTERN: Me, nothing. I'm acting for Doctor Moore. He has a score to settle with them, I don't know much why–they bother him–from what it appears–and his plans. And then, he's distrustful of Suzannah. Anyway, that's his business. I'm always working for the Doctor. He remains faithful to the traditions of the Family and that suits me. With him, at least, there's no fear of dozing off as a pickpocket and waking up as a soldier. Me, a soldier! Fie!

MR. GRUFF: You say!

BOB LANTERN: Suffice–you know what I mean.

MISTRESS GRUFF: Speaking of the Doctor–the flask?

BOB LANTERN (*pulling a flask from his pocket*): Here. Three drops–you know well enough–

MISTRESS GRUFF: I know, Mr. Lantern.

BOB LANTERN: No more, no less. How much time will it take for this business?

MISTRESS GRUFF: Give me an hour.

BOB LANTERN: What a woman you've got there, Mr. Gruff!

MR. GRUFF: I am quite overwhelmed, Mr. Lantern.

BOB LANTERN: Well, my dear lady, in an hour the boat will be here (*pointing to the Thames*) under the trapdoor–and we'll climb up through the window. That's agreed.

MISTRESS GRUFF: Yes–yes–it's understood!

BOB LANTERN: Ah! What a woman you have there! How sweet!

(*He leaves.*)

MISTRESS GRUFF (*to her husband*): Stay here. As for me, I am going to prepare the toddy for those little girls.

MR. GRUFF: Yes, my dove.

MISTRESS GRUFF: I don't need you to say yes.

MR. GRUFF: Right, my beauty!

MISTRESS GRUFF: I don't need you to say right either.

MR. GRUFF: Well! What should I say then?

MISTRESS GRUFF (shrugging her shoulders): Nothing! Just shut up!

MR. GRUFF (*with a sigh*): And when I think there are people who pity widowers!

(*Mistress Gruff leaves. Above, the two sisters are seated at the table. Suzannah is resting her head on her hand and dozes. Clary casts frightened glances around the room.*)

CLARY: How dark these walls are! (*goes to Suzannah*) Do you hear the wind from the Thames whistling through the window? Do you hear it, sis? (*Suzannah doesn't reply*) Sis! Suzannah! Since that good woman left–I don't know why–my heart is gripped with terror.
SUZANNAH: Our father will come.
CLARY (*pulling up a chair and sitting down*): Oh! Let him come quick. You don't want to chat with me? In that case, tell me what you're thinking? If you would talk to me, I think I'd be less afraid.
SUZANNAH: You're afraid? Child, we are in the midst of London–a short distance from the King's Theater.
CLARY: You don't hear any noises from the city. Everything here is dark and sinister.
SUZANNAH: I spent months in this house.
CLARY: And you weren't afraid?
SUZANNAH: I was very unhappy.
CLARY: Poor sis. (*rising, goes to window and shivers*) The wind resembles the cry of a dying man. What's beneath this window, Suzannah?
SUZANNAH: The Thames.
CLARY (*crossing*): And, on this side?
SUZANNAH: The alley by which we came.
CLARY: We're far indeed from the well-lit square of the King's Theater! I beg you, Suzannah, speak to me, so I'll forget to shiver. You don't want to? (*with prayer*) A word, sis. I feel myself becoming all icy.
SUZANNAH (*to herself, aside*): He's late–and each minute that passes is still precious. I must see Mary Trevor–I must.
CLARY (*begging*): Suzannah! My sister–

SUZANNAH: Crazy child! There you are, all pale and trembling.

CLARY: Oh! I'm afraid! I'm afraid.

SUZANNAH (*kissing her*): I tell you, we have nothing to fear.

CLARY: Really true?

SUZANNAH: Yes.

CLARY (*shivering*): If I was going to die before seeing father again–

SUZANNAH: Die? Don't worry, my poor Clary. Who would hurt you, so sweet and so pretty.

CLARY: That man who came to seek us. His look comes back to me. It seems to me that I saw him before–

SUZANNAH: One of our unfortunate compatriots.

CLARY: I saw his eyes shine like coals on fire behind his thick eyebrows! Oh! Why isn't our father coming?

SUZANNAH (*aside*): Time is passing!

(*Downstairs, Mistress Gruff returns and crosses the lower room with a bowl of toddy in her hand; then, she climbs the stairs.*)

MISTRESS GRUFF (*with a dark look towards Mr. Gruff*): Lazy! Always lounging around!

MR. GRUFF (*with a sigh*): And when I think there are people who pity widowers!

MISTRESS GRUFF(*turning*): What did you say?

MR. GRUFF: Nothing! I shut up!

CLARY (*above*): I hear steps!

SUZANNAH (*half-rising*): It's our father–

(*Mistress Gruff enters with a smile on her lips.*)

MISTRESS GRUFF: A cup to the health of dear Ireland. (the girls don't touch their cups.) No? Fine! As you like. You won't wait much longer. (*smiles and leaves*)

CLARY: We ought to ask her to stay.

SUZANNAH: Why?

Clary: When she's here and I see her smiling face, I'm no longer afraid.

SUZANNAH: I ought to be at Mary Trevor's. (*falls back into a daze*)

(*Mistress Gruff is back downstairs.*)

MISTRESS GRUFF: This Suzannah plays the lady, now.

MR. GRUFF: Ah.

MISTRESS GRUFF: She didn't want to drink.

MR. GRUFF: Ah.

MISTRESS GRUFF (*imitating him*): Ah. Ah. I swear, God has made you to punish me in this world! Can't you climb up and persuade these wretches–

MR. GRUFF: You told me to stay here and shut up.

MISTRESS GRUFF: And I tell you so again, Mr. Gruff! God in Heaven! I would give anything to learn what purpose you serve on this Earth. Think–what will happen if these girls won't drink. They'll remain as awake as cats–and what will Mr. Lantern say then?

MR. GRUFF: He will say–

MISTRESS GRUFF: Shut up! Did I ask you for a stupidity? Go quietly up the stairs and see if they're drinking. (*makes him go*)

MR. GRUFF: Yes, my dove.

(*Mr. Gruff rises and takes a few hesitant steps. Meanwhile, above, Suzannah, too, rises and goes to the door.*)

MISTRESS GRUFF (*watching Mr. Gruff*): An ox that walks– an ox from Dushain, my word! Mr. Gruff! Mr. Gruff! You make more noise than a regiment of horse guards.

MR. GRUFF: I'll try to be more circumspect, my dear Mistress Gruff.

CLARY (*above*): The odor of this toddy brings me back to Ireland. It seems to me that I see the bogs of Arleigh and my father returning home after the exhaustion of the day. Do you intend to drink it, Suzannah?

SUZANNAH: Did you notice the look of that woman?

CLARY: Oh! yes–good smiling eyes. It's since she came that I'm no longer afraid.

SUZANNAH: There was something strange in it.

CLARY: Heavens! Am I the bravest now?

SUZANNAH: I don't know–

CLARY: Ah-ah! Now it's you who's afraid!

SUZANNAH: No–but how long our father is in coming–

CLARY: Ten minutes have not passed. Meanwhile, see what a nice smell this toddy has! I'm thirsty, Suzannah.

SUZANNAH: Well! what's preventing you from drinking?

CLARY: I won't drink all alone.

SUZANNAH (*pouring a drink*): Child!

(*Mr. Gruff listens at the door above. He stealthily locks it. Suzannah looks at the door.*)

SUZANNAH: I heard–

CLARY: Nothing. (*eyes on her glass*) To your health, Suzannah.

SUZANNAH: To our father's health.

CLARY: How good this Irish toddy is.

SUZANNAH (*placing her cup down after having drunk*): I'm sure I heard–

CLARY: Scaredy cat!

(*Mr. Gruff comes down.*)

MR. GRUFF: They've drunk, the dear angels.

MISTRESS GRUFF: And old man Donnor doesn't suspect–

MR. GRUFF (*laughing*): As to that it's certain–that brave old man I would laugh so heartily if I were to see him at this moment!

(*The door opens and Donnor enters.*)

MISTRESS GRUFF (*aside*): The father!

DONNOR: Tell me, you had here a young girl named Suzannah for a servant?

MR. GRUFF: Why, sir–

DONNOR: Answer!

MISTRESS GRUFF: Yes. Well, and so what? Why are you questioning us?

DONNOR: Why?

MR. GRUFF: Yes, indeed! Why?

DONNOR: Because I'm her father.

MR. GRUFF (*aside*): I know the rest. This is bad! Very bad!

MISTRESS GRUFF: Miss Suzannah was, indeed, living with us for some time. She left–right after–an argument–

MR. GRUFF (*aside*): An argument. That's satisfying.

DONNOR: I don't care about that. After her departure, you haven't seen her again?

MISTRESS GRUFF: Never, sir–

DONNOR (*throwing himself in a chair*): It's like a curse! At the home where Clary was staying, they told me: "They left, they were looking for you." Mr. Percival must have seen them, but he escapes me as they do. I cannot find them. (*drying sweat from his brow*) I don't know why, but I have a foreboding in my soul of some great misfortune.

MISTRESS GRUFF: Sir, would you like a drink?

DONNOR: No. (*aside*) They're looking for me. Is it a trap or is it just chance? If it's a trap, I will know it. I'll question the first villain who enters here–with death on his mind–and if nobody comes, I'll take this innkeeper by the throat and drag him to the police station. Ah! I have only two daughters in this world and no one's going to take them from me! (*aloud*) I changed my mind, I'd like something to drink now!

CLARY (*above*): I was mad to be afraid! Just because the walls are dark! (*drinks*) I feel completely happy now–look, I'm smiling despite myself.

SUZANNAH: Clary! Clary! What about me? What's wrong with me? Clary! My God! She's gone to sleep. (*goes to the door*) Locked! It's a trap! Ah! If only I had something to write with! This kerchief. (*writes on the kerchief*) My head is heavy–my eyes are clouding. Help! Help!

(*A boat can be seen arriving on the river, with two men in it. It stops under the trapdoor.*)

DONNOR: What's happening upstairs? I thought I heard a scream.
MISTRESS GRUFF: Rowdy sailors, sir.
DONNOR: A *woman's* scream–
MISTRESS GRUFF: Soldiers sometimes give rendezvous to the ladies in the alley.

(*The men from the boat climb up outside, raise the window, and enter the room as Suzannah cries "help" for the last time. They seize the two girls and come down by the trapdoor.*)

DONNOR: That scream came from upstairs.
MISTRESS GRUFF: Upstairs–ah, no–that's our room–
DONNOR: Ah! It's your room.
MISTRESS GRUFF: Er, yes, it's our room. The gentleman doesn't need anything?
DONNOR: No.

(*Mr. Gruff and his wife leave.*)

DONNOR: That woman hesitated to answer me. Oh! There's something odd going on here. I'm going to find out what.

(*Donnor gets up, hesitates a moment, then rushes up the stairway. He pushes open the upstairs door. Looking all about, he finally sees the kerchief left by Suzannah on the table–he examines it and notices her writing.*)

DONNOR: This kerchief–words scrawled in blood–and–I–I can't read them.

(*Mr. and Mrs. Gruff return. Donnor seizes Mr. Gruff.*)

DONNOR: What's going on here? Answer me!

MR. GRUFF: Here? What do you mean, sir?

DONNOR: Something's wrong here. What is it?

MR. GRUFF: Nothing, sir.

DONNOR: You're lying. Do you have a reason to lie to me? Something horrible is going on. I know it. On your knees, both of you–you're going to die!

MR. GRUFF (*recovering*): But sir–

SUZANNAH (*screaming in the distance*): Father! Help, father!

DONNOR (*bewildered*): Suzannah's voice! It was them! My daughters! (*rushes toward the window*) A boat! (*to the Gruffs*) I'll find you again, you murderers! (*hurls himself in the Thames*) My God! Be with me!

CURTAIN

Act V

Scene IX

(*The Thames. The boat carrying the sleeping Suzannah and Clary has reached the middle of the river. One of the two oarsmen is revealed to be Doctor Moore, dressed as a sailor.*

(*Moore looks to his left and sees Donnor, swimming behind them, gaining ground. Donnor has almost reached the boat. The other oarsman rises, takes one of his oars in both hands and strikes a violent blow into the water. Donnor disappears and the two men resume rowing. After a moment, Donnor reappears on the other side of the boat; he seizes the oar with which the oarsman tries to strike him, pulls the man overboard and grapples his way aboard. Moore pulls out a knife.*)

DONNOR (*now on the boat*): Your knife will not save you, vile murderer! Give me back my girls!
MOORE: Not without killing me first.

(*The two men fight. Donnor snatches the knife from Moore and strikes him to the heart. Moore falls into the water.*)

DONNOR: Heavens–Suzannah–Clary (*gets on his knees between them*)
SUZANNAH (*in a weak voice*): Father–
DONNOR (*joining his hands*): They're alive. Be blessed, my God!
SUZANNAH: Ah! I remember–quick, to shore, father–I may still arrive in time!

Scene X

(*A salon inside Trevor Mansion. View of a balcony. Mary and Lord Trevor are seated. Mary is very pale. Lord Trevor cold. Suzannah, standing, has just finished the explanation of the kiss, thus completing Percival's mission.*)

LORD TREVOR: Is that all, Miss?

SUZANNAH: Yes, Milord, and I swear to you– (*to Mary*) Believe me, I have no wish to deceive you. Mr. Percival is innocent.

MARY TREVOR (*moved*): I believe you.

LORD TREVOR (*cold*): We believe you.

SUZANNAH: God be praised.

LORD TREVOR: Daughter, does what you just heard change your decision?

MARY TREVOR (*hesitating*): Father!

LORD TREVOR: Think of your reply! Despite Frank Percival's innocence, although he has not ceased to love you, do you still consent to marry the Marquis de Rio Santo?

MARY TREVOR (*drying a tear*): Yes, father.

SUZANNAH: What do I hear? You haven't heard what I said?

LORD TREVOR (*to Suzannah*): Indeed, we have, Miss (*to Mary*) Come prepare yourself for the ceremony, my daughter.

(*Lord Trevor rises and gives his arm to Mary, who follows, him, casting a look of profound distress to Suzannah. They leave.*)

SUZANNAH: I am dreaming. She doesn't love him! Yet. that glance she threw as she left– Oh! The hand of Rio Santo is still at work here.

(*Donnor half-opens the door.*)

SUZANNAH: Come in, father.

DONNOR: Everything has been said.

SUZANNAH: Everything

DONOR: Thanks, for him and for me, my girl. Now we can return to Mr. Percival and tell him–

SUZANNAH: Hold on, father.

DONNOR: Why?

SUZANNAH: I confessed everything–but Miss Trevor is still intent on marrying Rio Santo within the hour.

DONNOR (*recoiling*): Ah! Poor Mr. Percival!

SUZANNAH (*with sudden violence*): And me–and me, father!

DONNOR: Yes, and you, dear child. It's true, that man is our bad luck.

SUZANNAH (shivering): Here he comes.

DONNOR: I have to talk to him.

SUZANNAH (*bitterly*): He's already dressed for the wedding ceremony.

(*Suzannah withdraws, somber and mute.*)

DONNOR (*to Rio Santo*): Pardon, Milord, an instant, a few minutes of your time to speak to you of two poor children who are suffering–

RIO SANTO: Not now, not now–

DONNOR: Milord, one of those children is her. (*pointing to Suzannah*)

RIO SANTO (*shivering*): Suzannah! (*aside*) She kept her promise.

DONNOR: The other is called Frank Percival. He's waiting for a word of salvation and I have nothing to bring him except despair–

RIO SANTO: At the point we've reached, there's nothing I can do for either Miss Suzannah or Mr. Percival.

DONNOR: So, it's true, you are coming to marry Miss Trevor?

RIO SANTO: Yes.

DONNOR: I'm only a poor man, but I have gray hair, so you must hear me, Milord. God has not placed the mark of evil on your noble face, and in your looks, I see a good heart. What have they done to you, these children whose lives you are wrecking? Mr. Percival was young, strong and happy; yet, you crossed his path, the ball from your pistol pierced his breast. If that were all! But he's in love–he placed all his future and all his hope in his love. I am not speaking to you of my daughter. (*pointing to Suzannah*) At 20, unfortunate all her life, her sorrows have become mine–and I'd never ask pity for myself. Milord, this is not worthy of you! To marry by force a poor girl who doesn't love you! Because she doesn't love you, you know that well enough–

RIO SANTO: Love? It's a game for children–

DONNOR: No, Milord. Love is the greatest blessing from Heaven when it is shared and God blesses it. Milord, be generous; let your heart speak. Poor Mr. Percival! If you only knew how he was reborn to life as a little hope reentered his poor soul. If you only knew–

RIO SANTO (*stopping him*): Listen.

(*Eight o'clock strikes.*)

SUZANNAH (*aside*): In an hour, they'll be married.

DONNOR (*following him, entreatingly*): Milord! Milord, you haven't yet said to me a single good word–but I'm not discouraged. I will follow you, if necessary, to the foot of the altar–

RIO SANTO: Wait. (*writing*) "Our fate is about to be decided. If in an hour, you see me appear on the balcony, hand on my heart, it will mean happiness for you. In that case, come at once." (*seals the letter and gives it to Donnor*) Here, for Mr. Percival–immediately.

DONNOR: Oh! Thanks! Is it good news?

RIO SANTO: Perhaps. Go.

DONNOR: You wouldn't want to make me hope in vain. To make game of an old man! Pardon. Poor child. I didn't intercede for her at least.

(*Donnor leaves. Suzannah remains motionless.*)

RIO SANTO: Yes, our fate will soon be decided–but what's a delay of a few minutes? Fanny may yet come, and if she doesn't come today, will she come tomorrow? Oh! When one is in such haste to despair, it's because there's nothing more to want. Has this love made a coward of me? (*with anger*) A coward! A deserter! A traitor! (*getting control of himself*) No, by Heaven! These are hours of madness. But Rio Santo is awakening. This letter that I just wrote–what does anything matter? Despite all, despite myself, I will accomplish my work.

SUZANNAH: Milord–

RIO SANTO (*aside*): Yet another attack against my heart!

SUZANNAH: Don't fear that I will seek, at this supreme moment, to thwart your projects. No, Milord, I am coming only to address a final thanks to you for the kindness you have just now shown in listening to that poor old man, my father– and to leave with him a last glimmer of hope. But that hope which cradles him, I do not share. Milord, I attempted an impossible struggle against you–and I failed. I am vanquished, destroyed, annihilated–and I will never try to raise myself from my defeat. Poor madwoman! With ardent eyes fixed on you, I didn't see the abyss which separates us. Now, I see it, that abyss; it's awaiting me–and I know very well there's nothing left for me to do but die! So I will die! I repeat to you– I will die! That decision is too coldly calculated for any human will to change it.

RIO SANTO: Suzannah!

SUZANNAH: If I were to die by force, perhaps I would give way to the rage in my heart. But when one has really decided to appear before God, one is calm, resigned–one weeps, that's all. And one says to those who have done evil–be happy, be very happy–as for me, I will pray for you!

RIO SANTO: Suzannah!

SUZANNAH: Milord, now I cannot hold back my tears. My God, excuse me, a woman has only so much strength, and at this moment, I'm really weak and overwhelmed! When I'm no longer here, if by chance you think of me, tell yourself that my misfortune is not completely my own work, and that, perhaps, many torments would have been spared me if you had not said to me one day, "Suzannah, you will be my faith, my support, my courage! Suzannah, I will love you."

RIO SANTO (*impetuously*): And who told you that I don't love you?

SUZANNAH: Don't speak to me thus, you will drive me mad!

RIO SANTO: But I do love you! Do you understand plainly? I do love you.

SUZANNAH: Ah!

RIO SANTO: Yes, I do love you, do you get it? You haven't understood that your lamentations are tearing my heart apart? When you were speaking of dying, I was suffering a thousand deaths! Jealousy, violence–what does that matter to me? It's a fight, and in a fight, I'm strong. But your tears, your resignation, that trumps my plans, my oath, everything. Yes! When I saw you pale and overwhelmed–when I saw your burning eyes that could no longer find tears–my soul collapsed! My God! You are witness that I struggled with all my courage and all my strength! You are witness that, for a long while, I crushed under my pitiless will this love that engulfs both our lives! But still, it's too much to suffer! I'm only a man–my courage is vanquished, my strength is exhausted! Let my projects of ten years perish! Perish the ambition of my life, perish all that! Rather than our happiness– of a day, an hour, a moment. Suzannah, love me as I love you! For I do love you! I do love you!

SUZANNAH: My God! My God!

RIO SANTO: Let no one speak to me further of treasures, of ambition, of the future! The most precious of all treasures–

that's you! Ambition, the future, all that, for me, is in you, in you alone! What more do you still want? Well, we will flee far from this cursed city. This very night, right away, if you wish–fiancée, relatives, friends–for you I will abandon all! I will forget all!

(*Fanny enters.*)

FANNY: Even Ireland?
RIO SANTO (*aside*): Fanny! I no longer expected her.
SUZANNAH (*aside*): What a beautiful dream! Already the awakening!
RIO SANTO: Well, Fanny, what news? What have you to apprise me of?
FANNY: I don't know, Milord. The Liberator was not in Dublin. This letter addressed to you is the only result of my trip.
RIO SANTO: Give it to me.

(*Captain Paddy O'Chrane arrives.*)

PADDY O'CHRANE: Milord, the Gentlemen of the Night are assembled. They are awaiting your orders.
RIO SANTO (*who has just read the letter*): Heaven! Let them obey this one. Go!

(*He makes him enter an adjoining room, then runs to the balcony at the back of the stage. The church bells ring.*)

FANNY: Those bells–that crowd–Lord Trevor, Miss Mary, dressed as a bride– Ah! I remember.
SUZANNAH: What's she saying? Me, too, I remember. The bells–they're from the chapel. Ah!
FANNY (*coming to her*): Suzannah! Why are you staying here?
SUZANNAH: They're going to get married, right?
FANNY: Don't stay here, I tell you, come! Come!

SUZANNAH: No! My God! Thoughts are coming into my head which horrify me! Ah! Am I going mad? I'm not strong enough for this torture.

FANNY: Come, for love of him! Come–here they are!

SUZANNAH (*aside*): For love of him–yes, she's right. Am I not sufficiently rewarded? Don't let this mad passion cost him a sacrifice. Die, poor girl–sure that he loves you! Die without regrets!

(*Suzannah stabs herself.*)

FANNY (*calling*): Suzannah! What have you done? Help! Help!

RIO SANTO: Suzannah! Wounded–

FANNY: On my life, I'll answer for her life–

(*Lord Trevor enters, followed by Donnor, then Percival.*)

LORD TREVOR: What's wrong? What's the matter?

DONNOR: I want to speak to you, Milord. (*seeing Suzannah*) My daughter!

PERCIVAL: What's the happiness that this letter promises me?

RIO SANTO: O'Connell is no more! His last wish makes my struggle now impossible. (*to Lord Trevor*) You gave me the hand of your daughter, but henceforth she can be happy. I release you from your promise. (*to Percival*) Mr. Percival, I told you we would be friends. Be happy.

SUZANNAH: What about you, Milord?

RIO SANTO: I will be happy, too, since I am now yours– forever!

CURTAIN

Captain Phantom

Characters

Cesar de Cabanil, Captain of the 8th Dragoon Regiment, a.k.a. Captain Phantom
and in order of appearance:
The Widow Coutard, owner of the *Hôtel des Victoires*
Sergeant Jean Coutard, of the 8th Regiment, her brother-in-law
Pierre, a Dragoon of the 8th Regiment
Manoel de Cabanil
Baptiste, a servant at the *Hôtel des Victoires*
Sarreluck, a Dragoon of the 8th Regiment
Pont-Neuf, a Dragoon of the 8th Regiment
Petit Eustache, a Dragoon of the 8th Regiment
Doña Mencia, Contessa de Cabanil
Lieutenant Valverde, of the 8th Regiment
Lieutenant Hector de Cabanil, Cesar's brother
Urban Moreno, owner of the *Inn of the Dead Bull*
Barbara Moreno, his wife
Lazarillo, his servant
Lilias de Santa Cruz, posing as Maritana, another servant
Joaquina de Cabanil, Doña Mencia's daughter
Rodrigue, a servant at Castle de Cabanil
Andres, a Squire at Castle de Cabanil
A French Officer
General Arthur Wellesley's Envoy
A Mystery Man, possibly King Joseph of Spain
A Prison Guard in Toledo
A Spanish Officer
Two Gravediggers

Maria, a young Spanish girl
Macpherson, a Scottish Grenadier
Morin, an Infantry Sergeant
Sir Ned Wellesley, Commander of the Scottish Grenadier
Rodrigo, a Spanish guerilla
Guttieres, the inn-keeper of Gavila
Major Clinton, a British soldier

Bandits, peasants, soldiers, etc.

The story takes place in 1808, in France and in Spain during the Peninsular War.

Prologue

Scene I

(*Paris, 1808. The front courtyard of a large hotel–the* Hôtel des Victoires, *rue Montmartre. To the right, the entrance to the hotel, with the concierge's loge and a flight of stairs. To the left, a garden which with benches.*)

WIDOW COUTARD (*sweeping the courtyard*): My dear brother-in-law, don't go out yet. The air is too cool this morning.

COUTARD (*inside the lodge*): Have you seen my pipe, my dear sister-in-law?

WIDOW COUTARD: It's on the dresser–but smoke it in the corner, by the fire.

COUTARD: Come on! Pipe tobacco doesn't like to be shut in. It needs the Egyptian desert, the plains of Italy, the shores of the Rhine! Still, better yet to smoke at *Hôtel des Victoires*!

WIDOW COUTARD: Are you feeling well today?

COUTARD (*examining himself*): Not bad! That saber blow, still haunts me. Yet, that wound has had the advantage of entitling me to a convalescent leave during which I have enjoyed the hospitality of my family with open arms.

WIDOW COUTARD: Brother-in-law, be careful! Your 17th wound isn't yet cured.

COUTARD: My 17th wound! Ah, don't mention it to me–a nasty blow to the wrist. Speak to me rather of my second wound–a bullet in the stomach–or my 5th wound–a shrapnel in my left nostril–the result of which being a perpetual head cold.

(*Pierre, a Dragoon of the 8th Regiment, enters.*)

143

PIERRE: The Captain of the 8th?

COUTARD: At the rear, door to the left, three steps to climb.

(*The Dragoon leaves as instructed.*)

COUTARD: Speaking of the Captain, we're expecting another officer soon–a captain whom I had the honor to serve under when we were in the same regiment.

WIDOW COUTARD: Ah, yes, Captain Cabanil, who has a young brother–Hector.

COUTARD: Hector–Hector! I care less about him, who's a civilian, and a rash youth.

WIDOW COUTARD: Your Captain Cabanil came here earlier to see them.

COUTARD: Who, them?

WIDOW COUTARD: A lady and a gentleman. Spaniards, I think. She resides here, on the first floor.

COUTARD: And the gentleman?

WIDOW COUTARD: A splendid fellow–whom I wouldn't mind seeing again–but I'm babbling.

COUTARD: Very well, enough chatting, go attend to your business, and fetch me my morning cup to kill the damp.

WIDOW COUTARD: Ah! If only my late husband had health like that.

(*She goes inside.*)

COUTARD (*alone*): Spaniards!... Indeed, now that I think of it, I believe that Captain Cabanil is a bit of a Castilian himself–and that suffices to reconcile me with the hidalgos. I cherish him, my Captain–and to think that I will serve under another and no longer hear his thunderous voice shouting "Charge!" Well, now I'll work on getting rid of one of my vices. I'll spoke one pipe, no more, no less...

(*Manoel enters and addresses Baptiste, a servant who's just come in, carrying a cup on a tray.*)

144

MANOEL: You! Is the Contessa Doña Mencia de Cabanil in?

BAPTISTE: The Contessa is at church, but she should be back soon.

MANOEL: Then, I'll wait for her in the garden. Isn't she going out again later?

BAPTISTE: I don't know, Monsieur.

MANOEL (*giving him a coin*): Perhaps you could search your memory?

BAPTISTE: A Napoleon! Now, that's generous!

MANOEL: So, is she going out again?

BAPTISTE: She's ordered a carriage for 11 o'clock.

MANOEL: To go–?

BAPTISTE: To go to a pension on the Rue de Sèvres, where Mademoiselle Joaquina is being raised.

MANOEL: These ladies are not counting on returning to Spain soon?

BAPTISTE: The Contessa came here to find her daughter–and should indeed return to Madrid, if Captain de Cabanil, whom she is expecting, comes today.

MANOEL: That's fine.

(*He goes into the garden. Baptiste brings the hot cup to Coutard.*)

COUTARD: Thanks!

(*Sarreluck, a Dragoon, enters.*)

SARRELUCK: The Captain of the 8th?

COUTARD: Ah! Again? At the rear, door to the left, three steps to climb. (*looking at Sarreluck, doing a double-take*): Hey! It's you, Sarreluck!?

SARRELUCK: Hey! Doggone! Coutard!

(*Pont-Neuf, another Dragoon, enters.*)

145

PONT-NEUF: The Captain of the 8th–Coutard! Sarreluck!
COUTARD: Pont-Neuf!

(*Petit Eustache, yet another Dragoon, enters.*)

PETIT EUSTACHE: 73 Rue Montmartre, that must be here.
The Captain of the 8th–Coutard! The corporal of corporals!
COUTARD: Petit Eustache. Come here! Embrace your old
comrade! Sister-in-law! Sister-in-law! It's silly to get into
such a state for three old comrades! Sister-in-law!

(*The Widow Coutard appears.*)

COUTARD: Liquor with discretion here. Here's Sarreluck,
nicknamed Friendly, Pont-Neuf, the Parisian, and Petit
Eustache, also called the Bold– you don't know them, but
they're friends of mine!–but no matter, enough chat, no more
talk–just friends–
WIDOW COUTARD (to herself): Friends!
THE FOUR DRAGOONS (in chorus): Aye, Friends! (*they all
four hold hands*) For life, until death!
WIDOW COUTARD (*softened*): They are magnificent! You
are going to be served, my good men.
COUTARD: They don't make 'em like that woman anymore–
who belongs to me by the sacramental bonds of her legitimate
marriage with my brother. Ah! indeed–where are you coming
from, comrades?

(*They go to sit at a table and are served.*)

SARRELUCK: Me, from the 3rd Hunters Regiment, of Italy.
PONT-NEUF: And I, from the 3rd Hussars Regiment, of
Germany.
PETIT EUSTACHE: From the 7th Dragoons Regiment, of the
North.
COUTARD: And you've all been transferred to the 8th–
Bravo!

ALL: Bravo! (*They drink*)

PETIT EUSTACHE: Actually, no–not bravo. They're assigning me to the Cavalry again, me, Petit Eustache of Brittany, born to be an Admiral! I adore the sea which witnessed my birth, and they're condemning me to herd cows in perpetuity. I am well only on a boat and they stick me on a horse!

COUTARD: I've seen you under fire, Petit Eustache. You ride like a ball of wax–it's true, but you swing a mean saber. Stop your complaints, milksop that you are. What should I say, I who served under Dumourier and who's seen all my cadets promoted before me just because they knew how to read! And they say that all men are equal! No! It'll always be the same–

SARRELUCK: As for me, I regret only my Lolotte–we were engaged–she promised to wait for me, no matter how long it'd take.

PONT-NEUF (*aside*): They never do!

COUTARD (*to Pont-Neuf*): And you, skin and bones, do you also complain about remaining in the Cavalry?

PONT-NEUF: Me, complain? The horse and I were made as one. I was born on a horse. My mother was a circus rider and I learned riding before reading. I'd just debuted at the Circus of Monthabor when conscription came and took me away from the applause of an idolatrous public! Go for the service, I said to myself, I owe it to my country! When I first reported for duty, I told them that I was a complete man only with a horse between my legs or under my feet. So they transferred me to the 2nd Hussars Regiment. Our last piece of business was in Germany. We were facing a regiment of the Austrian Imperial Guard, giants, real Goliaths. The Army yelled at us "Charge at will!" "Great!" I thought to myself. So I made myself as tall as a tress, leaped on my horse and charged standing up in my saddle. Then, it was that the giants' turn to lift their noses to see blows which fell on them from the sky. My poor horse received a grapeshot from somewhere. I felt him give way from under me. I made a huge leap and landed with both feet on the back of an enemy Colonel. "Get out of my way!" I

147

shouted. We laughed a lot at things like that in the 2nd Hussars.

COUTARD: No reasons not to! Well, wise guy, in the future, you will use your wit for the benefit of the 8th Regiment.

PONT-NEUF: We'll do our best. But in the 8th, I won't be serving under my former Lieutenant–who's since become a Captain, by the way–and who was the most fearless man in the entire army.

SARRELUCK: Come on. We had one just like that in the 3rd Hunters.

PETIT EUSTACHE: And we, in the 7th Dragoons.

COUTARD: Shut up with all your Lieutenants–they're only foot draggers compared to my Captain. A real devil that one! But also my good angel. When I had my eleventh wound here–a blow from a bayonet in my full breast–they were going to leave me on the battlefield like an old carcass. But, no. "The little fellow's still alive!" shouted my Captain. On the spot, he picked me up, threw me over his shoulder and carried me half a league. Ah–Good Lord! I must drink to his health.

PETIT EUSTACHE: I want to be nice to you–also, because you're a corporal–but we'll also drink to my Lieutenant's health then.

SARRELUCK & PONT-NEUF: And mine–

COUTARD: Good Heavens! All together, if you wish–four brave officers–let's name them all together–

ALL: Yes–to their health!

COUTARD: My Captain–

PETIT EUSTACHE, SARRELUCK & PONT-NEUF: My Lieutenant–

ALL FOUR (*together*): –Cesar de Cabanil!

(*They remain speechless, looking at each other for a moment, then all four rise.*)

COUTARD: *Sacrebleu*! For that one, one toast isn't enough! To Captain Cesar–

ALL: To Captain Cesar.

PETIT EUSTACHE: Now that we've drunk our fill, take us to the Captain.
COUTARD: Follow me. I'll show you the way.

(*They climb up the steps and leave. The Contessa Doña Mencia de Cabanil, dressed in mourning, enters and heads slowly towards the concierge's loge. The Widow Coutard comes out.*)

DOÑA MENCIA: Captain Cesar de Cabanil hasn't come in yet?
WIDOW COUTARD (*in the doorway*): No, Contessa.
DOÑA MENCIA: His return was announced for today.
WIDOW COUTARD: Ah? I don't know, Contessa... The mailman just brought a letter for you.
DOÑA MENCIA: Give it to me–It comes from Spain. (*aside*) From my faithful Andres, no doubt (*opening the letter*) No, it's from Lilias de Santa Cruz–Joaquina's childhood friend. She's telling me that troubles are increasing, armed bands are roaming through the provinces, several castles have been pillaged and burned, and that the Marquis de Santa Cruz has had to arm his men to resist a likely attack. Lilias asks me not to return to Cabanil and to wait in France, or at least in Madrid, for this dreadful storm to abate. Dear Lilias! She doesn't know that, above all, I must obey the last wishes of a dying man. And it is only at the Castle de Cabanil that those wishes can be fulfilled (*to the Widow Coutard*) Madame–I am going to leave you my card, to be handed to Captain de Cabanil as soon as he arrives.

(*After taking the card, the Widow Coutard withdraws. As Doña Mencia is about to leave, Manoel returns.*)

MANOEL: I salute you, Doña Mencia.
DOÑA MENCIA: I fear I do not know you, Monsieur.
MANOEL: I'm Manoel.
DOÑA MENCIA: Manoel!

MANOEL (*harshly*): Yes–Manoel de Cabanil.

DOÑA MENCIA (*recoiling*): Señor–

MANOEL: Your husband, the Count de Cabanil, was my father. You know it very well. You took the place of my mother, who died from shame and sorrow. You bear a name which belonged to my mother. When he died, the Count–my father–bequeathed my title, my fortune to his nephew, Cesar de Cabanil, on the condition that he marry Joaquina, your daughter.

DOÑA MENCIA: All that is true–but the Count didn't forget you. He left you–

MANOEL: Alms–which I refused. I want–I only want my rightful inheritance. My mother has bequeathed me her hatred against you and yours. Doña Mencia, I'm afraid you'll have many more deaths to mourn in the future.

(*He bows deeply and leaves.*)

DOÑA MENCIA (*alone*): Ah! That man frightens me! Joaquina! My daughter! I tremble for her!

(*Baptiste enters; Doña Mencia calls to him.*)

DOÑA MENCIA: My carriage! Prepare my carriage!

(*He leaves to execute her orders.*)

DOÑA MENCIA (*alone again*): Ah! Why hasn't Captain de Cabanil arrived yet?

(*She walks into the hotel. Valverde enters from the right. He looks in a hurry.*)

VALVERDE: Madame Coutard! A round of drinks! I'm bringing news of a great victory.

(*Coutard comes rushing down the stairs.*)

COUTARD: A great victory? On whom?

VALVERDE: On the 6th Regiment. I went ahead of our dear Captain, Cesar, who just shouted at me before I left that he'd been reassigned to the 8th Regiment!

COUTARD: Ours! He's now our Captain! Ah! Good Lord! The Spaniards are in for some nasty surprises! Let's take care of that round of drinks!

(*Baptiste returns; Valverde calls out to him.*)

VALVERDE: You! (*handing him a note*) Quick! Take this note to Monsieur Hector de Cabanil, No. 37, Rue du Bac. You'll never get there fast enough because you're bringing good news–and you'll be well rewarded! Go!

(*Baptiste leaves by one side. Cesar de Cabanil comes in and is immediately surrounded by his fellow soldiers, who have followed Coutard, who press about him, congratulating him; he smiles and shakes hands.*)

VALVERDE: A toast to the triumphant hero!

ALL: A toast!

CESAR (*good-naturedly*): A triumphant hero who just got out of a nasty carriage which almost tipped over three times. I was lucky to get here in one piece.

(*The Widow Coutard comes out, bringing in a large punch bowl and glasses.*)

COUTARD: Have a drink, my Captain.

CESAR: Gladly. I have all the dust of the road in my throat. (*he sits down*) So, my old comrades, we're all going to be fighting together again on the battlefield! Tell me, Coutard, my old grumbler, are you still a Republican?

COUTARD: Always–Long live the Emperor!

CESAR: Good answer! Has anyone seen my brother, Hector?

151

VALVERDE: I just sent for him, Captain–but will he be at home? Hector's in love–(*toasting*) To your health!

CESAR (*toasting*): To yours! In love with who?

VALVERDE: I don't know. It's a secret.

CESAR: At his age, it's no great misfortune to be in love– (*to the Widow Coutard who has just shown him Manoel's card*) What's this?

WIDOW COUTARD: It from a lady in mourning.

CESAR: The Contessa of Cabanil. Ah, my noble aunt is in Paris.

WIDOW COUTARD: I'll rush to tell her that you've arrived.

(*She runs back inside.*)

VALVERDE: Your aunt is a Contessa, Captain?

CESAR: Why not? I'm a Count myself!

VALVERDE: You–a Count?

CESAR: From head to toe. It's not my fault. I never boast of it– (*with serious pride*) But I never hide it either.

VALVERDE: You may be sure that I didn't intend–

CESAR: To offend me? (*shakes his hand*) Perish the thought! On my arrival in France, Marshal Soult was not as good a Prince as you. When I said to him, "I want to be a soldier," he asked my name. "Count de Cabanil," I replied. He raised an eyebrow and grumbled, "To the Devil with Counts–where do you come from, Citizen?" That was under the Republic, you understand? "General," I told him, "I'm a foreigner." "A man without a country then," he said. "General, I know English, Spanish, Italian and German, but it's in French that I ask to serve, that I request a place in your army." He looked me in the whites of my eyes. "You will have it tomorrow, Citizen Count, and we shall soon hear what language you use with the enemies of France."

VALVERDE: We all heard it, by Jove!

COUTARD: I was there when the Citizen Count brought back two flags from the enemy!

CESAR: True, you were there. General Soult was always kind to me–and he no longer says "To the Devil with Counts" since the Emperor made him Duke of Dalmatia. (*he wipes a hand across his face*)

VALVERDE: What's wrong?

CESAR (*pensive*): The Contessa is in mourning! My uncle must have died and I'm now head of the family. Do I look like one? I don't even know what it is to be a landowner or a nobleman. I'm a soldier, I can only be–I only want to be–a soldier. It's quite enough for me to care for Hector–my brother–I could almost say my son, for I love him the way a father loves his child. And caution, which never enters my mind for myself, comes to me when it's about him–but bah! My uncle was a wise man–would he have chosen a fool to be head of the Cabanil family? Of course not! Drink up, comrades, drink up!

(*They drink. Doña Mencia enters and crosses the stage.*)

COUTARD (*to Cesar*): Captain, here's the Contessa–

CESAR (*shivering*): Huh? What? So soon! (*he sees her and sighs*) Gentlemen, I fear I've lived my last hours of freedom. I must now be alone. If there's a god for those who live life without a care, I commend myself to your prayers.

(*All rise and salute Doña Mencia as they exit. Cesar bows respectfully before Doña Mencia, takes her hand and kisses it, then invites her to sit down.*)

DOÑA MENCIA (*after taking a good look at* him): I didn't know you before, Cesar. But now that I've seen you, I understand the hopes of my late husband.

CESAR: My uncle, the Count Blas de Cabanil.

DOÑA MENCIA: He died in my arms, and if I came to France, it was to obey his final wish–Don Cesar, you are the last of our line.

CESAR: I have a brother, Doña Mencia.

DOÑA MENCIA: Much too young. Although your father chose to become French, the Cabanils of Spain are still–

CESAR: –The elder branch of my family, I know, Doña Mencia

DOÑA MENCIA: It's been two years since my daughter Joaquina came to Paris. We kept her out of Spain when the troubles began. Count Blas was the friend of France and of King Joseph, whom he called the Last Hope of Spain–his last wish is that you inherit his title, his rank of Grandee of Spain, with all its privileges and wealth.

CESAR (shocked): Doña Mencia! I can't–

DOÑA MENCIA: Wait! I haven't finished–all this on the condition that you agree to marry Doña Joaquina de Cabanil, our daughter.

CESAR (aside): This is madness! (aloud) Doña Mencia, Doña Joaquina doesn't even know me!

DOÑA MENCIA: She knows that the hand of a hero will be a safe and steady support.

CESAR (smiling): Quite a poor hero–who might not please her–

DOÑA MENCIA: Here's her portrait, Don Cesar (opening a medallion) And I affirm to you that her soul is even more beautiful than her face. (she gives the medallion to Cesar)

CESAR (surprised by her beauty): Heavens! I beg your pardon, Doña Mencia–I don't need this charming vision to agree to do my duty. I will do what Don Blas asked of me. Tomorrow, I will become the head of the House of Cabanil.

DOÑA MENCIA (extending her hand to him): I did not expect less from you, Don Cesar. My carriage is here. In an hour, my Joaquina will leave her convent. The Notary has been instructed and has drawn up the contract. Here's his name and address. In an hour, I will expect you there. Time is running short–tonight, we are leaving for Talavera de la Reina.

CESAR: In an hour, Doña Mencia. So be it (he kisses her hand)

DOÑA MENCIA: Till later–and thank you.

(*She leaves.*)

CESAR (alone): Now there's something unexpected. The Devil if I wanted to get married! On the contrary, I had a solid and well- established reputation as a bachelor–a condition which I intended to prolong– (*looks at the medallion*) Still, she is ravishing. Her eyes–her smile! Yes, Señora, your smile is enchanting–it will drive me mad if I ever get jealous–but in front of a Notary, it might give me pause. Me, married? It's absurd (*he looks at the portrait, smiling*)

(*The officers return and surround him, laughing.*)

VALVERDE: What's absurd?
CESAR (*hiding the medallion*): Can you picture me as a Grandee of Spain?
VALVERDE: Why not? You're a Count already!
CESAR: That's not all. I'm getting married.
ALL: Bravo!
VALVERDE: Is she pretty?
CESAR: A jewel!
VALVERDE: Rich?
CESAR (*shrugging*): She stands to inherit a fortune.

(*All burst into laughter.*)

VALVERDE: And you're not happy?
CESAR (*exploding*): By Jove! I'd like to see how you'd handle it! A royal dowry! Castles in Castille and Aragon, Galicia, Leon, Navarre–and other places.
VALVERDE: Hurrah!
CESAR: You'd marry her–wouldn't you?
VALVERDE: Twice!
ALL: Me, me, me, too.
CESAR: It's absurd!

VALVERDE: To be so unhappy about being burdened with a rich dowry and a pretty fiancée, you must already be in love, eh, Captain?

CESAR: Me? In love? Get out! Follies like that are for Hector! My word, no. I think I was once, though–for a whole hour–at least.

VALVERDE: Truly?

CESAR: It was two years ago. I'd asked for a leave to come and see Hector. On one fair spring day, I was strolling in the Bois de Boulogne. I was musing about a superb Andalusian horse that I'd just seen enter through the Porte de Maillot, ridden by a charming Amazon.

VALVERDE: Ah. You were also thinking of the Amazon?

CESAR: Perhaps.

VALVERDE: A young girl?

CESAR: Maybe. Maybe not. But charming nevertheless.

VALVERDE: Was she alone?

CESAR: No–an old man with a proud and noble face accompanied her. There had been, I surmised, a duel in the Bois–shots had been exchanged. The noise had terrified the horse. No longer obeying the Amazon's commands, he was carrying her away and, crazed with terror, almost threw her into a tree. I rushed to stop him.

VALVERDE: At great risk to yourself.

CESAR: I leaped out and stopped the beast, and contained it until the arrival of the old man, who was riding fast, shouting "My daughter! Save my daughter!"

VALVERDE: I see the picture. The beautiful Amazon had fainted in your arms.

CESAR: She didn't faint at all.

VALVERDE: Brave girl.

CESAR: Her father, now reassured, pressed my hand in his and asked my name. I saw no reason to hide it.

VALVERDE: No doubt, and you wished, in your turn, to know the name of the one you had just–

CESAR: No–I respectfully placed the bridle in the young woman's hand, I bowed and–

VALVERDE: And?

CESAR: –I left.

VALVERDE: Did you ever see this gorgeous Amazon again?

CESAR: Never.

VALVERDE: But you always think about her?

CESAR (*laughing*): Always, no–sometimes, yes.

(*Hector enters, excitedly.*)

HECTOR: My brother has returned! Cesar–pardon me for not being here ahead of you. If only you knew the joy your return causes me!

CESAR: My dear Hector!

HECTOR: My dear Captain!

CESAR (*looking at him*): Do you know that you're all grown up now! (*to the soldiers*) Gentlemen, we need to be alone.

VALVERDE: Again?

CESAR: My friends, when you're drowning, you grab whatever you can. Be nice! Let us alone for a moment. (*he motions them to leave.*)

(*The soldiers leave. Valverde lingers on behind.*)

VALVERDE (*aside, as he is walking away*): Is he going to try to find someone to take his place?

CESAR (*to Hector*): Come closer, brother!

HECTOR: You have something to say to me?

CESAR: Yes–but first of all let me hug you!

VALVERDE (*aside*): He's wheedling him.

CESAR (*to Hector*): I hear you're in love. With some little shop girl of the Galerie du Bois perhaps?

HECTOR: Who told you that?

CESAR: This is serious–at your age– by Jove! Very serious– (*aside*) He's as much a Cabanil as I am–what's to be done–

HECTOR (*annoyed*): I'm not in love with a shop girl.

157

CESAR: So much the better! (*aside*) He'll do the business of the Contessa as well as I– (*abruptly*) Are you going to hug me back?

HECTOR: I want to know what you have to say.

CESAR: I see that (*with spirit*) What you'll never know is how much I love you, my little brother!

VALVERDE (*in the distance*): It's heating up.

CESAR (*to Hector*): Look here–people get married young in Spain–

HECTOR: Ah?

CESAR: Word of honor! In France, it would seem ridiculous– but down there, it's the custom–take you, for example, little brother–you would be just the right age to get married.

HECTOR (*astonished*): Me?

CESAR: Exactly–wait a little longer and you'll begin to pass for an old bachelor.

HECTOR (*impatiently*): Why are you telling me this, brother?

CESAR: Word of honor! You'll understand soon. Since it's the custom of the country, it's necessary to conform to it, isn't it? And since you're not in love with a little shopkeeper–well– it's all very simple. We're going to marry you off!

HECTOR (*recoiling*): Marry me off! I'd sooner blow my brains out!

CESAR: Huh? (*aside*) Decidedly, we have no taste for marriage in this family. (*aloud*) You don't know what you're turning down, brother.

HECTOR: What does it matter?

CESAR: Millions.

HECTOR: I don't need millions!

CESAR: Titles

HECTOR: I only want to be a soldier, like you.

CESAR: A lovely wife.

HECTOR: I don't like lovely women.

CESAR: Oh! That can't be true (*showing him the medallion*) Just take a look!

HECTOR (*pushing the medallion away*): No.

CESAR: What the Devil! It doesn't cost anything to look.

HECTOR (*smiling despite himself*): I lied–I'm in love with a shop girl.

CESAR: Look anyway.

Hector: No.

CESAR (*grabbing him by the collar*): Look, I say! Or I'll beat you all the way to the barracks!

HECTOR (*looking, after a bit of wrestling*): Joaquina! Can it be?

CESAR (*stupefied*): Huh? You know her?

HECTOR (*seizing the portrait and carrying it to his lips*): I won't return this portrait to you except with my life!

CESAR: Wonderful! (*aside*) I've escaped beautifully (*aloud*) In that case, you know the way to the Rue de Sèvres?

HECTOR (*begging*): Cesar–my brother.

CESAR: Peace. I don't hear a thing! You're going to present yourself to Doña Mencia, Countess de Cabanil. Joaquina is leaving the convent as we speak. You will all three go to the Notary. Hold on, here's his name and address. I'll give up the girl, her millions, and in exchange, I sentence you to marriage in perpetuity. Go!

HECTOR: Oh, brother of mine, it's happiness you're giving me.

CESAR: And it's freedom you're giving me.

HECTOR (rushing to his arms): Oh! If you knew how happy I am–

CESAR (*effusively hugging him*): And me, too–go brother, go!

(*Hector rushes out. There's a great commotion at the back of the stage. The soldiers have returned, each with a slip of paper.*)

ALL: Captain Cesar! Captain!

CESAR: I did it! I swapped with him! I did it!

VALVERDE: So tomorrow we march on the enemy!

CESAR (*tossing his hat in the air*): No more weddings and celebrations!

(*The Widow Coutard enters.*)

CESAR: Madame Coutard, I remain a bachelor. I'm inviting everyone for dinner. Fix up a banquet of your finest foods. I have neither inheritance, nor monies, nor vineyards. I'm only a soldier–but I'm not without money. Twenty settings, 50 settings–

WIDOW COUTARD: I'm going to surpass myself for you, Captain.

CESAR: And some wine! Before food, we need a drink.

PETIT EUSTACHE: So it's true–you're our Captain again?

CESAR: Hold on! Hold on! My fat Petit Eustache! You've put on weight, Breton!

PETIT EUSTACHE: You're as frank as ever, Captain.

CESAR: And Sarreluck–my sensitive man. Is your Lolotte still in good health?

SARRELUCK: Perhaps, Captain.

CESAR: And Pont-Neuf, my Parisian urchin!

PONT-NEUF: Ready to get my head bashed in again for you, Captain.

CESAR: And Coutard, my old Coutard!

COUTARD: Who is recovering from his 17th wound, but nevertheless remains as ready as ever to fight for you.

CESAR: My guests, my old friends, drink, eat and be merry! Tomorrow, with men such as yourselves, we shall cause much distress amongst the enemy–let's drink to our first victory in Spain!

(*Manoel appears stealthily at the back.*)

MANOEL: So he's going to Spain! Heir of Cabanil, I shall be waiting for you!

ALL (*toasting*): To our first victory!

CURTAIN

Act I

Scene II

(*The interior of the* Inn of the Dead Bull. *To the right, mid-stage, there is a window opening onto the street and heavily grilled. Further back, there is a door leading outside. In the rear, there is an entrance stairway to the next floor. To the left, opposite the window on the right, there are tables, chairs, etc. Beyond is a kitchen door. Under the stairs, there a door leading to the cellar. Above all this is a wretched and dilapidated room reached by the stairway. At the back of this room is a bed–next to it is the door connecting to the stairway. To the right, there are another grilled window, a table, an armchair and a simple chair. To the left, mid-stage, there is a fireplace.*)

(*AT RISE, Barbara is straightening up the inn. Urban Moreno comes down the stairway.*)

BARBARA (*to Urban*): So?
URBAN: He was sleeping like a saint!
BARBARA: He's dead.
URBAN: Yes. And here's what he had on him–a full purse.
BARBARA: No jewels?
URBAN: No–no matter, the loot is good enough.
BARBARA: Call Lazarillo and take the body down to the cellar.
URBAN: I can't. He's on the second floor. Maritana might see us. We'll have to wait until night. But there's no rush.
BARBARA: Maritana! Why did we ever take this beggar into our home? She's good for nothing and she'll rat us out if she ever leaves.

URBAN: Bah! You're jealous, my dove–as if you were not the most beautiful woman on Earth. I'm interested in this girl and if any ill befalls her, I will hold you responsible.

BARBARA: It's good that fever will rid us of her, in that case.

URBAN: Don't try to assist the fever–that girl is pretty–she attracts travelers and inspire them with confidence.

BARBARA: Are you going into the mountains today?

URBAN: No–I'm expecting someone.

BARBARA: Who?

URBAN: The new head of insurgents in the Surza. He's just arrived in the province and already they only swear by his name– Manoel. They're sure that he's going to get a major command soon.

(*Someone raps three times on the door.*)

URBAN: That must be him–open up Barbara!

(*Barbara goes to open the door to the right, and Manoel, dressed in the picturesque costume of a guerilla chief, appears in the doorway–seeing Barbara, he stops.*)

URBAN: Be welcome, Señor. Wife, go make sure Lazarillo is there. Perhaps I'll need him later.

(*Barbara leaves by the door at the back. Manoel enters, locking the door behind him.*)

MANOEL: Are we alone?

URBAN: Yes, Excellency–the Galician is watching outside. Lazarillo, my servant, is grooming my mule in the stable and there's no one upstairs, except a poor serving girl who can neither see us nor hear us.

MANOEL: That's fine. Urban Moreno–we've already met.

URBAN: Yes, Excellency, I was at the attack on the Castle of Santa Cruz.

MANOEL: I noticed you only at the moment of plunder.

URBAN: I arrived a little late, it's true.

MANOEL: The junta had condemned the Marquis de Santa Cruz but none dared to execute the sentence–the job was a tough one. I wanted to try it, followed by bandits who had sworn to fight with me as soldiers. I attacked the castle, my men were falling around me, but those who remained held firm and won some ground. As the tide of battle began to turn in our favor, men like you entered the castle by a side less well protected. The Marquis fired his last cartridge against them, then remained disarmed. At this moment, a woman, pale with horror, rushed towards the old man, covered him with her body and took his sword, screaming "Father, I shall defend you!" I got there just in time to disarm and carry off the courageous young girl and prevent her from being slain over her father's body.

URBAN: I saw nothing of all that. I'd gone down into the cellars where, it was said, the old Marquis hid barrels of gold, but we only found barrels of gun powder. (*smiling*) But I've heard tales of the Señora Lilias de Santa Cruz who, rich and beautiful, had turned down the most handsome men in the Kingdom in order to not be separated from her father. She must no longer be so young today.

MANOEL: How gorgeous she was! Oh! For her, I'd sacrifice all my plans of revenge, all my ambitious dreams–perhaps I would forget and forgive everything.

URBAN: Ah. They took her back from you?

MANOEL (*his head falling into his hands*): She's dead.

URBAN: Dead!

MANOEL (*abruptly*): Let's talk about something else. Urban Moreno, I need you. It's a question of ridding myself of a man that I can't ambush in the mountains as I had planned. An order of the Junta forces me to leave at once with all my forces.

URBAN: Who is this man who troubles your Excellency?

MANOEL: A Frenchman, a Captain of Dragoons named Cesar de Cabanil. He's rejoining his regiment, which is part of General Dupont's army. I know which road he'll take; I've counted his stops–arriving here during the day, he must stop at your inn.

URBAN: And he must not leave?

MANOEL: This is for payment (*he gives him a roll of gold*)

URBAN: You pay like a prince, Señor. You will be honestly served.

MANOEL (*aside*): Between me and the inheritance of Count Blas de Cabanil, there are only two men–Urban will rid me of one, and I'll take care of the other one.

URBAN (*calling*): Hey, Lazarillo!

MANOEL: Who are you calling?

URBAN: My servant–my confident–

(*A small, weak, ill-featured man enters from the back.*)

LAZARILLO: Here I am, Master!

MANOEL (*making a face*): What can you do with such a man?

URBAN: Lazarillo has tried his hand at all trades–he's been a shepherd, a peddler, a smuggler–today he's my servant and purveyor–he goes in quest of travelers. Excellency–the description of the man I must–trifle with?

MANOEL: He's taller than I am, with black mustache. His expression is stern, his voice strong. He wears a white cloak on his Dragoon uniform, and sports the epaulettes of a Captain.

URBAN: Lazarillo, you've heard; you've understood?

LAZARILLO: Yes, master.

MANOEL: You'll recognize this man?

LAZARILLO: I will.

MANOEL: And you will bring him here?

LAZARILLO: I will.

MANOEL (tossing him gold): Here, this is for you. Urban, we will see each other again.

LAZARILLO (*picking up the coins*): Gold! (*aside*) With this, I will buy the medicine that Barbara is refusing the poor sick girl.

(*Urban escorts Manoel out, then returns.*)

URBAN: Are you still here?
LAZARILLO: I'm going and I won't return alone, I promise you!

(*He leaves through the large door than Manoel left open.*)

URBAN: A roll of gold, a well-filled purse–these French officers will make my fortune. Let's see what's in the purse...

(*He goes to close the door, empties the purse on a table and starts counting coins.*)

URBAN: One, two, four, eight!

(*There is a violent rapping at the door.*)

URBAN: Oh-oh! who's coming?–let's hide these first.

(*He puts the coins in his pocket and tosses the empty purse under the table.*)

COUTARD (*outside*): Hey! Anyone in there?
PONT-NEUF: What a wretched place!
PETIT EUSTACHE: Hello! Hello!
SARRELUCK: Ah, indeed–there isn't anyone there.
URBAN (*rising*): The French! My Captain perhaps? But will he be alone? Let's see anyway

(*He opens the door and the four Dragoons, covered with dust, enter.*)

URBAN (*aside*): Soldiers–bad business!

COUTARD: What an awful country! They have twice as many holes in the road to break your neck and when you fall, you've got to take a lousy inn by force to get it to open up!

URBAN: What do you want?

PETIT EUSTACHE: Your ugly sign out there proclaims you to be the *Inn of the Dead Bull*—one can drink and eat here, right?

URBAN: So?

PONT-NEUF: So, we're hungry and thirsty! Serve us quickly and promptly—if that's possible.

URBAN (*aside*): These folks are no good for business. (*aloud*) If my door was locked, it's because I haven't got any more room. You'll find another inn a short league from here.

COUTARD: We're all too familiar with the "short leagues" of Spain. We'll rest here.

URBAN: I'm the master here! I receive who I want—and I don't want you.

COUTARD, SARRELUCK & PONT-NEUF: By the Devil!

URBAN (*drawing his sword*): *Demonios*!

PONT-NEUF: He's calling us names bow!

(*Barbara enters from the back.*)

BARBARA: Mercy! What an uproar!

SARRELUCK (*looking at Barbara*): Now there's a very strong creature.

BARBARA: What do you want?

COUTARD: To drink

SARRELUCK: And to eat, in like manner.

PONT-NEUF: We pay in gold.

PETIT EUSTACHE: But we're not rich.

URBAN (*aside*): Ah! If there were not four of you—or if I had my men with me.

BARBARA (*to Urban*): Let me take care of it (*aloud*) We will serve you but it'll cost you a piastre per head and per day.

ALL: A piastre!

COUTARD: Great Lord–are you in the habit of catering to Kings and Princes?

BARBARA: That's our price (*low, to Urban*) See? They're going to leave.

PONT-NEUF (*awestruck*): A piastre!

PETIT EUSTACHE: Per head and per day (*aloud*) That's fine–serve us, we'll pay.

COUTARD (*low*): With what? We don't have a piastre between the four of us.

PETIT EUSTACHE (*low*): I'm good with numbers. I'll add up the bill.

COUTARD: Make it small–and do some subtracting, too.

URBAN (*low, to Barbara*): After all, if they pay... Perhaps it's not necessary to be rid of them... (aloud) Stay, then–I'm going to the cellar–

BARBARA: As for me, I'm going to start the service–

COUTARD: At last!

(*They sit around a table.*)

BARBARA (*calling*): Martina! Martina! Get down here, will you, lazy bones! We've got company–and I can't do everything by myself!

(*Lilias de Santa Cruz, who is hiding under the alias of Maritana, comes down. She is dressed in black and looks pale and tired.*)

BARBARA: Come on then, I need help! Quick, quick, some bread, cheese and onions!

PONT-NEUF: Onions, always onions–I'm weeping in advance!

(*Silently, Lilias prepares to serve the Dragoons, but as she approaches their table, she staggers.*)

COUTARD: Goodness! The poor girl is going to faint!

167

BARBARA: Pay no attention to her–she's had a fever but she's getting better. Come on, girl, take this! (*she gives her a big loaf to carry*)

PONT-NEUF (*taking the loaf of bread*): It's bigger than she is–

PETIT EUSTACHE: Oh! What pretty little hands!

SARRELUCK: And what eyes!

PONT-NEUF (*who's been putting the bread on the table*): And what a figure (he wants to take her in his arms)

LILIAS (*gently pushing him away*): Aren't you French?

PONT-NEUF: From Paris!

COUTARD: Why do you ask that?

LILIAS: Because I thought that, in France, you protected the weak and you respected sorrow.

PONT-NEUF: Forgive me!

COUTARD (*aside*): She said that like a princess. (*to Lilias*) You have nothing to fear, girl. (*to the others*) The first to disrespect this lady will have to answer to me! Enough said now–we won't speak of it further.

URBAN: Here's some wine.

ALL: Ah! Not a moment too soon!

LILIAS (*aside*): If I dared to trust these men–yes, I will do it, because I want to get away from here at all costs.

PONT-NEUF: Funny country. They have bottles made of goatskin.

COUTARD: Which naturally makes the wine taste like goat milk.

PETIT EUSTACHE: Well, we'll just nurse it, then. Never mind, let's drink our first glass to the health of our Captain!

ALL: To the health of our Captain!

URBAN (*aside*): Hmm... Could this be the Captain I'm expecting? (*aloud*) What's your Captain's name?

COUTARD (*drinking*): Cesar–

PETIT EUSTACHE (*who's swallowed*): –de Cabanil.

LILIAS (*aside*): Cesar de Cabanil!

PETIT EUSTACHE (*low to Coutard*): Sergeant, let's eat and drink, but not talk too loudly. I've got my suspicions.

LILIAS (aside): Cesar de Cabanil–yes, it's him!

URBAN: Your Captain's just rejoined the Army?

PONT-NEUF: How do you know that?

URBAN: I learned it from one of the officers who stopped here this morning.

COUTARD: Lieutenant Valverde–

SARRELUCK: In all likelihood.

PETIT EUSTACHE (*low*): Drink, drink, and let's get out of here!

COUTARD: Like us, the Captain is rejoining the 8th Dragoons Regiment.

PONT-NEUF: We're just hours ahead of him.

URBAN (*uneasily*): Do you plan to wait for him here?

PETIT EUSTACHE (*rising*): No–our quarters are at Bujarrabal–it's a good "short league" from here and we're going to have to get going soon.

URBAN (*aside*): Excellent.

PONT-NEUF: Already?

PETIT EUSTACHE: I have my reasons.

LILIAS (*aside*): If I leave, who will warn Cesar de Cabanil? I must stay.

PONT-NEUF: Let's be on our way then–

BARBARA: You're forgetting something.

SARRELUCK: What's that?

BARBARA: To pay your bill.

PONT-NEUF: Aie!

PETIT EUSTACHE: That's a distraction

COUTARD: Madame Innkeeper, handle this with the Breton– he's got a mind for numbers–you bet!

PETIT EUSTACHE (*gravely*): We said a piastre.

URBAN & BARBARA: Per head.

PETIT EUSTACHE: Yes, and per day, that's understood. Now's the time to use my arithmetic skills. One piastre per day–in every country on Earth, a day has 24 hours–a piastre is worth 24 maravedis. Look at your clock–we stayed three quarters of an hour–so then, per head, we owe you three quarters of a maravedis each. Almost a French *sou*.

BARBARA: You must be joking?

PETIT EUSTACHE: I never joke about money. I tell you what–we'll pay for the full hour–one maravedis each–a quarter of a maravedis extra–just to show our good will.

COUTARD (*laughing*): He sure has got a mind for numbers, our Breton!

PONT-NEUF: A most convincing reasoning.

SARRELUCK: Admirable.

BARBARA (*low, to Urban*): They're making fun of us.

URBAN (*low*): Their Captain will pay for them–but if ever I see them again...

PETIT EUSTACHE: Here are the four maravedis. Take care of yourself–

COUTARD: You see, we don't haggle–to your health!

SARRELUCK: And go (*unintelligible*)–

URBAN: What did he say?

PONT-NEUF: Here's what he said: (*making a rude gesture*)

(*The four dragoons leave, making rude mocking gestures. Urban puts his hand on his knife as if he was going after them, but Barbara stops him.*)

BARBARA: Stop–they're out of here–isn't that what you wanted?

URBAN: You're right. Better to deal with a single man than four.

LILIAS (*aside*): I was right.

URBAN: I'm thinking of another thing. Our inn is infamous enough. If Lazarillo hasn't met the Captain, he might not want to come here. I'll take down our sign–it might warn him.

(*Urban goes out.*)

BARBARA (to *Lilias, who is following Urban with her eyes*): What are you staring at, idiot? You're listening to us, spying on us? If you ever plot to betray us, you know what I promised you–and I'm a woman of my word.

(*Urban returns with the sign.*)

URBAN: Here! Maritana, put it away so that the man we're expecting can't see it. (*to Barbara*) Night's coming–bring your lamp, woman.
LILIAS (*aside*): He means, Cesar de Cabanil. I will remember.

(*Barbara lights a lamp which she places on a table near the window. Meanwhile, Lilias goes up the stairs with the sign and can be seen in the room above.*)

URBAN: Travelers will still the light through the windows. Hark! Do I hear the steps of a horse echoing on the cobblestones of the highway?
LILIAS (*listening*): It must be him. May God protect us. (*she gets ready to come down after placing the sign against a wall.*)
BARBARA (*going to open the door*): It's Lazarillo who's bringing us travelers.

(*At this moment, Cesar enters; he is wrapped in his great white cloak and supports Lazarillo–pale and hardly able to walk.*)

URBAN: No, dear wife, it's the traveler who's bringing Lazarillo.

(*Lilias has come down the stairs, without being noticed by the two innkeepers, and watches Cesar.*)

URBAN: What's wrong with this imbecile?

(*Lilias goes to help Lazarillo; she makes him sit down and forces him to drink something.*)

CESAR: There, there–don't scold him!

LILIAS (*aside*): It's really him.

CESAR: This man offered to guide me just as night was approaching, so I accepted his services. He walked in front of me, stopping sometimes to pick some herbs and flowers. At a corner where the road borders on a precipice, he saw a plant he was seeking–he tried to go down but the ground was wet and the grass slippery, so he lost his footing and fell. I leapt down from my horse and I saw him already halfway down, lying by a dead tree. I couldn't leave him there. I did my best to hold on to bushes and branches, and eventually, I got to him. I plucked him from his tree and brought him down. Only, he was half-broken from his fall and couldn't walk anymore. I hoisted him up onto my horse. Thanks to the rays of moonlight, I was able to find my way to your inn–which, if you don't mind my saying so, is the ugliest inn I've ever seen.

LAZARILLO: Excellency, I owe you my life.

CESAR: Bah! You don't owe me anything at all.

LAZARILLO: And the herbs I picked–

CESAR: –Must be precious, for you to have clung to them during your fall. I kept them, here they are. (*giving him a handful of herbs*)

LAZARILLO (*to Lilias, her back now turned to Cesar*): Take this, Maritana–it will cure your fever.

URBAN: A good night on a pallet of hay will restore Lazarillo. We're concerned only with you, Señor Captain. The fog is penetrating this evening. Maritana, quick–a fire to warm up His Excellency!

CESAR: It's true that that fog froze me to the bone.

BARBARA: Give my your cloak, Señor.

CESAR: There, good woman. It weighs a ton, I warn you. (*under the cloak, Cesar has a saber and two pistols in his belt.*)

URBAN: Now, wife, to the kitchen and prepare for His Excellency the best meal we have in the house–I'll select the wine myself–I want to choose a wine worthy of our guest.

(*Barbara leaves by the door to the left, leading to the kitchen.*)

CESAR (*to Urban*): You must have lodged a young officer of my regiment–Lieutenant Valverde–
URBAN: An officer? No, no, Excellency.
CESAR (*puzzled*): His route was to take him through Bujarrabal to reach Siguenza. Aren't we in Bujarrabal?
URBAN: Yes, indeed. We're a poor county, but honest and God-fearing.
CESAR: And you have an Alcade, don't you?
URBAN: Yes–yes, Your Excellency
CESAR: Good. I carry an order for that honorable civil servant from the General governing the province–it concerns one Urban Moreno.
URBAN (*aside*): What?
CESAR: It's about hanging an innkeeper who's a bandit and confiscating his inn, which is a lair of cut-throats.
URBAN (*aside*): Now there's an order you will never deliver.
CESAR (*looking around him*): A place very much like this one, I suppose. So, what's on the menu? I warn you: I'm famished.
URBAN: A slice of lard fried on the stove, a lard omelet and a corn cake.
CESAR: With lard, I bet. Not much variety.
URBAN: Well, the wine will be better than the food. I have a sherry–you won't drink it's like again. I'll bring you a bottle while Maritana sets your place. (*to Lilias*) Come on, girl! Leave the fire alone. Take care of the Señor while I go down to the cellar, since Lazarillo isn't good for anything tonight.

(*He leaves by the back.*)

CESAR (*aside, watching Lilias*): Heavens, I hadn't noticed the girl. (*to Lilias*) Thanks for the fire you made, Señorita. (*he sits by the fire while Lilias sets the table*)
LILIAS (*low to Lazarillo*): Will you let the one who saved your life be murdered?

LAZARILLO: What can I do?
LILIAS (*low*): Help me.
CESAR: This fire is doing me a world of good.

(*Barbara returns carrying a platter of food.*)

BARBARA: Here's a dish that they wouldn't serve at the King's table. (*she puts the plate on the table.*) Would you like to take off your sword and pistols?
CESAR (*sitting*): Thank you, but no, they won't bother me.
BARBARA: As you please, Señor–I was only thinking of your comfort.
CESAR: Why, this meat is excellent, my word of honor–but the cake is choking me a bit–and since the wine hasn't arrived, give me a glass of water.

(*Lilias takes the jug and pours it, avoiding showing her face to Cesar.*)

CESAR: By Jove–to hide your face so carefully, you must be famously ugly. (*after having drunk*) Well, not every girl can be pretty. (*taking her hand*) Eh, eh–a fine hand, delicate and white–a charming arm–Goodness, that makes me want to see your face.

(*He gently forces Lilias to look at him in the face.*)

CESAR: Hell's bells–why, you're not ugly!
BARBARA: You're doing too much honor to a serving girl by bothering with her, Señor.
CESAR (*looking at Lilias*): It's strange. I've seen her somewhere. Ah, I remember–but, no, it's impossible! You've never been to France, have you?
LILIAS: Me?
BARBARA: Her? To France! She's a beggar!
CESAR: That's true! (*looking again*) Still–the same look, the same features–the resemblance is incredible.

174

(*Urban returns, a bottle in hand.*)

URBAN: Here's the sherry.

CESAR (*aside*): I must be mistaken. That's not possible. (*aloud, to Urban*) There you are, at last! What took you so long?

URBAN: I had to find the right bottle for the Captain (*low to his wife*) One of our "special" bottles.

CESAR: And you say it's good?

URBAN: The best!

CESAR: Strong enough to revive the dead, right?

URBAN (*aside*): Quite the opposite, in fact. (*aloud*) I guarantee it.

CESAR: Well then, give the first glass of this nectar to this poor lad who's as pale as a clown.

URBAN (*aside*): The Devil–I can't serve it to Lazarillo–it'll kill him!

BARBARA: Your Excellency must be joking. A wine like this isn't meant to be drunk by a servant.

URBAN (*to Lazarillo*): Come on, time to earn your keep! While we're serving His Excellency, take his luggage upstairs. And after that, bring in his horse, which is freezing outside, and put him in the stable.

CESAR: Good idea! Yes, take care of my horse, my good man.

LILIAS (*low to Lazarillo*): Don't unsaddle it so it'll be ready to leave.

LAZARILLO (low): I understand. Whatever I can do for you and him, I will do.

(*Lazarillo takes the luggage upstairs; he enters the room and sets to work, silently, to remove the bars on the window.*)

BARBARA: Excellency, will you allow me to fill your glass?

URBAN: Look at that wine! What golden reflections–a true ray of sunshine!

175

CESAR (*aside, looking at Lilias*): That resemblance can't be the effect of chance–or a play of my imagination (*taking his glass*) To your beauty, girl!

LILIAS (*as he brings the glass to his lips, low*): Don't drink!

CESAR (*looking at her*): What?

LILIAS (putting a finger to her lips): Don't drink.

URBAN: Wife, you've forgotten the cheese–cheese makes the wine taste better (*low to Barbara*) That'll make him drink.

(*After Urban has spoken to her, Barbara leaves; meanwhile, Lilias seizes the glass and empties it in the fireplace.*)

CESAR (*low to Lilias*): What are you doing?

LILIAS: Hush!

(*Urban turns and sees the empty glass.*)

URBAN: Ah! You've drunk–that stuff burns a bit going down, but it's the taste. Another glass, Excellency! (*he pours*)

CESAR: That wine has a charming color.

URBAN: That it has, Your Excellency

(*Barbara returns with a plate of cheese; Urban runs to help her. Meanwhile, Lilias again takes Cesar's glass and empties it in the fireplace.*)

URBAN: Hurry up, will you! (*seeing the empty glass on the table*) You're getting a taste for it–so much the better. Empty the bottle–it won't cost you any more. (*pouring*) Come on– another glass–to my wife's health. The Captain is too gallant to refuse.

(*Supplicating gesture from Lilias.*)

CESAR (*aside*): Decidedly, there's something fishy about this wine. By Jove!–I'm going to know (*aloud*) Very willingly, my good man, but this time, we will drink together–I insist!

URBAN: Ah.

CESAR: A glass for your husband, my dear woman.
BARBARA: Er, no point in it–my husband only drinks water.
URBAN: Yes, Your Excellency–it's a vow that I took.
CESAR (*rising*): Damnation, my host, you will drink with me or else–

(*In the room above, Lazarillo has finished unscrewing the window bars.*)

LAZARILLO: At the first effort, these bars will fall and he can escape.

(*He leaves the room. Meanwhile, Lilias picks up the purse Urban tossed under the table earlier and excitedly gives it to Cesar.*)

LILIAS: Is this your purse, Señor Captain?
CESAR: Mine? No–no. (*aside*) This is Valverde's purse–if so, it means he stayed here–and this man is lying.

(*Lazarillo comes down the stairs.*)

LAZARILLO: The Captains' room is ready.
BARBARA (*lighting another lamp*): If Your Excellency has finished his supper, we'll escort him to his room–right above this one.

(*Lazarillo leaves by the cellar door after having given a sign to Lilias.*)

LILIAS (*low to Cesar*): Accept (*excitedly, in a loud voice, taking Barbara's lamp*) I'll show you the way, Captain.
CESAR: I always follow pretty girls.

(He begins to go up the stairs, lit by Lilias.)

CESAR: Goodnight, water drinker.

URBAN: Goodnight, Your Excellency.
CESAR: I'll be leaving tomorrow at dawn.

(*Cesar and Lilias disappear up the stairway.*)

URBAN: In an hour, he'll be sleeping the sleep of the dead–literally.
BARBARA (*who's moved close to her husband*): No, he won't.
URBAN: Come on! With all the sherry he drank.
BARBARA: He didn't drink any–while I was lighting the lamp I saw–over there–in the fireplace.
URBAN: What?
BARBARA: The wine he threw away. Look!
URBAN: My word, it's true! Then he suspects.
BARBARA: We've failed.
URBAN: Come with me into the courtyard–there I will tell you what threatens us and what I intend to do about it–were he the Devil in person, I swear that Captain won't leave here alive!

(*He leaves by the backdoor with Barbara after having extinguished the lamp. The room below remains dark and empty. Cesar enters the room above with Lilias, who puts the lamp down on the small table.*)

CESAR: So, girl, will you now tell me–
LILIAS: Don't go to sleep.

(*She leaves, shutting the door behind her.*)

CESAR (*alone*): What will I do if I don't sleep. Ah–I'm not even sure of being in my right mind. I recognize under the rags of a servant girl the angel of my dreams–and this poor Cinderella is protecting me–me, whom she doesn't know. Come on, I need a good night sleep to–but sleep, like wine, is forbidden. She very clearly said in her sweet voice: "Don't sleep!" Will she come back and explain herself later? (*he removes his sword and pistols*) Here is some paper and ink– Why don't I write a letter to Hector? "Dear Hector, I suppose you're now in Castle de Cabanil, near your charming fiancée, counting the days, the hours, for Joaquina's mourning only ends in three months. Dear brother, you won't have long until you savor the delights of the honeymoon. A Cabanil must be a soldier and King Joseph has promised me to give you a Lieutenancy." (*stopping*) It's raining in here. A large drop of water just fell on my hand–Why, no!–It's a drop of blood!– falling through the ceiling–onto my letter. That's the Devil is going on here? (*there is a soft rapping at the door*) Maybe I'll finally get an explanation for all these mysteries.

(*He grabs his pistols, goes to open the door and finds Lilias, who enters quickly with a small suitcase in hand.*)

LILIAS: Quick, lock your door!
CESAR: Will you tell me–
LILIAS: Everything.
CESAR: Good!
LILIAS: Don't walk around, don't speak, except in a low voice. They mustn't suspect my presence here otherwise they won't leave me enough time to save you.
CESAR: What do you mean? I'm quite capable of taking care of myself!.
LILIAS: You don't know where you are–look! (*she turns over the sign placed against the wall*)
CESAR: *The Dead Bull*! Then, my host is–
LILIAS: Yes! Urban Moreno!
CESAR: And I told him I was carrying the order for him to be hanged! But why are you risking your life to save me when you don't know me?
LILIAS: But I do know you, Señor Cabanil.
CESAR: What? You've seen me before?
LILIES: Yes, once.
CESAR: In France?

LILIAS: Yes, in France.

CESAR: I knew it! It was you who–But no, that's impossible–you are not, you can't be–

LILIAS: The happy girl you saved and placed in the arms of her father? Yes, the serving girl of Urban Moreno is in reality the daughter of the Marquis de Santa Cruz–

CESAR: You!

LILIAS: –Of the Marquis de Santa Cruz, who until his last breath, blessed Cesar de Cabanil–

CESAR: The old Marquis is dead?

LILIAS: Murdered by a gang of bandits. The leader of these wretches carried off dying. When I came to, that man offered me his protection. I rejected him with horror and scorn, so he left me alone, but still took care to lock me up. With the help of a dagger, I managed to escape. I found myself in the middle of the night in the Sierras, running away from my pursuers. I kept going all night; it was only at daybreak that, exhausted, I fell on the side of the highway. It was there that Lazarillo found me. He brought me to this horrible house. At first, they refused to take me in. The fever was burning me; only Lazarillo's care and remedies brought me back to life–and I thank God for it, for now I'm able to repay my debt to you. Oh! I will save you, Señor de Cabanil!

CESAR: And this man–the leader of the bandits?

LILIAS: His name was Manoel–he must have thought me dead, my body rotting in the Sierras.

CESAR: Manoel! It's strange–we have the same enemy, Señorita. For I'm told this same Manoel has sworn the ruin of the House of Cabanil, but mercy, finish your tale–this blood that just now reddened my hand?

LILIAS: That blood is that of the officer who preceded you– I wasn't able to warn him.

CESAR: Lieutenant Valverde, right?

LILIAS: That purse was his. His body is still stretched out on the floor just above.

CESAR: Oh–I will avenge him. But first of all, let me thank you.

180

LILIAS: Señor de Cabanil, in lieu of strength, I swear to you, I will have energy and courage

(*Suddenly, a stone is thrown into the room and falls at Lilias' feet.*)

CESAR: Watch out! That stone almost hit you.
LILIES: There must be a paper attached to it.
CESAR (picking it up): Yes there is.
LILIAS (*taking the paper*): It's advice from Lazarillo. (*reading*) "The master, knowing he won't find the Captain asleep, has called the bandits from the mountains–and they've just arrived."
CESAR: My pistols will easily kill two men. My sword will do the rest.
LILIES (*reading*): "They are in the cellar, planning their attack. They've locked all the doors, but the Captain can leave by the window–I cut two bars."
CESAR (*going to the window*): He's right! (*he pulls out the two bars*) It's good to have friends everywhere, especially at Urban Moreno's.
LILIAS (*reading*): "I've slipped out of the house. Let the Captain hasten and I will serve as his guide as far as Bujarrabal."
CESAR (*looking*): Fifteen feet, at least. But with the help of these curtains, it'll be easy getting down. (*he tears the curtains from the bed*) They'll be strong enough to bear you, Señorita.
LILIAS: Me?
CESAR: You've got to go first. (*he attaches the curtains to the bars that remain in the window*) I know you're courageous and determined–you won't hesitate.
LILIAS: To show you the road, no–for we must leave this house at all costs!

(*At this moment, downstairs, Urban and his bandits emerge from the cellar.*)

URBAN: I fear I've lost my inn; they'll take it from me tomorrow. Better to burn it today, with the dead officer and the living one.

ALL: Yes!

URBAN: Barbara and the others will keep watch outside and try to find Lazarillo, who's sneakily abandoned me. Have the rest of you brought the wood?

BANDIT: Yes.

URBAN: We'll build a pyre on the stairs. To work, quickly!

(*The bandits pass bundles of wood from hand to hand. Urban grabs them and places them on the stairs.*)

LILIAS: Hurry up–I hear some noise on the stairway and this bolt won't resist very long.

CESAR (*looking outside again*): I don't see anyone. Go down, go down quickly–but be careful.

LILIAS: Don't be afraid for me–worry only about yourself.

(*She climbs down the improvised rope and disappears.*)

URBAN (*on the bottom step*): Give me the torch now.

(*He disappears with the torch up the stairway.*)

CESAR (*at the window*): Good! She's on the ground. But, by Jove, that's not the way I'm going to take. They're planning to surprise me. (*taking his arms*) But it's I who's going to surprise them–by charging them when they expect it the least! Forward!

(*He opens the door, and recoils from the torrent of flames which Urban has now ignited.*)

CESAR: Oh, the bastards–they want burn me alive. Impossible now to get down the stairs.

LAZARILLO (*outside*): Help! Help.

BARBARA (*outside*): Ah! Traitors–we'll get the two of you now!

LILIAS: Cesar, don't come down!

CESAR: That's the Señorita de la Cruz!

(*He rushes to the window and is greeted by a fusillade which forces him to move away.*)

CESAR: I can't leave that way either. It would be hopeless, with all those bandits shooting at me. I don't want burn here–but how to get out? (*seeing the chimney*) That way! (*grabbing the loose bars, he uses them as crowbars*) Yes!

(*He starts pulling bricks out to make himself an escape route passage. Downstairs, Barbara is dragging Lilias away with her as the brigands threaten Lazarillo.*)

URBAN (*looking up the stairs, in flame*): It's a real fire from Hell! (*laughing out loudly*) Ah! Ah! You weren't expecting that, eh, my French Captain?

CESAR (*shouting back*): True.

URBAN: We've got you.

CESAR: Not yet.

URBAN: Bah! The stairs are like a furnace now.

LILIAS (*to Barbara*): Oh, please! Show mercy to the Captain!

BARBARA: We won't be merciful–either to him or to you. You've betrayed us and you know what I promised you. (*she pulls a dagger from her belt and knocks Lilias over, preparing to strike her.*)

LILIAS (*on the ground, screaming*): Help! Captain! Help!

URBAN: Too late, little fool! No one can help you anymore!

(*Suddenly, Cesar, who had vanished inside the flue, reappears out of the downstairs fireplace, in the midst of the bandits.*)

CESAR: Not so!

(*He fires both his pistols, and the two bandits holding Lazarillo fall. One gets up. Cesar runs him through with his sword. Lazarillo hurls himself at Barbara, whom he disarms and knocks over. Urban, wounded by a blow to his head, falls over. The bandits flee. Cesar grabs Lilias.*)

CESAR: You're free, Señorita! Now on to Bujarrabal, Lazarillo, to Bujarrabal!

CURTAIN

Act II

Scene III

(*A large gothic hall at Castle de Cabanil. In the rear, there is the door of a corridor leading to the chapel. The drapery of this door, when lifted, reveals a perspective ending with the gothic doorway of the chapel.*)

JOAQUINA (*to Lilias*): You will end up making me jealous with all these stories you tell about Cesar's exploits.
HECTOR (*smiling to Joaquina*): Beloved Joaquina, the opportunity will come to show you that there is more than one hero in the House of Cabanil. (*to Lilias*) Thank you, Señorita– for the tender affection which unites you to my fiancée–and also because I owe you my brother's life. Now, I'll jump on my horse and run to meet Cesar. Till later!

(*Hector leaves.*)

LILIAS (*to Joaquina who has followed Hector with her eyes*): You love him so much?
JOAQUINA (*who goes to take a bouquet*): Oh! yes!
LILIAS: Are we going back to see Doña Mencia now?
JOAQUINA: My poor mother, who greeted you with so much joy, can't endure any more uproar around her bed of sorrow, and if you don't mind, we'll finish dressing my marriage crowns here.
LILIAS: I understand.
JOAQUINA: Cesar will find Hector greatly changed. Did you notice how pale he is? His head is always burning and sometimes his hand is icy. (*she lets the flowers go*)
LILIAS (*working*): Is he ill? Does he complain?

185

JOAQUINA: No, he doesn't complain, but I'm certain that he is ill... (*after a pause*) Why do you tremble when I mention Cesar?

LILIAS: See how beautiful this flower is!

JOAQUINA: Beautiful amongst flowers as you're beautiful amongst women. (*she takes Lilias' garland, puts it down, then takes Lilias' hands in hers*)

LILIAS: What are you doing?

JOAQUINA: I want to feel your hands in mine, to look into your eyes. Tell me, Lilias, do you love Cesar?

LILIAS: Joaquina, we've been friends since childhood–I want to remain discreet–You mustn't question me–

JOAQUINA: Then you mustn't display your feelings so clearly.

LILIAS: Let's continue making your wedding garlands. You're happy, that's all I need.

JOAQUINA: Still, you do love him, don't you?

LILIAS (*begging*): Joaquina, please–

JOAQUINA: Oh–say it!

LILIAS (*explosively*): Yes! I do love him! With all the strength of my heart! God has brought us together twice. The first time, he threw himself between me and death. The second time–blessed be the Virgin Mary–it was I who threw myself between him and death! As for you, Joaquina, you love a noble and dear child. Me, I love a soldier. You've asked my secret! I've just told you–and as I speak, I am confessing it to myself as well. Look into the depths of my heart that I haven't dared fathom–see my love, my only love–which is now my life. Yes, I'm in love, dear Joaquina. I weep sometimes–burning and delicious tears–I think that I will die, killed by happiness, were some Heavenly voice to tell me: Lilias you are loved too!

JOAQUINA: But you *are*, Lilias.

LILIAS (*taking her two hands, going pale*): How can you be sure? Who told you that?

JOAQUINA: No one, but I'm sure of it.

LILIAS (*listening*): Hush–someone's coming–it's Rodrigue.

(*The door opens and a servant–Rodrigue–enters.*)

RODRIGUE: Señoras, a monk from the convent is soliciting a donation from the Cabanils on the occasion of the marriage.
JOAQUINA (*to Rodrigue*): Show him in. It's getting late and I'm late dressing up. Come, Lilias, let's get ready.
LILIAS: Let's not make the good monk wait.

(*They both leave.*)

RODRIGUE: The "good monk!" Ha! The Devil rather. Come in.

(*Manoel enters, dressed as a monk.*)

MANOEL: My son! (*he looks all around him*)
RODRIGUE: We're alone.
MANOEL (*pulling back his hood*): I'm not happy with you, Rodrigue–you promised me that this odious marriage would never take place.
RODRIGUE: I've done what I could–the young man is very pale.
MANOEL: But he still lives! He's going to infuse new strength and vigor into the Cabanils. I paid you well and chose an infallible poison.
RODRIGUE: Someone's been keeping a careful eye on me–the old squire–Andres–follows me around like a shadow–perhaps my trembling hand betrayed me!
MANOEL: Someone is certainly protecting them, these accursed Cabanils! Where is your post for the ceremony?
RODRIGUE (*pointing to the large door at the back*): Here.
MANOEL: What's beyond that door?
RODRIGUE: The gallery of honor leading to the chapel.
MANOEL: What's your role?
RODRIGUE: I oversee the four servants who are to hold the wedding crowns over the head of the bride and groom.

MANOEL: They're not yet wed–they will die before they reach the altar! I will give you four of my men to replace your porters of the crowns. Others will be posted inside the chapel. The bells will toll for the wedding–I can't stop that!–but they'll be our signal to act–and the cursed Frenchman who is stealing the name of Cabanil will hear them upon his dying breath.

LILIAS (*outside*): Hurry, Joaquina–we mustn't make the good friar wait–

MANOEL: That voice–Who is this?

RODRIGUE: La Señorita Lilias de Santa Cruz.

MANOEL (*awestruck*): You said–Lilias de Santa Cruz?

RODRIGUE: Yes.

MANOEL: Lilias alive! (*to Rodrigue, excitedly*) Leave us and remember my orders!

(*Rodrigue bows and leaves as Lilias enters.*)

LILIAS: Father, allow me to–

Manoel (*taking a step toward her*): Lilias!

LILIAS (*recognizing him, afraid*): Manoel! You! Am I to be again the victim of your insults and threats?

MANOEL: Is it an insult to a woman to declare one's love on one's knees? Is it a threat to place the adoration of a strong and valiant heart at her feet? Lilias! Oh! Lilias–do not reject me! You're the only woman who ever made my heart beat– Let me love you as a slave.

LILIAS (*aside, regaining her self-control*): I shouldn't be frightened in this house where I'm surrounded by friends and servants. (*to Manoel*) You dare say you love me, you whom I saw commanding a gang of murderers. You dare touch my hand–you whose hand is stained with my father's blood.

MANOEL: Your father and I were two soldiers, facing each other. I did not kill the Marquis de Santa Cruz, and if it is necessary to beg your forgiveness for my past actions, I will gladly do so. I have grown, Lilias–the simple soldier has become the head of an army. The name Manoel is heard far

188

and wide today–it is a name that's feared by our enemies. You are a daughter of Spain, Lilias de Santa Cruz, why do you curse a man who is merely defending his–and your–country?

LILIAS: I admire the true defenders of Spain, but I have only scorn and contempt for the bandits who shelter under its flag.

MANOEL: Hear me then. Behind the name of Manoel, there is another name–a title even–for I am the last of the Cabanils.

LILIAS: You, a Cabanil!

MANOEL (*forcefully*): I will be made a grandee of Spain– King Ferdinand himself had recognized my claims.

LILIAS: Lies! Lies!

MANOEL (*seizing her hands*): That's enough, Señora. I love you. I would give my life for you. I once thought you dead and wept for you, but now that I see you alive, I swear that you will belong to me–to Manoel de Cabanil.

LILIAS: Never!

(*Suddenly, a great uproar is heard outside.*)

VOICES (*off*): Honor to Captain Cesar de Cabanil!

LILIAS (*joyfully*): Ah! Cesar has returned! You won't dare threaten me anymore now.

MANOEL: I understand everything, Lilias. All that was lacking was for this man to become my rival. Your love will kill him more surely than my hate!

(*He leaves quickly, raising the tapestry in the back. Andres enters from the left.*)

ANDRES: The Contessa is asking for the Señora.

LILIAS: Andres, you're devoted body and soul to the Cabanils. Look over there– (*she points to the tapestry which Andres lifts*)

ANDRES: There's no one in the gallery.

LILIAS (*aside*): No one. But knowing that Cesar's in the castle, Manoel won't dare– (*aloud*) No matter then–keep a look out, and may God bless the Cabanils.

(*She leaves.*)

ANDRES: God has sure blessed them by sending us Captain Cesar.

(*Cesar and Hector enter.*)

CESAR (*hugging his younger brother*): I'm so happy to see you!

HECTOR (*introducing Andres*): Brother–I present you our family's oldest servant–Andres–who played as a child with our uncle, Don Blas de Cabanil, and who followed him onto all his battlefields and closed his eyes when he died.

CESAR: Such servants must be friends. Andres, your hand.

ANDRES (*bowing*): Señor Captain.

CESAR: Would you be so good as to announce us to our noble aunt, Doña Mencia de Cabanil?

ANDRES: Yes, Your Excellency (*low*) But first, I need to speak to you.

CESAR: To me?

ANDRES: To you alone, before the marriage ceremony–it's about your brother.

CESAR (*low*): About my brother? Well, then–after he leaves–

ANDRES (*bowing*): I will return.

(*He leaves.*)

CESAR: Come here, so I can look at you–you're pale, emaciated–

HECTOR: I've been ill for weeks–but I'm better now–much better now. Your journey down from Tarragone went well?

CESAR (*smiling*): Well enough.

HECTOR: What happened?

CESAR (*hugging him, then looking at him*): Nothing to worry you about–Decidedly I find you very pale.

HECTOR: I tell you, I'm fine.

CESAR: Not a cloud in your sky, then? You're happy?

HECTOR: Yes, very happy–but tell me–did an accident befall you during the journey?

CESAR: Nothing, I tell you.

HECTOR: I want to know.

CESAR: I can't say no to my little brother. (*he hugs him*) Here is what happened. I was galloping down from Tarragone. At a rest stop, I ate a snack while they were getting me a new horse–one which I'd picked myself–and I know horses–when I heard some commotion outside. I went out and I saw a fellow who was unsaddling my horse to hitch it up to his own post chaise.

HECTOR: So you quarreled with him?

CESAR (*arranging himself in the mirror*): Naturally.

HECTOR (*uneasy*): You challenged him?

CESAR (*the same*): I should say so!

Hector: You wounded him? You killed him?

CESAR (*abandoning the mirror*): I'm afraid I might have! Listen, little brother, I've got something far more serious to tell you–

HECTOR (*in an altered voice*): Who was that man?

CESAR: I don't know–an idiot–a Colonel in the Spanish Auxiliary army.

HECTOR (*fearful*): A Colonel.

CESAR: One who had the gall to claim he outranked a French Captain.

HECTOR (*grasping Cesar's hand*): You fool, there's a new edict–from the King–

CESAR: Even if there were 20 edicts, that won't resuscitate that villainous chap. Let's leave that Colonel where he is and talk.

HECTOR: The King's edict establishes a single hierarchy for the French and Spanish troops.

CESAR: So what? It was a proper duel–no big deal.

HECTOR (*sorry*): But the King's edict imposes the death sentence–

CESAR (*angry*): Damnation! Do you intend to listen to me, yes or no? I tell you, I've got a serious matter which I need to discuss with you, now that I feel reassured about you–you did tell me everything is going well here?

HECTOR: Yes, everything.

CESAR: Then, let's talk about me.

HECTOR: What about you?

CESAR: I don't very well know to tell you–you won't make fun of your big brother, eh? Well, here we go: I'm madly in love. There. Were you expecting that?

HECTOR: Perhaps–besides, am I not in love, too?

CESAR: Oh, but you're in love properly–you proclaim it–I heard you–you're getting married. I don't know how you can do it. I admire you–my word of honor. But I don't think I will ever dare confess my secret to her.

HECTOR: I didn't realize you were such a timid character.

CESAR: Yes–with the women I'm not in love with, I'm not clumsy–that goes without saying–but her–I adore her! Do you understand? Speak up! How happy the four of us would be! Two little households–blond heads in the cradles–who would I love more–your daughter or my son? But you will perhaps have the son! As for me, it doesn't matter. Go for the girl. We'll call her Lilias–you know–cross godfathers and godmothers. Lilias and I for your little Grandee of Spain, you and Joaquina for my little girl. Come on, it's agreed–pop the question for me.

HECTOR: But–

CESAR: What? Do you want to be happy all alone?

HECTOR: No, of course not.

CESAR: If she refuses (*passing his hand across his face*) But she won't refuse–my heart tells me so. Besides, you know how to talk to women. Oh! If I dared–but I don't. Go on, little brother, be clever, be eloquent, be seductive, but do it as if it were for yourself.

HECTOR: You're not giving me much time to prepare.

CESAR (*with deep tenderness*): You can't imagine the joy I'd feel if I owed you my happiness.

(*He presses him against his heart and pushes him out.*)

CESAR (*alone*) Dear boy–since he's gotten so pale, he resembles our mother even more.

(*Andres enters.*)

ANDRES: He's still fighting the poison.
CESAR (*grasping his arm*): Poison! Did you say poison? Someone's tried to poison my brother?
ANDRES (*lowering his head*): Yes–I'm sure of it.
CESAR (*violently*): Who?
ANDRES: I don't know. The poison is only one of the weapons threatening Hector.
CESAR (*shocked*): But who? Who?
ANDRES (*coming closer*): There's a strange danger in this castle, which grows larger every day–a danger that surrounds your brother, that watches at his bedside–mysterious, fatal. I was waiting for you, Lord, to warn you: "Watch over Hector de Cabanil. Protect your brother."
CESAR: Indeed, it's to protect him that I'm here, but first of all–how did he get poisoned?
ANDRES: In a pomegranate.
CESAR: Given by whom?
ANDRES: Picked by him–in front of me–on a tree even.
CESAR: You freeze my blood.
ANDRES: That's not all–or rather, there's more. There's a scar under his hair, by his right temple.
CESAR: A scar–
ANDRES: The mark of a bullet, the flew in from God knows where, through a broken window of his bedroom.
CESAR: At night?
ANDRES: At night. I no longer sleep. I slide, I prowl, I search, my eyes are open–my ears extended. Yesterday evening, I saw two shadows under the porch and overheard

these words: "When the bells toll–when the betrothed enter the chapel–"

CESAR: So the bells will be the signal–but the sword is powerless against assassins who skulk in darkness. And I only know the sword. I'm helpless. I see Manoel's hand in all this. What failed yesterday might succeed tomorrow–today perhaps. It's not Hector he wishes to kill–it's whoever marries Joaquina–whoever becomes Don Blas' heir. Ah–I gave my brother a funeral gift when I told him to court her. That bell shall not toll–that wedding will not take place. It wasn't Hector that Don Blas had designated to become the new head of our family–it was me. Well, I'll do what he ordered–if it preserved my beloved brother's life. My God! Let Hector live!

ANDRES: Someone's coming!

(*He leaves. Lilias enters.*)

LILIAS: Doña Mencia now wishes to see you, Captain, but she's really sick and weak. Your brother told me–

CESAR: Hector–let's talk about him, let's talk only of him. Hector is more than my brother.

LILIAS: Yes, I know.

CESAR: And he's going to die.

LILIAS: Die!

CESAR: Because of me.

LILIAS: Because of you?

CESAR: Yes. It's not that boy they seek to kill, it's whoever becomes the heir of Cabanil. I was that heir, but I put him in my place–and now Manoel's hatred is directed towards him.

LILIAS: Manoel was here just now.

CESAR: In this house?

LILIAS: In this very room.

CESAR: I knew it!

LILIAS: We must save Hector.

CESAR: The danger which threatens him is hard to fathom. But if I face it myself, it'll be forced to reveal itself, and I can fight it! Lilias, the heir of Cabanil is meant to be killed when the bells toll and the betrothed appear at the altar. I therefore intend to be the betrothed of Joaquina–whatever happens, she won't be harmed. I will cover her with my own body if need be. You've grasped what I intend to do?

LILIAS: Yes.

CESAR: So, go and warn Joaquina. If God is with me in this supreme battle, I will succeed. Lilias, you know the secret of my heart. Say to me, "Cesar, I could have loved you."

LILIAS: Cesar, I do love you.

CESAR: Oh! With a single word, you've doubled my strength and my courage–let's hope still, Lilias.

LILIAS: I will never abandon hope–not in God, nor in you!

(*She leaves. Coutard enters.*)

COUTARD: Ah, pardon, Captain, but a messenger has just brought a letter. For the groom

CESAR: For Hector. Give it to me.

COUTARD: Here it is! Stamped by the Quartermaster.

CESAR: A stamp can be faked; a letter can be poisoned. (*breaking the seal*)

COUTARD: It's true that Spain is the country of arsenic and *vert-de-gris*–they use them everywhere.

CESAR: It's a commission–as Lieutenant.

COUTARD: A nice wedding gift.

CESAR: An order to rejoin his regiment.

COUTARD: The honeymoon will be short.

CESAR (*aside*): Once in the army, Hector will have nothing more to fear from Manoel. (*aloud*) Hector will have to go.

COUTARD: Not before tomorrow, I suppose.

CESAR: No. He will leave today–right away.

COUTARD: What about the wedding–are you canceling it, Captain?

(*Andres passes at the back.*)

CESAR: Where are you going?

ANDRES: To take to Count Hector his cloak of a Grandee of Spain–and this sword.

CESAR: Leave them here. Where is Hector?

ANDRES: In his room, dressing for–

CESAR: How many doors to that room?

ANDRES: Just one–and a single window.

CESAR: Which gives on–?

ANDRES: On the moat of the Castle–and it's barred, like all the windows which give on that side.

CESAR: That's fine. The hour is approaching. Go tell the ladies they should hasten. The ceremony will take place. I will answer for everything.

(*Andres leaves.*)

CESAR: Coutard, listen carefully to your instructions.

COUTARD: There's a service to be performed?

CESAR: Take this commission to Hector.

COUTARD: I understand.

CESAR: Then, lock his door from the outside with a double lock.

COUTARD: To keep the groom locked up? Now, I don't understand.

CESAR: You'll stand guard before this locked door, you and your comrades–you will not heed any threats or entreaties.

COUTARD: The Lieutenant will want to leave.

CESAR: If he leaves, they'll kill him. Do you understand now?

COUTARD: I do. He won't leave.

CESAR: Even if you hear the sound of fighting inside the castle, don't leave your post. Hector's life is worth more than mine–and you will answer for it to me.

COUTARD: Yes, Captain.

(*Coutard leaves as Andres returns. The chapel bells begin to toll.*)

196

ANDRES: I hear the bells.
CESAR (*to Andres*): Give me that cloak

(*Andres hands him the cloak, which Cesar puts on; the Captain grabs the sword.*)

CESAR: This sword will be my battle sword.

(*The guests start arriving, then the bride enters, completely veiled. The draperies open, revealing a perspective of lights leading to the chapel. All along this perspective are servants bearing torches. At the entrance, the bearers of the dais await, headed by Manoel who is wearing Rodrigue's uniform.*)

CESAR (*walking towards the bride*): Courage, Joaquina.
LILIAS (*lifting her veil to him*): Do I need anyone to tell me how to be brave?
CESAR (*astounded*): Lilias! You?
LILIAS: I tricked Joaquina–if it's a question of dying with you–I've taken her place.
CESAR (*with spirit*): My love! United in this world or in the next. I gave up the Cabanil inheritance to my brother, Hector–I hereby take it back. Today, I am the Count de Cabanil!
MANOEL: Oh, this one is worth ten times the other! (*they step forward*) To the chapel! Let the deed be done!

(*Suddenly, a French officer, sword in hand, enters, accompanied by soldiers.*)

OFFICER: Monsieur de Cabanil, in the name of the King, I arrest you.
MANOEL: He's going to escape us!
OFFICER: For having killed a superior officer, Colonel Mendez, in a duel.
LILIAS (*low*): The King's edict saves us.
CESAR (*to Lilias*): Perhaps (*he smiles and surrenders his sword to the Officer*) I must follow you, Monsieur–but in so

doing, I place under the protection of the King Lieutenant Hector de Cabanil and the ladies of Castle de Cabanil.

Scene IV

(*A prison in Toledo. A bed, two chairs and a table with a lamp on it.*)

CESAR (*alone, seated on the bed in undershirt*): From Cabanil to Toledo, six hours by carriage–interrogated, tried and sentenced, all in 48 hours. Lilias, by invoking her father's memory, was able to obtain a temporary stay of my execution. They wait for the return of King Joseph, but he will confirm my sentence–reason of State demands it. (*pulling a letter out and rereading it*) If I wished to live, I could–I could be free today if I wanted to. King Joseph doesn't suspect that. This letter from General Wellesley makes me an offer–the General has good spies who keep him informed of what's happening. He's put to profit the events of the past week and has me an interesting offer. This letter tells me that his own personal Envoy will come here to receive my answer. Here! These Toledo prisons aren't very well guarded–and have terrible service. (*he is about to tear the letter, but stops*) Wait! I can use the back to write to Lilias and say my good-byes. My poor Lilias, whom I'll never see again. And to my brother, who's still angry at me but who must now learn the truth–now that he's safely under the protection of our flag. (*he begins to write*) Someone's coming! Ah! For goodness sake! Can it be General Wellesley's Envoy already?

(*The door opens. The British Envoy enters, a bit out of breath.*)

ENVOY: Sir, I don't have a minute to lose.
CESAR: As for me, I don't have a minute too many.

ENVOY: The letter you received told you about me.

CESAR: Ah, yes–in that case I know whom I have the honor of addressing.

ENVOY: I've come, sir–

CESAR (*interrupting him*): No need to–you're leaving, sir.

ENVOY: But the General–

CESAR: A man of talent

ENVOY: The General directed me to–

CESAR: I know–yes, Lord Wellesley knows me by my reputation–but he knows me ill–for any French officer, an offer like this is an insult. But your General is English. That's his excuse. Please tell him, sir, that I don't wish him ill for it. (*he turns his back on the Envoy*)

ENVOY: Are you aware then that King Joseph has returned–that this very night–

CESAR: Ah! It's for tonight?

ENVOY: It must be.

CESAR: The twelve bullets I shall receive in my breast are a matter between my country and I. It does not concern the General.

ENVOY: That's you last word?

CESAR (*smiling*): My last word will be to order them to fire.

ENVOY: Your escape is prepared.

CESAR: Don't tell me about such things. I would be forced to make a report against the guards of this prison. (*politely*) Excuse me, sir, if I turn you away, but I have some small affairs to put in order before my departure–my compliments to your General (*bowing and pushing him out*) And would you kindly tell those who let you pass that I am henceforth not at home to anyone.

(*The Envoy leaves and Cesar goes to shut the door, but it reopens, letting Coutard in.*)

COUTARD: Not even for me, Captain?

CESAR (*moved*): Coutard! As for you, it's different! Come in! I haven't seen you since Cabanil.

COUTARD: We were relieved of our watch by an officer of the King who made the Lieutenant leave with him and left a detachment to garrison the castle.

CESAR: Yes. He'd promised me to do that.

COUTARD: After what had happened, there could no longer be any talk of wedding. We headed to Toledo and, upon arrival, learned–damn it all–that we were only allowed to visit you one at a time. The others are at the door.

CESAR (*offering his hand and shaking it several times*): This is for them.

COUTARD: Thanks. That will please them. But we're really embarrassed Captain...

CESAR: Why?

COUTARD: About deserting

CESAR (*frowning*): Deserting–my dragoons!

COUTARD: We reached an agreement, me, Sarreluck, Pont-Neuf and Petit Eustache, to leave the regiment all together.

CESAR (*impatient*): But why? Tell me why?

COUTARD (*lowering his head*): Because we were ordered to do something that we can't possible do.

CESAR (*indignant*): Refuse an order!

COUTARD: This particular order, yes, Captain.

CESAR (*smiling*): Ah. I think I understand.

COUTARD: Yes, Captain–you understand

CESAR: You're part of the squad which will shoot me at dawn?

COUTARD: Actually, we're the whole squad–all four of us.

CESAR: That's not proper.

COUTARD: They will issue us cartridges in the courtyard and we will have to load our guns before the Royal Commissioner. That way, there's no way of avoiding the order.

CESAR (*thoughtful*): These are singular precautions.

COUTARD: That's why, the comrades and I said to each other–if that's the kind of work for which they've made us return hurriedly, we won't do it.

CESAR: You will do it.

COUTARD: But Captain–

CESAR: I insist–I command you–

COUTARD (*hesitating*): Damn!

CESAR: You will do it–and you'll do it properly. It's the last service you can render me, my brave friends. I'm counting on you. Be a brave heart, but let your eyes be dry and your hands steady.

COUTARD: Captain! (*he makes a strong effort to control himself*) We've never disobeyed you.

CESAR: Everything is the way it should be, my old friend. I have to hug you, for yourself first (*pulling him to his breast*) then for the others. For Hector, a good brotherly kiss–and for Lilias–you will know how to perform this errand?

COUTARD (*drying his eyes*): All the same–

CESAR: You will say to her–

COUTARD: I will say to her: "He loved you proudly."

CESAR (*choked up, too*): That's it. Everything is settled. Now, old chap, leave me alone.

COUTARD: You can't leave us like that!

CESAR: Bah! We'll meet again–on high–someday–after some battle.

COUTARD (*gravely*): We'll do our best, Captain.

(*He gives a military salute and leaves.*)

CESAR (*alone*): Loyal and worthy hearts... (*looking at the letter*) The English General might have saved me. Go over to the enemy to save one's life. He offered it to me like a glass of wine. And a good pay to boot–with the rank of Colonel. (*he listens*) Someone else's coming. Was there ever a prison like this one? (*loudly*) I said I wasn't here for anyone!

(*A man draped in a huge cloak, his face hidden in the shadow of a large hat, enters.*)

MYSTERY MAN: I'm here on behalf of the King.

CESAR (*rising*): That's different.

MYSTERY MAN (*after a pause*): Captain Cesar de Cabanil, the King thinks you're too young to die.

CESAR: Before the enemy, one is never too young–but in the courtyard of a prison, yes, I share His Majesty's opinion.

MYSTERY MAN: France needs all its soldiers. (*Cesar nods*) Are you prepared to continue to serve France?

CESAR: I will do everything in my power.

MYSTERY MAN: Everything?

CESAR: Unless it's contrary to honor.

MYSTERY MAN (*haughtily*): I'm a soldier like yourself, Captain. (*a pause*) The King knows you, Monsieur. You're the adopted son of Count Blas de Cabanil, who was a faithful friend of the King. The Duke of Dalmatia told the King your worth. (*Cesar opens his mouth*) I beg you to not interrupt me. In a few more years, with a few more heroic deeds, you might become a General.

CESAR (*gravely*): I had my hopes. I can have my regrets. But neither one nor the other will ever influence my conduct. You've told me that you've come on behalf of the King. What does His Majesty desire?

MYSTERY MAN: The King wants to give you back your freedom–and your life.

CESAR: Without conditions?

MYSTERY MAN: On one condition

CESAR: I am listening.

MYSTERY MAN: Captain de Cabanil your unfortunate duel was a blow to the King's policies.

CESAR: Which is why I'm prepared to die without begging for mercy.

MYSTERY MAN: Still, you could do the King far more good than the harm you've caused him.

CESAR: In what way?

MYSTERY MAN: By accepting General Wellesley's offer. (*Cesar is startled*) Yes, the King knows everything and it's he who allowed the British Envoy to reach you. Do you understand what the King is asking of you?

CESAR: I do.

MYSTERY MAN: Do you accept?

CESAR: Before replying, I demand to see a proof of your request.

MYSTERY MAN: That's only fair. (*he rises, takes the lamp in one hand while raising his hat with the other.*) Do you trust me now?

CESAR: I do. (*he bows respectfully*)

MYSTERY MAN (*putting the lamp back on the table*): Monsieur de Cabanil, you've had proof of the importance of this matter. Let's speak frankly. The King remembers your bravery in the service of France and in no event, will he let you die here. Your life is your own–would you like your sword back? You're hesitating–

CESAR: I'm asking myself if any of my ancestors purchased his right to bear a sword at this price.

MYSTERY MAN: Your ancestors were fearless knights, yet none of them ever had a more heroic mission than the one asked of you today. Where the King is sending you, you will be alone against thousands of enemies. Death will be all around you–everywhere.

CESAR (*getting excited*): True indeed, but–

MYSTERY MAN: One word stops you–your mouth doesn't even wish to utter it–thsat of "spy." But you won't be a spy, Captain. (*gesture of denial by Cesar*) No, I affirm it to you on my honor! English gold has raised Spain against us–plunged it into chaos. Its parts no longer have a common brain, its arms are unaware of its head. You, alone, can help put that giant back together again–it's great work, Monsieur, sanctified by a terrible danger.

CESAR (*deeply moved*): A terrible danger–a great work. Tell His Majesty that I will do it.

MYSTERY MAN: Thank you. The King in turns swears to watch over all those whom you love. A horse–the best in the Royal Stables–will be placed at your disposal tonight. We know that the four Dragoons who were with you at Castle de Cabanil are devoted to you body and soul. These men will be allowed to rejoin you and will henceforth report only you. Here are your instructions and your full authority.

CESAR: But promise me that at the first sign of battle, I will be able to charge at the head of my regiment.

MYSTERY MAN: Monsieur, in the name of the King, I promise you that.

(*He leaves. A prison guard enters and slips Cesar a note.*)

GUARD: Read this fast. They're coming to get you.

CESAR: It's from Lilias (*reading*) "I waited for the King. I threw myself at his feet but was not able to obtain your grace. He even refused me the kindness of seeing you one last time. They are preparing your execution. You are doing to die while God condemns me to live–my tears are choking me. I love you and I pray."

GUARD: Here's the firing squad.

(*The firing squad–four men–enter.*)

CESAR (*aside*): Are they my Dragoons? (*looks at them*) No–these soldiers are Spaniards. They will shoot me. All this is very confusing–has the King change his mind?

SPANISH OFFICER: Señor, we are waiting for you.

CESAR: I am ready. (*to the guard*) My cloak? (*a large white cloak is placed over his shoulders*) In any event, the die cast. Now I'm either going to play the lead in a comedy or a tragedy. In any case, I must make a good figure. Let's go and God protect me.

(*He places himself in the midst of the squad and marches out with them at a sign from the officer.*)

Scene V

(*A cemetery outside Toledo. The walls surrounding it are all in ruins and reveal large holes through which country fields can be seen in the moonlight. Near the audience we see a ruined chapel and some trees. Two Gravediggers enter from the left with shovels on their shoulders.*)

FIRST GRAVEDIGGER: When the handsome Captain who was shot tonight arrives here, he'll find his bed all prepared. We've spent almost the whole night working and all for nothing.

SECOND GRAVEDIGGER: You're mistaken, my friend. We'll be paid–and well paid.

FIRST GRAVEDIGGER: By whom?

SECOND GRAVEDIGGER: By a young lady ,veiled in black, who promised me 20 douros.

FIRST GRAVEDIGGER: Twenty dourous? For what?

(*Lilias, wrapped in a black cloak, enters through the large hole at the back.*)

SECOND GRAVEDIGGER (*pointing to her*): You're going to find out. (*to Lilias*) You got here first, Señora.

LILIAS: I will wait.

FIRST GRAVEDIGGER: You won't have to wait for long

SECOND GRAVEDIGGER: It's true, I believe they're coming.

FIRST GRAVEDIGGER: They mustn't see the Señora.

SECOND GRAVEDIGGER: We're going to hide you until we're alone with the body–but first– (*he holds out his hand*)

LILIAS (*handing him a purse*): Here are your wages.

SECOND GRAVEDIGGER: Quick! Hide in there! (*he shows her the ruined chapel*)

LILIAS (*hesitant*): In there?

FIRST GRAVEDIGGER: You aren't afraid to walk down into that chapel?

LILIAS: If necessary, I would walk down to Hell.

SECOND GRAVEDIGGER: Hurry–they're getting closer.

(*Lilias disappears into the ruins of the old chapel, as the Mystery Man arrives.*)

MYSTERY MAN: Everything is ready?

SECOND GRAVEDIGGER (*taking his spade*): Yes, Your Excellency.

MYSTERY MAN: Then leave your spades here and go away–finish your other work.

SECOND GRAVEDIGGER (*low, to his comrade*): And the veiled lady? What's going to become of her?

FIRST GRAVEDIGGER: She likely heard the–it's not our fault–our douros were well-earned.

(*The two gravediggers leave by the hole at the back. Then, on a sign from the Mystery Man, the four Dragoons enter, carrying Cesar's body on a stretcher, hidden under his long white cloak. They stop before the chapel at a sign from the Mystery Man.*)

MYSTERY MAN: Two of you will remain with the body–the other two, take these spades and follow me.

PONT-NEUF (*aside*): First, executioners down there–now, gravediggers here–nice work.

MYSTERY MAN (*looking at his watch*): Everything must be finished by four o'clock. We have only a few minutes left–let's hurry.

(*He disappears to the left, followed by Pont-Neuf and Sarreluck.*)

COUTARD: To love a man the way we loved our Captain!

PETIT EUSTACHE: And to shoot him with our own hands–almost at point blank range.

COUTARD: Oh! If he hadn't ordered it himself, I'd never have fired.

PETIT EUSTACHE: Me neither. Our dear Captain–did you notice how he smiled at us when he saw us ready to take over from the Spanish soldiers by order of the King.

COUTARD: Still–he was pretty pale.

PETIT EUSTACHE: And when the King's Aide-de-Camp went close to him and whispered in his ear, the Captain had something like a moment of hesitation.

COUTARD: But when he looked at us, he became calm again. "Shoot for the heart," he told me–and he fell, as if thunderstruck. The Aide-de-Camp threw his great cloak over the body immediately. After all the Spanish soldiers had gone, they brought a stretcher and they told us to carry the body to the cemetery–and here we are. (*choking back a sigh*)

(*Lilias comes out of the chapel.*)

LILIAS: Sergeant Coutard!

COUTARD: Huh? Who is calling me?

PETIT EUSTACHE: It's the phantom of our Captain, who's returned from the dead!

COUTARD: Imbecile–do you believe in ghosts?

PETIT EUSTACHE: I believe in everything.

LILIAS: Petit Eustache?

PETIT EUSTACHE: The phantom knows my name–he's calling me by my name.

COUTARD: Who goes there?

LILIAS: It's me, Lilias.

COUTARD: Ah! I should have guessed–you had his last thought–you're coming to say a last prayer over him.

LILIAS: I want to see him alone–go away.

COUTARD: We would be failing the order which was given us–but it seems to me that it's still he who commands us with

207

your voice. We'll stand watch over there to make sure that no one surprises you.

(*They walk to the side, Coutard to the left, Petit Eustache to the right. Lilias kneels by the stretcher and prays.*)

LILIAS: My God–why didn't you take me with him? Why didn't you give us the same tomb? You alone know how much I loved him–how proud I was of loving him, so noble, so valiant, so good. I couldn't tell him all that was buried inside my heart when he was alive. Now, I am going to die to the world, find refuge in a convent, to live with only his memory. Lord God, pardon me–it's to you that I pray–but it's of him that I think.

(*Pont-Neuf appears on the left.*)

COUTARD (*stopping him*): Stop. Why are you back so soon?
PONT-NEUF (*low*): This is very strange. I don't know what's going on. The Aide-de-Camp just ordered us to fill a grave that had already been dug. Then, once that was done, he left with Sarreluck.

(*The bell sounds the hour. Liias, who hasn't heard a thing, pulls back the cloak and bends forward, preparing to kiss the body.*

LILIAS: When my mother died, I piously placed a kiss on her face–to you, too–my final goodbye–to you, I give the kiss of death.

(*But instead, Cesar rises and it's he who places a kiss upon her lips.*)

CESAR: My beloved–forever mine!
LILIAS: Oh! It's a miracle! Cesar! You're alive!

(*Coutard, Petit Eustache and Pont-Neuf turn around and see Cesar.*)

ALL: Oh! Captain! The Captain is alive!

(*At the same moment, Sarreluck appears at the back with a horse. Cesar runs to it and jumps into its saddle.*)

CESAR: To all, except to you, my friends, Cesar de Cabanil is dead. Now, I am only–Captain Phantom!

(*He spurs the horse gently and disappears.*)

CURTAIN

Act III

Scene VI

(*The Fountain Saint-Julian. The countryside is to the rear. To the right, there is the fountain with its stone basin. Trees and bushes are near it. To the left, there are ruins in the midst of shrubs and wild plants. In the far back, one can see the escarpment of a road that twists and turns as far as the eye can see. Coutard and Sarreluck, dressed in local garb, are resting in the shadows of the trees, talking to some Spanish peasants.*)

COUTARD: We are, like all good Spaniards, devoted to the holy cause. Our guns have often shot at the French, whom they say have all been excommunicated, and at the British, who are all heretics.

MARIA: Really? But I thought the British were our friends?

COUTARD: The British are nobody's friend. (*pointing to Sarreluck*) If my comrade here could speak, he would undoubtedly agree with me.

MARIA: Why can't he speak?

COUTARD: Because he's mute

PEASANTS: Mute!

MARIA: From birth?

COUTARD: Not at all–it was an accident–quite ridiculous. Here's how it happened–this lad spoke his native Biscayne ravishingly, but the English silenced him.

MARIA: How did that happen?

COUTARD: A stray bullet went full into his mouth and broke his palate–it's still lodged inside his throat. It liked it so much there that it refused to leave. Show her the bullet. (*he makes Sarreluck come forward and place his finger on his throat*) There it is–do you see it–down there?

210

ALL: Yes–yes!

COUTARD (*to Maria*): You can even touch it–

MARIA: And the bullet prevents him from–?

COUTARD: Absolutely. A bullet in the gullet hampers the conversation.

MARIA: He can't just swallow it?

COUTARD: Never. Try again–you see, it keeps returning to the same place.

MARIA: No longer able to speak... (*she pulls a dagger from her belt*) I'll try removing it.

SARRELUCK (*pushing her away*): Damn!

(*Coutard steps on his foot, but too late.*)

ALL: He spoke!

COUTARD: No, no, he just swore–he can still swear, but he no longer speaks in full sentences. And yet, he made a pilgrimage to San Pancracio...

(*Petit Eustache, hidden under a monk's robe, with a long beard and a tonsure on his head, appears at the back.*)

PETIT EUSTACHE: San Pancracio–why, he's my patron saint.

COUTARD: Heh! There's a monk with a well-filled purse–or so it seems to me.

PETIT EUSTACHE: Why, yes. There are still charitable souls left in this country.

COUTARD: Supper will be good this evening.

PETIT EUSTACHE: Not for me, brother. I've vowed to mortify my poor body. I abstain from all things. I live only off dry biscuit and clear water, and permit myself only one meal during the week.

MARIA: Poor man–even on Sundays?

PETIT EUSTACHE: On Sundays, I fast, sister.

MARIA: Shouldn't you be a lot thinner then?

PETIT EUSTACHE: Quite the contrary, I'm getting fatter–another blessing from San Pancracio.

(*There is loud noise outside; women and children enter from the back, looking terrified.*)

MARIA: What's going on?
ALL: A mad bull–see–down there!
MARIA: Holy Virgin. There's a man on that bull.
ALL: A man!
COUTARD: My word, it's true.
MARIA: God preserve us! The bull's coming towards us!
COUTARD (*readying his musket*): I'll get him when he gets in range
PETIT EUSTACHE (*low*): Don't kill the man.
COUTARD (*low*): I should say so–it's Pont-Neuf.
PETIT EUSTACHE: I knew it!
COUTARD: Watch out! (*he fires*) Good–there's the bull rolling!
PETIT EUSTACHE: And the man?
MARIA: He fell, too.
COUTARD: Yes, but he's getting up now–he wasn't hit because he's starting to run.
MARIA: He must be a *picador*.
COUTARD: Rehearsing one of his stunts, no doubt.

(*Enter Pont-Neuf, dressed as a picador, covered with dust.*)

PONT-NEUF: Well, now there's a shock! Who is it who shot my bull–who was only a mad cow?
COUTARD: It was me.
PONT-NEUF: Good shot! (*low*) Thanks, Coutard.
MARIA: Was the cow truly mad?
PONT-NEUF: Scared out of its wits, that's all.
MARIA: Scared of you?
PONT-NEUF: By right of conquest. I'd taken it from the British.

ALL: From the British!

PONT-NEUF: Who were counting on making it into a roast this evening–now you can grill it–I leave it to you–but hurry up, because the Scots I left behind will soon be here with their prisoners. I heard an order to hurry up and make camp at the Fountain Saint-Julian.

MARIA: Let's all hurry then!

PONT-NEUF: Yes, cut it and chop it, and may your steaks be tasty.

(*Maria and the others leave, running to the left.*)

COUTARD (looking around): Now we're alone.

SARRELUCK (*with his usual Alsatian accent*): Finally I can speak! What a villainous role being mute is!

COUTARD: You can't play any other since you can't get rid of your accent

SARRELUCK: I hardly have any. Besides, I'm sure it wouldn't be noticed.

PETIT EUSTACHE: In Strasbourg, no.

COUTARD: Now, Pont-Neuf is going to tell us how–and why–he got here.

PETIT EUSTACHE: Atop a cow.

COUTARD: Yes. That's not a suitable mount for a Dragoon of the 8th Regiment.

PONT-NEUF: I was lucky to find it. I came across it when I was returning to our lair, that cave found by Lazarillo, that brave lad devoted body and soul to Mademoiselle Lilias de Santa Cruz–

PONT-NEUF: Who uses him to correspond with–the Captain.

COUTARD: So you were returning to our lair?

PETIT EUSTACHE: Where we keep our disguises–

SARRELUCK: And our arsenal–

COUTARD: Why will you shut up, blabbermouths!

PONT-NEUF: When, suddenly, I heard a powerful volley–instinctively, I ran toward the fire–

COUTARD: It's in the blood–go on, friend, you've got me interested.

PONT-NEUF: I got to a height from which I could see everything

COUTARD: So you saw the fighting–describe everything.

PONT-NEUF: They was no more fighting. Four hundred Scottish troops had ambushed, surrounded and wiped out an infantry squadron of 40, commanded by a young Lieutenant–ten to one odds–our men surrounded. Oh, if only the four of us had been there! But I was alone–by myself–what could I do to help our comrades. I was biting my fists. I then noticed a herd of cows which was following the Scots–you know the British–theyt never go anywhere without their beef. I had the idea of frightening them into a stampede so that in the inevitable brouhaha, some of our men might escape. So I slipped unobserved into the herd. I had two packs of cartridges. I set them on–bang–bang–and the cows started to run.

COUTARD & PETIT EUSTACHE: Very clever!

PONT-NEUF: Yes–very clever–up to a point. Because here is when things started to go wrong. The fattest of the herd, instead of going the same way as his friends, turned nasty and headed right for me, head lowered. Fortunately, I saw what was happening in time. I made a feint and, as he passed me, I jumped on his back. To rid himself of me, he started to jump and prance, but I was nailed to him, fastened tight–then, he left at a gallop. Finally, thanks to Coutard, my crazy ride came to a stop. By luck, the cow brought me here. Now that it's over, I'm quite pleased to know that I'm as good on a cow as a horse.

COUTARD: Our comrades, prisoners–here–near us!

PETIT EUSTACHE: If only the Captain knew.

(*Lazarillo emerges from the ruins.*)

LAZARILLO: He does know it!

ALL: Lazarillo!

LAZARILLO: The Captain knows–moreover the young Lieutenant commanding that squadron was none other than– Hector de Cabanil.

ALL: His brother!

COUTARD: Then–damn it!–we're going to have to launch an attack!

LAZARILLO: I've got orders from the Captain–

COUTARD: Silence in the ranks.

LAZARILLO: He said, return to the cave, feed the horses, load your muskets and, at midnight, be in the saddle–ready for battle. And be sure to each have your trumpet.

COUTARD: Understood–we know the trick!

(*In the distance, we hear the sound of Scottish bagpipes.*)

PETIT EUSTACHE: The Scots are coming.

SARRELUCK: We'll soon give them something to play about.

PETIT EUSTACHE: Tonight–a general free for all.

COUTARD: To the cave, my friends, to the cave!

(*They all leave by the right. Then, the Scots Grenadiers enter from the west, with their French prisoners.*)

MACPHERSON: Platoon! Halt! Front! Rest arms–break ranks (*all orders are executed*)

MORIN (*sadly*): To stop here or further, that's all the same to me. Beaten by the Scots–but it wasn't the fault of our little Lieutenant–he fought like a lion, but there were too many of them.

ALL: Long live our Lieutenant!

MACPHERSON (*to the Scots*): Setting up the kitchens now!

MORIN: We won't be the ones turning the spit. Remember that we've been the conquerors of Europe Morin, Sergeant let's be dignified and let us do without food in silence.

MACPHERSON (*to Morin*): My Commander has ordered me to treat you same as us, so I'll be serving you first. While the soup is heating up, have some rum. That whets the appetite. (*he offers a gourd*)

MORIN (*taking the gourd*): I guess the Scots aren't like the British after all. (*to Macpherson*) Comrade, if the opportunity comes, we'll remember this.

MACPHERSON: If you are thirsty, make grogs. There's some wood–get water from the fountain (*the Scots offer gourds and cups to the French soldiers*)

SCOTTISH GRENADIER (*off*): Who goes there?

CESAR (*off*): General Arthur Wellesley's Courier!

MACPHERSON: Ah! It's Pedro de Tomas and his horse who can outrun the wind.

(*All the soldiers turn to greet Cesar, who remains on horseback. He is dressed like a Spaniard–with a beard and long hair–and is quite unrecognizable.*)

ALL: Hello, Señor Courier–

CESAR: Greetings to you all, gentlemen.

MACPHERSON: It's a long while since we've seen Sidi-Alazan, the King of Horses.

CESAR (*jumping down from his horse*): My cup of port, if you please.

MACPHERSON (*offering a large cup*): Here, Señor Courier.

CESAR: The first cup to the health of the Scottish Grenadiers. (*he drinks, then holds out his cup to be refilled*) The second to Sidi-Alazan (*he washes the horse's nose with port*) You've had some business today?

MACPHERSON: A skirmish.

CESAR: You've taken some prisoners from what I see.

MACPHERSON: A few infantry commanded by a little Lieutenant, as brave as his sword. which he didn't want to give up. and that our Commander, Sir Ned Wellesley generously left him.

CESAR: And this Lieutenant, where is he?

MACPHERSON: Hold on, there he is–the one coming this way, talking with Sir Ned who's trying to console him.

CESAR: Wounded–he's wounded.

MACPHERSON: Oh–just a bayonet scratch–nothing, nothing at all.

(*Ned Wellesley enters from the back with Hector de Cabanil, leaning on his arm. Hector, pale, defeated, wears his left arm in a sling, tied to the hilt of his sword. Cesar follows his wounded brother with his eyes.*)

MACPHERSON: Señor Courier, I've prepared a superb stable in these ruins especially for Sidi-Alazan.

CESAR: I'll take him there. (*aside, looking at Hector who slowly comes forward*) Poor Hector, he made me weep before and he's making me weep again. Later, brother, until later.

(*He disappears into the ruins on the left.*)

NED WELLESLEY (*to Macpherson*): Macpherson, tell the men to set another setting at the table. (*to Hector*) Monsieur, you can't refuse to do us the honor of dining with us.

HECTOR (*sadly*): I'll be a sad company, sir.

NED WELLESLEY (*to Hector*): I will say this to you, Monsieur: there are ancient friendships–relatives even– between France and Scotland. Our beautiful Queen Mary Stuart was almost French. Each of us, as soldiers, we've done our duty–but now–here–there is no longer a victor or a vanquished. Please see nothing more in me than a comrade who's offering you his hand and who would be esteemed by you, as much as he esteems you.

HECTOR (*shaking his hand*): I accept.

NED WELLESLEY (*to the soldiers*): The gentleman is one of us.

MACPHERSON: Good!

(*They bustle about Hector whom Ned has led to the table at the left. In the back, the French infantry and the Scottish Grenadiers are eating and drinking fraternally.*)

217

NED WELLESLEY (*to Macpherson*): I see another setting there. For whom is it?

MACPHERSON: For the Courier from the general.

NED WELLESLEY: Ah, yes. Don Pedro de Tomas–the best, the boldest cavalier I've even known. My uncle, Sir Arthur Wellesley, esteems him greatly. Where is the Señor Courier?

(*Cesar returns, steps forward and bows.*)

CESAR: At your orders, Your Excellency.

NED WELLESLEY: Be welcome as always. Please sit with us.

(*Cesar sits next to Macpherson, facing Sir Ned and Hector.*)

NED WELLESLEY: Where are you coming from this time?

CESAR: From Toledo.

NED WELLESLEY: Did you ride around the French lines?

CESAR: No, Excellency, I went through them.

NED WELLESLEY: We know you're a clever man–but how are you always able to pass with impunity through the midst of our enemies?

CESAR: Perhaps one day I'll be caught and shot. If the title of scout is much honored amongst you, gentlemen, on the other side of the pond, they don't display much sympathy for that useful profession–instead, they call me a spy. I'm sure that the gentleman who is French (*indicating Hector*) will no longer grant me the honor now of clinking his glass with mine.

HECTOR (*coldly*): I am not your judge, Señor. You rest only with your conscience.

NED WELLESLEY (*gaily*): What's the talk in Toledo, Señor Courier?

CESAR: They're talking a lot about Captain Phantom.

NED WELLESLEY: Ah, bah! That ridiculous story has already resounded too much in our ears. Our brave soldiers now believe in the existence of a supernatural being, a fantastic cavalier, dressed in the uniform of a French Dragoon and hiding his features under a black mask which hides his face, but for his eyes.

CESAR: Exactly the portrait of Captain Phantom as drawn by those who have seen him.

NED WELLESLEY: Ah, indeed? So you believe in ghosts, Señor Courier?

CESAR: Allow me to say this: there are ghosts and then, there are ghosts

HECTOR (*aside*): Why does the voice of this man make me shiver?

NED WELLESLEY: What is that supposed to mean?

CESAR: I don't know if the flesh he wears is wholly natural, but it suitably fills his uniform; he rides his horse like Saint George; he fights with a saber which chops and stabs like any mortal weapon. I don't know what face lurks beneath the mask, but his eyes burn with fearsome energies. In times of desperate peril, he charges at the head of his former Dragoons, strikes down his enemies and kills them all. To your health, Sir! At the battle of Las Navas, the Captain who had taken over the command of the 8th Dragoon Regiment had been struck dead–

HECTOR (*raising his head*): The 8th Dragoon?

CESAR: The lieutenants had also been killed. The soldiers no longer had any officers to lead them. Suddenly, Captain Phantom appeared, brandishing his saber, and he led the men to victory as ably as their former Captain, Cesar de Cabanil, would have done–had he been alive.

HECTOR: My brother

CESAR (*bowing*): Your brother–I saw him in Toledo–the very night when–

HECTOR: You've seen my brother?

CESAR: Yes–and he said much to me about you.

HECTOR: Of me!–Oh, Señor, you will repeat his words to me?

NED WELLESLEY (*rising and giving a sign to his officers*): We'll go smoke our cigarettes outside and inspect the encampment. (*to Hector*) Monsieur de Cabanil, you nobly bear a noble name. Come on, gentlemen.

(*They go out.*)

HECTOR (*aside, watching Cesar*): That voice, those eyes–oh!–that's impossible–it'd be madness.
CESAR (*low*): No more impossible, no more mad than the very existence of Captain Phantom, charging at the head of his Dragoons in the battle of Las Navas.
HECTOR: It *is* you! Cesar, my brother–
CESAR: Take care. They may be watching us. They mustn't see you embrace me–that is, if you still want to embrace me.
HECTOR: O, brother, I know only one thing, and that is that everything in you is noble and great. What you have done had to be done.
CESAR: Now, listen–moments are precious. When you were ambushed, were you making your way to the Fountain of Saint-Julian?
HECTOR: Yes
CESAR: There, you were supposed to meet a man who, forewarned of your visit, would have shown you a seal bearing the Royal Arms and an order signed by King Joseph himself.
HECTOR: Correct.
CESAR (*showing him*): Here's the seal and here's the signed order.
HECTOR: Indeed, this is it.
CESAR: To the one who was carrying this seal and this order, you were to deliver a message, also sealed with the King's Arms. Give me that message.
HECTOR (*obeying*): Here it is.
CESAR (*reading*): Indeed, it's what I thought. A supreme effort. A message to deliver to Marshal Soult–he shall have it tomorrow.
HECTOR: Marshal Soult is near?
CESAR: Yes.

HECTOR: But separated from us by General Wellesley and his three armies?

CESAR: I will cross his lines and pass through the midst of his armies.

HECTOR: And the distance?

CESAR: That's Sidi-Alazan's business. That horse's my greatest asset. To him, space is nothing–it's he who's given me wings–it's thanks to him that I've managed to keep the various French forces in Spain in touch with each other. Thanks to Sidi-Alazan, I will reach Soult tomorrow evening, and then I will carry his reply to the King the following day. When I have kept all my promises, perhaps the King will keep his and at last give me my reward–my place in battle. (*taking up his cape*) We must separate.

HECTOR: You're going to be on your way?

CESAR: First, I'm going to busy myself with you, brother–tonight, by favor of a diversion, I'll lead an attack on this camp and you and your men will be freed.

HECTOR: Brother, don't try anything for me–every of your hours is precious. Besides, as you can see, they left me my sword–I'm a prisoner upon my word–I don't have the right to escape.

CESAR: Oh, I'll save you despite yourself if necessary.

(*In the distance, one hears Macpherson issuing orders. The soldiers hastily take their arms and line up.*)

CESAR: What's happening?

MACPHERSON: A so-called Spanish "general" with his guerillas–they call it a "brigade." Sorry auxiliaries they're sending us.

(*Manoel, wearing the uniform of a Spanish General, enters, accompanied by Sir Ned, and followed by his men. The Scottish Commander is holding a letter.*)

CESAR (*aside*): Manoel!

MANOEL (*to Ned*): This order comes from the Commanding General, as you can see.

MANOEL: You must leave here immediately–before day-break–and head for Cabanil. You and your Grenadiers will garrison at the castle. You won't allow anyone to leave–no one at all. Finally, you are to deliver to me any prisoners you've taken and who might slow down your march.

NED WELLESLEY: Deliver my prisoners to you?

MANOEL: Such is the will of your Commanding General. (*to one of his men*) Rodrigo, relieve all the sentinels. We're going to be taking over from these gentlemen. Let the watch be doubled. (*noticing Hector*) Why has that man kept his sword?

NED WELLESLEY: Monsieur de Cabanil is a prisoner upon his word.

MANOEL: That's improper. All prisoners, officer or soldier, must be disarmed.

NED WELLESLEY: I won't suffer it.

MANOEL: Sir, you're no longer in command here. I alone am responsible now. (*to Hector*) Give me your sword.

NED WELLESLEY: Señor–

HECTOR (*to Ned*): It's the rule of war. One doesn't always meet adversaries like you, Sir.

(*Hector delivers his sword to Manoel, who looks at its hilt.*)

MANOEL: I see you're mourning for your brother–you are the last of the elder branch of the Cabanils. (*aside*) This time, you won't escape me. (*he places the sword on the table.*)

MACPHERSON (*to Ned*): Everything is ready for the departure, Sir!

NED WELLESLEY (*looking at the order*): I must obey. Come, gentlemen. (*low to Hector*) Monsieur de Cabanil, I release you from your word.

(*They shake hands. The Scots have been replaced by the Spaniards. Sir Ned and his officers leave.*)

CESAR (*low to Hector*): Do you still refuse the freedom I wish to secure for you?
HECTOR (*low*): No more. At what signal are we to attempt to get our weapons back?
CESAR: You'll be informed soon. Now, I must leave, too.

(*Rodrigo makes a sign to Hector to come forward. Hector goes and sits by the fountain. The French prisoners occupy the rear of the stage. As Cesar passes Manoel, the latter stops him with a gesture.*)

MANOEL: And who are you?
CESAR: Sir Arthur Wellesley's courier, Señor. I was on a mission and I am now returning to General's headquarters.
MANOEL: Ah yes. You're Pedro de Tomas, aren't you?
CESAR: Yes, Your Excellency.
MANOEL: I've often heard of you–I'm pleased to make your acquaintance. You will carry, if you please, a letter from me to General Wellesley–only a few lines.
CESAR: Yes, Señor–but please, write it quickly, because my time is not my own.
MANOEL (*sitting at a table*): Finish your cigarette while I write.

(*Cesar rolls a cigarette.*)

MANOEL: I've heard of your marvelous deeds. You're a bold and tireless man. Ah–and you smoke excellent tobacco.
CESAR: It was destined for Marshal Victor. Will Your Excellency do me the honor of smoking one of my cigarettes?
MANOEL: Gladly. (*he takes a cigarette from Cesar*) You're not worried about meeting a party of French soldiers?
CESAR: No, Señor
MANOEL (*laughing*): Or even Captain Phantom! Ah! Ah! Surely, you don't believe that ridiculous fairy-tale. This Captain Phantom exists only in the imagination of my guerillas.

CESAR: I'm sorry to contradict you, Señor, but man, ghost or demon, Captain Phantom does truly exists

MANOEL: Come on!

CESAR: I've seen him.

MANOEL: You–?

CESAR: With my own eyes. Just as I'm seeing you.

MANOEL: And he does wear the uniform of Captain of the Dragoons?

CESAR: That's what he wore at the battle of Las Navas.

MANOEL: How do you know that?

CESAR: I was there.

MANOEL (*striking the table*): Then it must be *him*!

CESAR: *Him*, Señor?

MANOEL (*low*): Cesar de Cabanil.

CESAR: It can't be, Señor. He was shot in Toledo by order of King Joseph.

MANOEL: And buried at Campo Santo. It's true, I am mad. The thought of that man pursues me everywhere.

CESAR (*noticing Hector*): That young officer is his brother, I believe?

MANOEL: Yes?

CESAR: Whose life was guaranteed by the Scottish Commander.

MANOEL: You're mistaken. He is to be shot.

CESAR: Ah. When's that?

MANOEL: At daybreak. A light, if you please (*Cesar approaches Manoel, who finds himself face to face with him.*) This is odd.

CESAR (*purposefully misunderstanding*): This is tobacco from Havana. It doesn't always light up properly.

MANOEL: No, it's not that. I've seen Cesar de Cabanil only twice in my life–first at Paris, then at Cabanil–and his features, his expression, have remained etched in my memory.

CESAR: Yes, there are striking faces one never forgets. Do I, by chance, resemble the late Captain?

MANOEL: You do have some of his features–especially his look.

CESAR: You flatter me, Señor, for I understand that, while he lived, Captain de Cabanil was, as they say, a very presentable cavalier. Is your letter written?

MANOEL: Yes. Here it is.

CESAR: Nothing else for General Wellesley?

MANOEL: Nothing.

CESAR: Do I have your leave to go now, Señor?

MANOEL: Yes, Señor Courier.

CESAR: Good-bye, General Manoel. Come on, Alazan! Let's go!

(*He salutes Manoel and leaves.*)

MANOEL (*near the table, calling*): Rodrigo!

RODRIGO: Excellency?

MANOEL: Double the watch for the night. We must be on guard against all surprises. Don't let them lose sight of that young man. (*gesturing towards Hector*) You will answer to me for him.

RODRIGO: Yes, Excellency. They've laid out a place for you to sleep in these ruins. (*pointing at the ruins*) It's almost suitable.

MANOEL (*to Hector*): Monsieur, by order of the Junta, all French officers must be shot. Prepare yourself to die in the morning.

HECTOR: A soldier is always ready, Señor.

MANOEL: Well said.

(*He leaves with Rodrigo.*)

HECTOR: Now, Cesar must either save me or avenge me.

(*At this moment, Lazarillo appears between the basin and the fountain.*)

LAZARILLO: Señor de Cabanil.

HECTOR: Who's calling me?

LAZARILLO: A friend. Listen carefully. Your men's rifles are here, in the ruins, guarded by this guerilla–and you'll soon hear the signal which was mentioned to you.

HECTOR: What will it be?

LAZARILLO: The explosion of the ammunition wagon! Almost immediately, you'll hear a charge being sounded and the camp will be attacked on four sides. The guerillas will be hit from every direction. At that time, hurl yourselves on the guards, grab your weapons and take your revenge. I've already warned your men.

HECTOR: Who sent you?

LAZARILLO: Captain Phantom.

(*Lazarillo disappears. Morin slips close to Hector.*)

MORIN: It seems as if we won't be getting any sleep tonight, Lieutenant.

HECTOR: We'll either be killed–or we'll be free.

MORIN: Agreed.

(*Then, an explosion is heard. As the guerilla on guard turns toward the noise, Lazarillo rises up from behind him and strikes him unconscious.*)

HECTOR: To arms, Comrades! Grab your weapons!

ALL: To arms!

MANOEL (*running*): Fire on the prisoners!

(*Some of the men trip up the guerillas guarding them, others run into the ruins. Hector has grabbed his sword and prepares to fight. From four different sides, one hears the charge being sounded.*)

GUERILLAS: The French! The French!

MANOEL: We are going to deal with them! Regroup!

(*Rodrigo returns, in panic.*)

RODRIGO (terrified): It's Captain Phantom!
MANOEL: Him!

(*Manoel seizes a rifle and, noticing Cesar on horseback, wearing the uniform of a Captain of Dragoons, his face hidden beneath a black mask, fires on him.*)

MANOEL: I'll kill you, Cesar de Cabanil

(*The shot misses. Captain Phantom rushes at a gallop and sabers the guerillas, who are also attacked by Hector and the French soldiers. Finally, they flee, dragging Manoel with them. Cesar cuts down the enemy flag with his sword, tosses it to Hector, then disappears.*)

ALL: Victory!

CURTAIN

Act IV

Scene VII

(*The Inn of Guttieres in the town of Gavila occupies the better half of the stage. The other half forms a square where the streets of Gavila intersect. At the left, we see an alley behind a house. There is also a street arcade. Inside the Inn, a door and a window give onto the square, while a backdoor leads to another street.*)

(*AT RISE, Lazarillo is sitting in the inn, drinking. Young Maria is looking through the window. Outside, Guttieres, the inn-keeper, stands by the door. Major Clinton, surrounded by his officers, stands on the square, filled with villagers of both sexes. Military trumpets blare.*)

CLINTON (*signaling the trumpets to stop*): Citizens of Gavila! Last night, Captain Phantom freed prisoners entrusted to General Manoel. During the battle, the mask which covered the Captain's face fell and General Manoel is now convinced that the Courier Pedro de Tomas and Captain Phantom are one and the same man. I've been given the task of pursuing and catching that traitor. Because he had quite a headstart, we haven't been able to stop him from reaching the Portuguese border. But we will indeed prevent him from carrying to King Joseph the reply from Marshal Soult. The Alcade of this town was a French supporter and, no doubt, Captain Phantom's accomplice. He's been arrested–and this very day, he'll be replaced by a new Alcade one more devoted to the Junta. This man will arrive soon. He will have discretionary power–and the order to hang anyone who gives refuge or protection to Captain Phantom.

(*Commotion in the crowd.*)

MARIA (*at the window*): They want to hang Captain Phantom. What a shame–he's such a fine cavalier!
LAZARILLO (*drinking*): Bah! They've got to catch him first!

(*Outside, Clinton gathers his officers.*)

CLINTON: Now, gentlemen, let's begin the hunt. We don't want the honor or the profit of capturing Captain Phantom to go to General Manoel– To the horses!
OFFICERS: To the horses!

(*They leave by the street to the left. The townsfolk form animated groups around the square.*)

GUTTIERES (*in the doorway, to the townsfolk*): Folks, let's be very careful. We're going to be getting a terrible Alcade.

(*He opens the door and steps back inside*).

LAZARILLO (*aside*): I'm supposed to be waiting in Gavila, at Señor Guttieres' Inn–so here I wait.
MARIA: If all the world was like me, the brave Captain Phantom would have nothing to fear.
GUTTIERES: Peace, girl! Go get us wine–these English–they're making me forget my guest–an old companion.
MARIA: Here's the wine–as for me, I'm going to go out and get news.

(*She leaves.*)

GUTTIERES (*to Lazarillo*): So, you're no longer a smuggler, Lazarillo?
LAZARILLO: No, my friend, I'm not.
GUTTIERES: When we knew each other–those were good times. (*sitting*) Today, on the other hand–

LAZARILLO: Today is bad. (*pouring him a drink*)

GUTTIERES: The profession is lost! The French burn the British's goods. The British confiscate the French's merchandise–and the Spanish take all that is neither confiscated nor burned.

LAZARILLO: That's the end of commerce.

GUTTIERES (*pounding the table with his fist*): And my luck is bad! By chance, Gavila suddenly finds itself without an Alcade. I am *de facto* the only authority left in the village. It would have been the perfect time–

LAZARILLO: To reopen your store?

GUTTIERES: You remember Pablo?

LAZARILLO: One-Armed Pablo?

GUTTIERES: The same! He's brought me 300 pistoles-worth of French merchandise. The goods are carried by four mules and they're waiting in the woods outside the walls.

LAZARILLO: The Santiago woods?

GUTTIERES: Exactly!–but now, with the coming of this devil of an Alcade–

LAZARILLO: Armed with discretionary powers–

GUTTIERES: With the order to hang anyone–

LAZARILLO: I see your problem–it'll be hard to bring in the bags.

GUTTIERES: Officially, through the gates, yes. But there's another way–

LAZARILLO: Ah?

GUTTIERES: Pablo knows it–the other way–and if this cursed Alcade could only be delayed for an hour or two– would you help me, Lazarillo?

LAZARILLO: With all my heart–but wait!–something's happening outside!

(*We hear a great commotion outside.*)

CROWD (*shouting*): The new Alcade's here!

GUTTIERES (*in despair*): Already? No! That can't be him!

(*Maria rushes in.*)

MARIA: The new Alcade's here! With his clerk. They make you afraid to look at them. He's fat and red, like a barrel. The clerk's all pale and thin like a candle! They're talking of hanging half the town already! (*she collapses into a chair*)
GUTTIERES: Quick, my lance! I'm a sergeant of Saint-Hermandad! I've got to present arms to the new Alcade, may the Devil take him.
MARIA (*to Lazarillo*): You're not running away?
LAZARILLO: No–I'm more curious than cowardly. (*he sets calmly by the window*)

(*Outside, the crowd moves uncertainly. Petit Eustache appears, mounted on a richly-harnessed mule. He's dressed in a Spanish style and wears a large, extravagant hat. Pont-Neuf follows him on foot, also dressed also in Spanish style and wearing an even more extravagant hat. Guttieres comes out to welcome them.*)

GUTTIERES (*shouting*): Long live His Excellency, the new Alcade!
CROWD (*noticeably lacking in enthusiasm*): Long live the new Alcade!
PETIT EUSTACHE: That lacks enthusiasm–wave your hats, people. Let the highest-ranking man in town hold my stirrups.
LAZARILLO (*at the window*): Ah! This is a fine-looking Alcade indeed.
GUTTIERES (*holding the stirrups*): Your Excellency–
PETIT EUSTACHE: Citizens of Gavila, I have the power of life and death over you–don't you forget it. Listen religiously to the orders of the Supreme Junta, which speaks to you in my voice. My first command is for all citizens to go back to their homes, to not station themselves in the streets. I hereby order the portcullis to be raised and the gates to be opened!

(*They rush to comply.*)

GUTTIERES (*timidly*): If I may–

PETIT EUSTACHE: I am the Law here!

PONT-NEUF (*to Guttieres*): Who are you to dare speak to His Excellency?

GUTTIERES: Guttieres, innkeeper and sergeant of Saint-Hermandad.

PETIT EUSTACHE: Guttieres (*low*) That's the name! (*aloud*) That inn of yours–where is it?

GUTTIERES (*pointing*): Why, just here–for His Excellency's convenience.

MARIA (*recoiling from the window*): That monster–the clerk–he's looking at me.

PETIT EUSTACHE: Ah! ah! (*to Pont-Neuf*) That's the rendezvous place!

PONT-NEUF (*to Petit Eustache*): I see Lazarillo at the window.

PETIT EUSTACHE (*to Guttieres*): I'll do you a great honor. I'll stay at your inn–with my clerk.

GUTTIERES (aside): What about my merchandise?

PETIT EUSTACHE: See to the execution of the orders I've just issued. Soon, I'll inspect the streets–with my clerk. If I find even a spaniel there–not a Spaniard–ill luck to you. I'll make a frightful example of this town. (*loudly*) Citizens of Gavila–go home and tremble!

(*He heads toward the inn, followed by Pont-Neuf*)

PONT-NEUF (*marching in lockstep*): Tremble!

GUTTIERES: I'm ruined (*he orders the crowd to evacuate the square*) Quicker! Now I'm responsible–

MARIA (*to Lazarillo*): They're coming in here. I no longer dare go home. Oh–that clerk especially frightens me.

LAZARILLO: Go then–I will serve them.

MARIA: Thanks!

(*Maria rushes up the stairs just as Petit Eustache and Pont-Neuf open the door. Outside, the square is now empty and Guttieres disappears with the last residents. Lazarillo goes to the newcomers and looks at them with admiration–then, he carefully closes the door and window.*)

LAZARILLO: Now that we're alone, I'd like to know–

(*Pont-Neuf starts pouring himself a drink, but Petit Eustache grabs the cup.*)

PETIT EUSTACHE: Me first! You're only my lowly clerk.
PONT-NEUF (*grabbing another cup*): This one is to the clerk. (*drinking, then to Lazarillo*) You want to know how we profited from the information you gave us? Nothing simpler–we waited for the new Alcade and his clerk, whom we knew were unknown to the inhabitants of Gavila. We saw them coming from a distance–the Alcade on his mule, the clerk following on foot
PETIT EUSTACHE: We drew straws for which of us would have the mule–
PONT-NEUF: And I lost
PETIT EUSTACHE: Naturally, since I won. The trouble was to find a safe place to lock up the clerk and the Alcade.
PONT-NEUF: I opted for a brick oven. I took the Alcade by the leg–
PETIT EUSTACHE: I put my leg out for the clerk–they were both undressed–
PONT-NEUF: We robbed them–
PETIT EUSTACHE: We tied them up–
PONT-NEUF: And we stuffed them properly in the oven! After that, we got dressed in turn–
PETIT EUSTACHE: And came to Gavila–the gates of which are henceforth wide open, with empty streets that will not hinder the Captain. He will cross the town at a gallop.
LAZARILLO: Do you have news of him?

PONT-NEUF: Coutard and Sarreluck are keeping watch at the pass of Pareja.

PETIT EUSTACHE: The Captain should be here in a quarter of an hour.

LAZARILLO: Coutard–Sarreluck–two brave men, but Clinton has a squadron, and Manoel a whole army.

PONT-NEUF: Bah! Once he's crossed Gavila, the worst part is over–and the Captain is unstoppable!

PETIT EUSTACHE: Tonight, King Joseph will have Marshal Soult's message.

(*There is a noise outside.*)

PONT-NEUF: Hush!

PETIT EUSTACHE: Could it be the Captain already?

(*Fearful faces are seen at the corners of the square.*)

LAZARILLO: It's only Guttieres. Back to your roles.

(*Guttieres enters, hat low, bowing almost to the ground.*)

GUTTIERES: Señor Alcade–

PETIT EUSTACHE (*terribly*): Are the streets empty? Is the square deserted?

GUTTIERES: On the contrary, it's full of people.

PETIT EUSTACHE: Demons! They dare disobey me! I'll punish you all!

GUTTIERES: Wait–I'm bringing some good news–

PONT-NEUF: Speak!

PETIT EUSTACHE: Yes, speak. I absolve you–for the moment–

GUTTIERES: The army has arrested two gypsies–

PETIT EUSTACHE: Where?

GUTTIERES: At the pass of Pareja. These gypsies fired on General Manoel.

PETIT EUSTACHE (*with authority*): Hum! Hum! Bring these two scoundrels to me.

GUTTIERES: What? Here? (*aside*) I'd hoped to get these two out of here and far away.

PONT-NEUF: Didn't you hear?

GUTTIERES (*embarrassed*): It's just that–wouldn't it be more convenient if you went–

PETIT EUSTACHE: No. I'm fine right here–I'm staying–go and do what I told you.

(*Guttieres steps aside.*)

GUTTIERES (*aside*): Impossible to tell Pablo to bring in the goods. I'm ruined!

LAZARILLO (*to Guttieres*): Can I help you, old friend?

GUTTIERES (*excitedly, taking Lazarillo's hands*): Yes! Run to the Santiago woods and tell Pablo he can't come here tonight–at nine–as we'd agreed.

LAZARILLO: He was coming here at nine (*naively*) through the gates?

GUTTIERES: No–through the other way.

LAZARILLO: What other way?

GUTTIERES (*suspicious*): You don't need to know. Go!

LAZARILLO (*aside*): Pablo will tell me

(*As he and Guttieres leave, the soldiers bring the two gypsies– Coutard and Sarreluck in disguise.*)

PONT-NEUF (*who has looked through the window*): It's Coutard!

PETIT EUSTACHE: With Sarreluck?

PONT-NEUF: Yes.

PETIT EUSTACHE: To your post. (*he sits at the table and takes up his large hat*) They'll see what I'm made of!

(*Guttieres returns, leading Coutard and Sarreluck.*)

GUTTIERES: Here are two accomplices of Captain Phantom.
PETIT EUSTACHE: Leave–I'll question them myself.
GUTTIERES: Leave you alone with these two bandits?
PETIT EUSTACHE: I have my clerk. Go! Go!
GUTTIERES: What a man!

(*He leaves. Outside, the soldiers and the people are spread all over the square. Inside, Pont-Neuf checks that the door and the window are well shut. Then, they all shake hands.*)

PETIT EUSTACHE: What news of the Captain?
COUTARD: Some good, some bad. For the first time in my life, I'm afraid.
PETIT EUSTACHE: You, old Coutard?
PONT-NEUF: Things must be getting pretty hot then.
SARRELUCK: Even more so than you think!
COUTARD: Fear for him–we were keeping watch at the pass of Pareja–a crook of a trench where two men like Pont-Neuf couldn't walk side by side–nothing to see, not a soul on the heights, or in the gorge. Suddenly, Sarreluck spots a little cloud of dust from the west. Then, another, much larger behind–far behind. It was the Captain–and he had a pack of red coats after him. The cloud got larger, then the Captain appeared, flying like a swallow–Alazan wasn't running, my holy word, no!–he was flying. It was superb to see!
SARRELUCK: Yes, truly superb!
COUTARD: I was going to give the agreed signal that the pass was free. As a matter of fact, if I had, I would have killed my Captain–for that signal would have meant certain death. There were 40 muskets hidden in that pass, and we hadn't seen the ambush. Manoel and his men were hidden under the rocks. Manoel, impatient as ever, revealed himself and let his villainous mug be seen. His guerillas swarmed in the thicket. You know what they say? A rifle shot is better than a warning shout. So I targeted Manoel and had him in my sights–but he leaned forward to give an order, and my shot popped off his lieutenant's head instead. Sarreluck bunked down another

236

officer. Hearing the sound of our two shots, the Captain turned around. Manoel ordered all his men to fire–it shook the rock under our feet. When the smoke had dissipated, we saw the Captain galloping in the distance, now hunted by two packs of dogs instead of one. But he had the lead on them and waved his hat, as if to say " 'Till soon, my friends, 'till soon."

PETIT EUSTACHE: What a tale!

PONT-NEUF: None are so bold as our Captain!

SARRELUCK: But Alazan–

COUTARD: You imagined it!

SARRELUCK: I saw Alazan limping after the shots were fired–and if Alazan is wounded, the Captain is lost!

COUTARD (*with enthusiasm*): The Captain is never lost!

SARRELUCK: They've captured us–

COUTARD: We're not the Captain!

PETIT EUSTACHE: And it's we who've got you, friends.

COUTARD (*laughingly*): And you won't shoot us, will you, Señor Alcade?

PETIT EUSTACHE: No, but we'll shoot others, won't we, old Coutard–

(*There is a lot of noise outside. Suddenly, Manoel appears on the square, followed by more of his men.*)

MANOEL: Watch all the streets! Captain Phantom managed to get through the mountain.

COUTARD (*looking through the window*): Manoel!

MANOEL: He's coming here! But with Clinton on one side and my guerillas on the other, we'll trap him here–he'll be caught in a wolf's trap. Shut the gates!

PETIT EUSTACHE: The devil (*The Dragoons look at each other*)

GUTTIERES (*outside*): Impossible!

MANOEL: Why?

GUTTIERES: The new Alcade has forbidden it under pain of death–

MANOEL (*shrugging*): You're joking?

GUTTIERES: He says he has his orders from the Junta.
MANOEL: Fine. I'll talk to him–where is he?
GUTTIERES: With his clerk, inside–but he's asked not to be disturbed.

(*Commotion amongst the Dragoons.*)

PONT-NEUF: This is going badly
GUTTIERES (*standing in front of Manoel*): You cannot enter!
MANOEL (*pushing Guttieres aside*): I go wherever I want!
PETIT EUSTACHE: Now there's a hostage that our good angel is sending us.

(*Manoel enters. Immediately, Pont-Neuf locks the door behind him. Manoel turns and finds guns pointed at him. He recoils but realizes he is surrounded.*)

COUTARD: One noise and you die like a dog.
MANOEL: You would dare?
COUTARD: Four against one–that's not our habit, we're French. So we're not going to harm unless you force us to. The gates will remain open. If the Captain must ride over the bodies of your men–then so he will.
PONT-NEUF: We're going to do with you what we did with the Alcade.

(*They tie him up.*)

PETIT EUSTACHE: Bound.
COUTARD (putting a gag on Manoel): Gagged.
SARRELUCK (carrying him): And packed!

(*They deposit Manoel in a room at the back and lock the door behind them. Suddenly, outside, Clinton enters the square, followed by his own soldiers.*)

CLINTON: Victory! We've caught him.

238

GUTTIERES: Who?
CLINTON: Captain Phantom!
GUTTIERES: You've taken Captain Phantom?
CLINTON: We've killed him! He's dead
DRAGOONS (*inside*): Dead!

(*Suddenly, Cesar comes out of an heretofore-unseen trapdoor.*)

CESAR: Captain Phantom–always killed, never dead!
DRAGOONS: The Captain!
CESAR: Hush! (*lowering the trapdoor and talking to someone below*) Thanks, Lazarillo. Hold my horse and the four mules ready.
PONT-NEUF (*jumping with joy*): The Captain's back!
GUTTIERES (*outside*): You're quite sure of it?
CLINTON: We searched the body and in its belt, we found a letter from Marshal Soult to King Joseph.
CESAR (*low to the Dragoons*): A trick. I'll explain.
CLINTON (*reading*): "I advise the King not to engage in a decisive battle, for it's not in my power to undertake the diversion that His Majesty expects of me. Soult." Is that clear? To headquarters, gentlemen!
ALL: To headquarters!

(*The British soldiers leave.*)

CESAR: My ruse succeeded. The Marshal wrote two letters from–one to deceive the enemy, the one Major Clinton found– and the other–the real reply–which I'll take to the King.
PETIT EUSTACHE: How were you able to get away?
CESAR: There were thirty of them chasing me. Alazan was wounded. With a final effort, I rushed into the cleft whose trees could put the rogues off the track, but a bandit better mounted than the others was gaining on me. I took a shot and hit him square in the face. He fell, dead, disfigured, unrecognizable. I dressed him up with my clothes–leaving the

misleading letter in the belt–and switched costumes. I leapt on his horse and rode away like the wind. I reached Santiago woods where Lazarillo was waiting for me. But when I learned what else had happened here, my friends, I decided to come to your aid–as you have so many times come to mine. At the agreed-upon hour, I will be in camp, I will embrace my brother and I will go to meet you at Cabanil. Secure the ferry boat there, hide–and wait for me–it's now a question of saving Lilias. To Cabanil, my brave friends, to Cabanil!

(*They all disappear down the trapdoor.*)

MANOEL'S VOICE (*from the back room*): Help! Help!
GUTTIERES (*just outside the door*): That's the voice of general Manoel–is he ill in there?
MANOEL: Help!
GUTTIERES (*trying the door*): It's locked from within–it's got to be broken down.

(*They break it in.*)

GUTTIERES (*entering*): Nobody?

(*After being freed by his men, Manoel emerges from the back room.*)

MANOEL: The wretches tried to murder me! Find them! Arrest them! I must have them–dead or alive!
ALL: Dead!

(*They rush about in all directions–great commotion.*)

CURTAIN

Act V

Scene VIII

(In the midst of a swollen river, a boat sways, lit by rays of moonlight. Its rear is facing the audience, who sees it from three sides. Lilias is seated at the rear, Manoel and Rodrigo are in the front.)

MANOEL: Anything in sight?

RODRIGO: Nothing between Talavera de la Reina and the front lines of King Joseph.

MANOEL: The river is flooded–it's a veritable sea out there.

RODRIGO: A riverboat can't resist this terrible current. Even the ferry boat has remained moored at the foot of the rocks of Cabanil.

LILIAS *(aside)*: The ferry boat. I saw men there, half-hidden in the shadows/ I'm sure of it–one of them even got up and bowed to me during the passage–who could that man be?

MANOEL: General Wellesley has surprisingly issued a safe conduct to the ladies of Cabanil–but a later order placed them at my discretion. They now belong to me. I've been merciful to them. The most precious treasure of Cabanil is Lilias–and she's mine now. Rodrigo, keep our men at the front of the ship. *(heading toward Lilias, who remains seated)* Lilias, do you now believe in my love?

LILIAS: I've sold you my life–it's yours, take it.

MANOEL: Nobody plays with impunity with my love.

LILIAS: What belongs to Cesar, a hero, can never belong to Manoel, a bandit. How could you ever believe that I would give myself to the murderer of my father, the murderer of my lover. One who does not fear death can defy all–as I defy you, Manoel.

MANOEL: Brave words which won't stop me.

RODRIGO: Ship under sail–coming straight for us.

MANOEL: A ship?

RODRIGO: Manned by five men who are rowing against the current. I recognize it–it's the ferry–

LILIAS: Ah! You deceived me. Cesar still lives–he must be aboard!

MANOEL: Cesar will be quite dead this time–and those men–whoever they are–won't have the opportunity to board us. Rodrigo, prepare to sink them!

LILIAS: My God! Protect those who are coming to help me!

MANOEL: Is their ship within range?

RODRIGO: Yes, Your Excellency.

MANOEL: Then fire!

(*The cannon fires.*)

RODRIGO: I hit them. They're sinking!

MANOEL: Excellent! The wind is rising–let's leave.

RODRIGO: The anchor is heavy–and we don't have a full crew.

MANOEL: I'll help you.

(*Rodrigo and Manoel turn their backs on the public to weigh anchor. On the other side, Cesar appears out of the water with his four Dragoons. They reach the starboard, hoist themselves onto the bridge with the aid of hanging ropes and rush Manoel and his men, who have come out from below bridge.*)

LILIAS (*joyfully*): Cesar!

MANOEL: Not him! It can't be him!

CESAR (*to his Dragoons*): Comrades–all these men–into the sea–and quickly!

COUTARD: There are only seven of them.

PONT-NEUF: It's too easy.

(*After a short struggle, Manoel and his men are tossed into the sea.*)

PETIT EUSTACHE: There–the bridge's been swept clean.

(*Noise of cannon fire in the distance.*)

CESAR: The battle of Talavera is starting–and our good angel is with us. To the battle, comrades!
ALL: To the battle! Long live Captain Phantom!

(*The sail takes the wind–the ship turns and the cannon fire increases.*)

CURTAIN